The DOG PARK Detectives
Bone of Contention

Blake Mara is a pseudonym of Mara Timon, author of Second World War thrillers *City of Spies* and *Resistance*. She started writing as a child; mostly short stories, but when an idea caught her imagination, she followed one 'what if' after another until her first (and second, and third . . .) novel emerged.

Mara is a native New Yorker who moved to the UK about twenty years ago. When Covid hit, she went cliché and got a pandemic puppy – a miniature dachshund with a massive personality. This opened her eyes to the canine-loving community that blossomed around the local dog park, and who became the inspiration for *The Dog Park Detectives*, the first book in her cosy crime series. But while her dog park pack have tackled some local crimes, they haven't found a dead body in the park . . . yet.

For more information, follow Mara at her website or on social media:

www.blakemara.com
X @TheBlakeMara
BlakeMaraAuthor
@mara.timon

Writing as Mara Timon: *As Blake Mara:*

City of Spies   The Dog Park Detectives
Resistance

The DOG PARK Detectives
Bone of Contention

Blake Mara

SIMON & SCHUSTER

London · New York · Amsterdam/Antwerp · Sydney/Melbourne · Toronto · New Delhi

First published in Great Britain by Simon & Schuster UK Ltd, 2025

Copyright © Blake Mara, 2025

The right of Blake Mara to be identified as author of this work has been asserted in accordance with the Copyright, Designs and Patents Act, 1988.

1 3 5 7 9 10 8 6 4 2

Simon & Schuster UK Ltd, 1st Floor
222 Gray's Inn Road, London WC1X 8HB

For more than 100 years, Simon & Schuster has championed authors and the stories they create. By respecting the copyright of an author's intellectual property, you enable Simon & Schuster and the author to continue publishing exceptional books for years to come. We thank you for supporting the author's copyright by purchasing an authorized edition of this book.
No amount of this book may be reproduced or stored in any format, nor may it be uploaded to any website, database, language-learning model, or other repository, retrieval, or artificial intelligence system without express permission. All rights reserved. Inquiries may be directed to Simon & Schuster, 222 Gray's Inn Road, London WC1X 8HB or RightsMailbox@simonandschuster.co.uk

Simon & Schuster Australia, Sydney
Simon & Schuster India, New Delhi

www.simonandschuster.co.uk
www.simonandschuster.com.au
www.simonandschuster.co.in

The authorised representative in the EEA is Simon & Schuster Netherlands BV, Herculesplein 96, 3584 AA Utrecht, Netherlands. info@simonandschuster.nl

Simon & Schuster strongly believes in freedom of expression and stands against censorship in all its forms. For more information, visit BooksBelong.com.

A CIP catalogue record for this book is available from the British Library

Paperback ISBN: 978-1-3985-2426-2
eBook ISBN: 978-1-3985-2427-9
Audio ISBN: 978-1-3985-2428-6

This book is a work of fiction. Names, characters, places and incidents are either a product of the author's imagination or are used fictitiously. Any resemblance to actual people living or dead, events or locales is entirely coincidental.

Typeset in the UK by M Rules
Printed and Bound in the UK using 100% Renewable Electricity at CPI Group (UK) Ltd

*For the best pack a girl could hope for:
Cláudia (Preta's Mum), Kalpna (Rolo's Mum),
Jen (Cava's Mum) and Jay (Cava's Mum).*

*And for the short, shouty, stubborn and most
beloved boy that has brought us all together.*

Love you all!

Meet THE PACK

Louise Mallory and her dachshund **Niklaus** (**Klaus**) moved to the neighbourhood after her divorce. Klaus is a pandemic puppy, and Louise's introduction to the dog park community. Klaus doesn't think he's a miniature doxie – he thinks he's a slightly short Rottweiler. Louise used to be called the same in the office, but she's now stepping back from the company she founded and has inadvertently discovered that she has a talent for sleuthing.

Irina Ivanova lives in the building next door to Louise. Her accent reads like a map of Eastern Europe, but since the Ukrainian War began, she plays down the fact that she's from Moscow. She is having an on-off affair with Tim Aziz, referring to him as 'As Is' when they're on, 'As Was' when they're off. She thinks no one knows, but everyone does. Despite working in law, her superpower is internet stalking. Her Scottish terrier, **Hamish**, is Klaus's best friend and a canine trash compactor who will eat anything (and then get sick).

Ex-convict **Gav MacAdams** looks older than he is, thanks to a dozen years in prison for GBH. He has a wonky hip but can still handle himself in a fight. He told his daughter he wanted a Dobermann pinscher but she (mistakenly?) bought him an Affenpinscher, **Violet**. On a good day, Violet looks like a demented Pomeranian; on a bad day, she resembles Gru's dog from the Minions movies. Gav and Violet are usually inseparable, though Gav doesn't like to take her to the pub (she gets ugly when no one gives her beer, and uglier when they do). While part of the dog community, Gav is more comfortable drinking with his East End mates at the George and Dragon pub.

Jake Hathaway recently moved in across the canal from Louise with his grey-and-white Staffordshire terrier, **Luther**. Jake is a dark horse, with no online presence. Louise is attracted to him, but can't seem to find out much about him. He's continued to defy Irina's stalking skills, maintaining a consistent and (to Louise) frustrating air of mystery.

Ejiro is a soft-spoken gentle giant from Birmingham, who is often the voice of reason within the Pack. His smart-mouthed partner **Yasmin** is petite and energetic. They have a boxer, **Hercules**, who is ball-obsessed.

Fiona ('**Fi**') is a good friend of Louise's, and her cocker spaniel, **Nala**, is very fond of (and submissive to) Klaus. Fi is an attractive Australian redhead who doesn't take much seriously, including herself. She's a financial analyst with one of the City firms.

Claire is a journalist for the local rag, *The Chronicle*. She's Irish and has a French bulldog ('Frenchie') called **Tank**. They both have a tendency to brazen their way through stuff, even if Tank sometimes does randomly barf (it's a Frenchie thing).

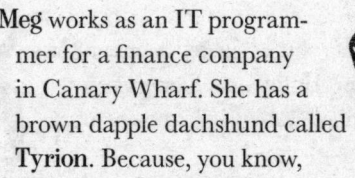

Meg works as an IT programmer for a finance company in Canary Wharf. She has a brown dapple dachshund called **Tyrion**. Because, you know, what better name would you give a feisty and clever little fiend? All dogs love Meg; she's a goldmine for treats. She's dating **Ethan** (aka 'Cat Boy'), who has a crotchety cat called Marlowe, and sometimes dog-sits her neighbour **Frances**'s long-haired daxie, **Phoebe**.

Tim Aziz and his girlfriend **Sophie** have a Jack Russell called **Loki**. Tim's the local Lothario and, perhaps because of that, Sophie dabbles (a lot) with Botox, fillers and other bits of cosmetic work. It's unclear how much Sophie knows about Irina and Tim's dalliance, but she and Irina do their best to avoid each other, a situation made difficult by how much Hamish and Loki love each other.

Paul and his partner **Ella**, the local French ex-pats, have two black Labrador retrievers: **Bark Vader** and **Jimmy Chew**. Jimmy is notorious for stealing other dogs' toys (and breaking the squeakers). Vader likes mud puddles.

Dr Indira ('Indy') Balasubramanian has a Romanian rescue called **Banjo**. Banjo looks to be part border collie, part corgi and 100 per cent street dog. He's come a long way since he was adopted, but isn't overly interested in engaging with the other dogs.

Kate Marcovici is an artist new to the area. She has two rescue beagles, **Perseus** (**Percy**) and **Andromeda** (**Andy**).

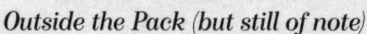

Outside the Pack (but still of note)

Andy Thompson and **Scott Williams** are detective constables with the Met Police, who met the Pack last June while investigating the murder of Phil Creasy. Andy is smart, ambitious and, despite her blowing hot and cold, fancies Irina. Scott thinks Irina's bonkers. Both, though, have a (sometimes grudging) respect for the Pack.

Gav's mates **Jono** and **Norma** own a café in Poplar and have a mastiff cross called **Rocco**. While a lot of mastiffs and American bulldogs are owned by neighbourhood thugs (and become part of the problem), Rocco has been trained and socialised, and is quite gentle.

Barbara ('Babs') Lane is Louise's very capable second-in-command at the consultancy firm she founded.

Annabel Lindford-Swayne works for one of the property management companies developing the area around Partridge Park, thanks to her father **Robert Lindford-Swayne**'s connections. She's Louise's friend as well as her go-to person when Louise has questions about the official side of Partridge Park's gentrification.

Caren 'Not Karen' Hansen and **Benny Bryce** are local hairdressers.

Mo is the owner/manager of the News-N-Booze off-licence, and a good friend of Gav's. **Zed** works at News-N-Booze as a cashier.

Angela is one of the local doggie daycare providers.

Tanzima runs the charity shop on the high street.

Dave Najafi owns Cluckin' Good Chicken, the new chicken shop where Village Vets used to be, as well as a string of cut-price perfume and shoe shops.

Dr Geoffrey Baggott is a retired entomologist and Louise's next-door neighbour.

Prologue

JONNY

Jonathan Tang looked out his window and winced. They were down there again. A pack of young men milling about outside the new chicken shop. What was it about chicken shops that seemed to attract yobs? This group didn't look like they were drinking, but The Bells was just across the street, and the men that hung out in there did. At closing time, it would kick off. Again. Two groups of idiots, one powered by booze, the other by skunk and nitrous oxide. Different ethnicities, but both fuelled by racism and xenophobia. He knew, from the words both groups had flung at him.

It was his own fault. His parents had suggested he buy a flat in Canary Wharf itself, to be closer to work. Travelling alone, late at night, could be dangerous, they'd said.

He hadn't realised at the time how right they were. Instead, lured by magnificent views and the understanding that money was being poured into the area for regeneration, he'd convinced himself that this place was a good investment. The flat was bright and spacious. The balcony might overlook a main street, but it was large, perfect for hosting cocktails on a summer evening. The estate agent had convinced him that it'd be like New York City's Meatpacking District, which had gone from a centre of drugs and prostitution to a trendy des res with boutiques, restaurants and nightclubs.

That balcony now boasted a lovely wicker set that he'd bought from John Lewis, and plants his mother had chosen; herbs that she'd claimed even he couldn't kill. She'd been wrong. In a country where it never seemed to stop raining, he'd still managed to kill the plants, not realising how much more water they still needed. He simply hadn't gone outside enough to notice. Not until they were already dead.

The magnificent city skyline seemed to be overshadowed by more and more new builds almost by the day, no longer distracting from the squat pub across the street. A Mecca for the pathetic sods who wasted their days at the betting shop down the street, it should have been demolished years ago.

And yet, it was symbolic of a neighbourhood that was still clinging on to dinge with bitter fingertips. As were the charity shops and businesses that he'd never seen a single customer in. How had they remained open? Money laundering?

For a short time, he'd convinced himself that the neighbourhood was changing. Things had seemed to be improving when the vets moved in, but they hadn't lasted long. From what he'd heard, even they were dirty, poisoning pets to make money 'saving' them. Seems one of them was even a murderer. Vets, for heaven's sake. Poisoning dogs. It was pathetic, even for this neighbourhood.

And now they'd been replaced by yet another fried chicken shop. Cluckin' Good Chicken.

Cluckin' Grim, as far as Jonny was concerned. He sighed and closed the window, shutting out the stench of weed and fried food. He hadn't understood how the owners had managed to get approval for it, when there was a chicken shop on every block; when people like him would have given anything for an independent restaurant. Sushi, or maybe tapas. Something decent, where you could go to have a nice meal to save yourself having to cook or order in.

Instead, he smelled frying chicken 24/7, even from the ninth floor. He suspected they piped their exhaust fumes into the flats' ventilation systems. Maybe to be expedient, or maybe to make people hungry enough to order from them?

The jeers from the men outside reached a crescendo, and despite himself, Jonny turned back to the window. A young woman with fair curly hair was walking her dog down the street, attracting the men's attention. He knew her; had seen her and her dog face off to the thugs more than once. As long as any confrontation was verbal, she'd be fine. That one, she could hold her own in most situations.

Most. But those men ... they wouldn't just stick to insults, would they?

And that dog. He was muscular, sure. A bulldog, of

sorts – the French variety. Ten, maybe twelve kilos, tops. He'd protect the woman to his last breath, if he had to.

But he shouldn't have to. Because one little French bulldog wouldn't do much against a half dozen full-grown men. Not if they were carrying knives, or worse. And as far as Jonny could tell, the building managers, police and council had little – if any – interest in curbing any type of antisocial behaviour. Every call, every email he sent fell on deaf ears.

Jonny sighed, slipping his jacket on and picking up his keys. He was running late and there wasn't much he could do that he hadn't already tried. Only, he couldn't stand by and watch something happen without at least trying to help.

He just couldn't.

Monday

1

YAZ

Partridge Bark

Fiona (Nala's Mum)

> Happy morning, everyone! I had a chat with Pete, the bartender at The Bells. Seems they're planning on installing CCTV this week.

Irina (Hamish's Mum)

> Bit late to catch the vet who killed Alfie's dad. What do they hope to see

> now? The squatters who took over the old print factory? Or CGC's new clients flirting – and I use that term loosely – with whoever walks past?

'I never thought I'd agree with the Tsarina,' Yaz said to her brown-and-black boxer dog as she guided him along the high street and down the ramp to the canal's towpath. It was not long past 7:30 a.m., but both she and Hercules needed a run. It was her usual morning route, but they'd been starting later as the days grew shorter, and with the clocks going back next weekend, she'd have to move from the towpath to the streets; the canal paths just weren't safe in the dark. Even with a big dog.

A shout from the far side of the water made its way past the music playing in her earbuds. Before getting a dog, the music had been amped up, but now she found herself more concerned with staying aware of the sounds, for Hercules's protection more than her own.

On the other side of the canal, the two men lounging on a picnic bench raised their cans in a salute. They were the usual tramps, and she'd seen them there every morning since she'd moved to the neighbourhood. They guzzled cheap beer and cider, and sometimes screamed comments that she couldn't understand, but they seemed by and large harmless.

'As far as you know,' her partner Ejiro had cautioned, though when it came to her, he saw muggers and rapists behind every bush. Hence his insistence on a big dog when Yaz would have preferred a pretty cocker spaniel, like Nala.

'Not that I'd trade you for anyone,' she assured Herc. He didn't appear to notice, trotting happily at her side. He looked at her and seemed to smile, jowls jiggling. *All good, Mumma.*

She raised her hand, giving the tramps a brief wave, and mused aloud, 'On the other hand, having that CCTV is better late than never. Although they should put it on the towpath. Bet you that'd work better to deter the drug dealers than removing the rubbish bins.'

That was something Tower Hamlets Council had done a few years ago. Yaz had lobbied for them to reinstate the bins, arguing that removing them only inconvenienced responsible people and would do little to deter the dealers, who used them as drop boxes. Needless to say, the council had no plans to reinstate the bins.

'Bingate,' Ejiro had laughed. In return she'd pointed to the cans, bottles, crisp packets and bags of dog poo that lined the path. Bags of dog poo, for heaven's sake. Someone had already done the messy work of picking it up, only to find nowhere to pitch it and leaving it there after all. Utterly ridiculous.

'The council is next to useless,' she added.

Hercules didn't answer, and that was what she liked about him. He was good company, and didn't judge her pre-caffeine ire.

Pre-, post- or peri-, if she was being honest. So much was irritating her these days — something the runs helped with.

With a sharp bark, Herc upped his pace, jolting her out of her reverie.

'Easy, boy,' Yaz panted, feeling the strain of the running belt around her waist as she struggled to keep up. It was exactly what Ejiro had warned her about when she'd bought the damned thing. 'He's gonna chase a goose, and you're gonna end up in the canal, Yaz.'

'At least I'm up to date on my tetanus shots,' she'd retorted. Only it wasn't funny now. She scanned ahead, but there weren't any geese or ducks that might have set Herc off. No squirrels either. 'Herc, STOP!'

Either he was pretending not to hear, or he was so focused on whatever damned thing he'd seen that he didn't care. They reached the paving stones by the bridge and Yaz's toe caught on an exposed edge. For a few moments she was airborne, flying on dog power, arms uselessly flailing.

She landed hard on the stones with a string of curses.

Herc pulled her for a foot or two, then stopped and doubled back, looking at her and nudging her shoulder with his nose. *Why'd you stop, Mumma?*

'Jesus flipping Christ, you big oaf!'

She gave herself a moment to catch her breath. Took a mental inventory and figured nothing was broken. One last deep breath, and she looked at her hands. Between them was a condom. Used, of course. She scrambled back, pulling a protesting Herc with her. Beyond the condom was a second one.

'Gross,' she muttered. 'Someone clearly had a good night. You'd think the weather would be too brisk for an al fresco shag by now, wouldn't you?'

Hercules barked at her. 'Don't you bark at your mother,' she scolded. He should at least have looked contrite. Instead, he gave her another nudge and looked over his shoulder, towards the far side of the tunnel.

'No concern about Mumma's bleeding palms, huh?' she grumbled, picking a pebble out of one of them. 'Or her shredded new Lululemon leggings.' Feeling every one of her thirty-six years, Yaz got to her feet. 'Bloody near miss. I could have fallen on those condoms.'

Stifling a gag, she brushed herself off and limped through the tunnel after Hercules. On the far side a man slouched on a bench, a filthy red cap pulled down over his eyes. On the bench beside him was a can of lager and a red box from Cluckin' Good Chicken. The blasted place had been open less than a month and their branded litter was *everywhere*.

Yaz barely got to the chicken bones before Herc did, and only because she pulled his lead to the side, frantically kicking any discarded bones within reach into the canal. 'Chicken bones? That's what you were so focused on that you made me fall? Seriously?'

She turned to the sleeping man. 'Hey arsehole, can't you at least clean up after yourself? Put your litter back into the box and bin it when you leave? Jesus, if my dog ate that bone, it could have splintered and killed him!'

The man didn't even look up.

A red rage passed over Yaz's eyes, and she took a step

forward, careful to keep her body between Herc and whatever bones might still be out of sight. 'You stinking idiot. What gives you the right to throw your crap everywhere? You got your own servants to come and clean up after you or something?'

He didn't respond. Didn't even move.

And that was the flag. *He didn't move.*

Not a twitch. Not even the gentle rise and fall of his chest.

'Oh no.'

She took a step backwards. 'No, no, no.'

A wave of nausea raced up from her belly, burning her throat. She turned and, bracing one raw palm on an equally raw knee, vomited into the canal. When the heaving stopped, she caressed Hercules's ears with a soft apology and took out her phone to call 999.

2

LOUISE

Yaz (Hercules's Mum)

> If you're awake, can you come down here – I'm at that bench just across from where the drunk guys hang out all day.

> We're up – at least I am. What's up?

> Can you meet me here? I need you.

> Of course – are you OK?

> Just hurry up. And bring a bottle of water, will you?

It wasn't like Yaz to ask for help. Not from me, and not this early in the morning. I pulled a heavy sweatshirt over my PJs, slid my feet into a pair of ballet flats and looked at my dachshund. He'd moved to my side of the bed as soon as I'd vacated it and curled into a little ball, brown eyes watching me, maybe wondering why we weren't having the usual morning cuddles.

'Sorry, my love. Time to get up.'

Klaus blinked, unconvinced.

'Our friends need us,' I said, gently lifting him into my arms and settling him over my left shoulder. 'You'll get to play with Hercules, how's that?' I slipped a knit jumper over his long body and set him down gently on the floor by the door to clip on his collar and lead. After checking that there were enough poo bags in the container hanging from the handle loop, I tucked a bottle of water under my other arm. I hadn't realised before I'd got a dog that leaving home with a dachshund was a bit of a production.

'Come on,' I urged, knowing Klaus always loved going out to see his friends. 'Shall we go see Herc? Yes! Hercules!' It was enough. Klaus scratched at the door and marched me to the lift.

We descended to the ground floor, and Klaus led the way across the street, cantering down the ramp to the towpath. He gave me a brief glance, as though to confirm that I was still keeping up; something made more difficult than usual by the lack of caffeine in my system. Then he veered to the grassy bit at the side and lifted his leg.

I'd read somewhere that small dogs wee higher than big ones. If that were true, the clear exception had to be sausage dogs. It was a feat of engineering that they didn't tip over when they weed.

Job done, he was content to follow me along the path towards the bridge. Once he saw Hercules at the far end of the tunnel, he pulled ahead with a happy bark.

Yaz was standing beside Herc, looking smaller than normal, and lost – an expression that didn't sit naturally on her. Sweat-darkened hair wrestled to escape its elastic band, and her knees were bleeding through her pale blue running tights, only intensifying her dishevelled look.

'What happened?' I asked, closing the distance between us. 'Are you all right?' I handed her the bottle of water, expecting her to use it to clean herself. Instead, she glugged a mouthful, gargled and spat it into the canal. Repeated that twice more, and guzzled the rest.

'Pick Klaus up, there's a lot of bones around.'

I did as she said, although Klaus knew better than to go for a chicken bone. He'd point them out to me, only to walk past them. That's not to say he didn't try to scavenge; discarded rice and miscellaneous meaty bits appeared to be a delicacy.

Yaz still hadn't given me any sort of explanation. 'What's going on? You should have told me you needed plasters. Or a first aid kit.'

'Too late for that,' she sighed, glancing over her shoulder. 'What I need is moral support.'

'Why?'

'Him.' She jerked her thumb in the same direction.

'Hercules?'

'No.' She stepped out of the way so I could see. 'The dead man on the bench.'

Oh no, not again...

I felt sick to my stomach, fighting down bile as well as the knee-jerk response to turn and run away. 'Are you sure?' If Yaz heard the tremor in my voice, she didn't comment on it.

'Well, the bluish skin is a giveaway. As is the lack of breathing.'

'You didn't touch him, did you?'

'Hell, no.' Yaz looked horrified at the thought. 'I'm not gonna touch a dead body.' She looked down at her trainers and then somewhere over my shoulder. A flush rose on her olive skin. 'But I did yell at him,' she admitted.

'I don't think he'd have heard you.' I looked at the man and shook my head. 'You should have called 999, not me, Yaz.'

Her brow lowered, her expression reminding me of her partner's. 'Do I look stupid to you, Louise? I did call them. The Incident Response team is supposedly on its way. But I don't want to do this by myself, and you've done it before.'

This past June, I – or rather Klaus – had found a dead body in Partridge Park. The dead man, Phil Creasy, had been someone I'd known through the dog park. He'd been working to shine a light on the dodgy vets who had been operating in the neighbourhood, and had been killed for his efforts. I was still mildly proud that our dog park pack had managed to find justice for our friend.

But I knew that even with my so-called experience, I wasn't Yaz's first port of call in a crisis. 'Ejiro is away?' I guessed.

'In New York for business. Flew out yesterday.'

'Great.' I took my phone out to text the detective we'd worked with on Phil's case. Andy Thompson hadn't quite joined the Pack, but he had been getting chummy with my Russian friend Irina, before she'd binned him for reasons she still wouldn't admit to. She wouldn't be impressed that I'd kept his number, but in this neighbourhood, having a detective's contact details could be useful. And besides, I liked him. Irina could have done far worse, and in fact, usually did.

I hit send and looked up. Yaz had her own phone out, taking photos of the scene.

'What the ...'

Her face was grim when she answered. 'When the response team comes, they'll check to make sure he's alive. Things'll move, maybe. I want to make sure it looks the way it did when I found him.'

'Why?'

'Well, you know ...'

'No.'

'Just in case ...'

'*No*, Yaz.'

'Well, we did a good job last time.'

'We're not getting involved, Yaz.'

She gave me an eyeroll and put her phone back in her pocket.

Klaus wriggled, trying to get down. I moved him to my right shoulder. He moved back to the left. Typical. It was always the left.

'But to get back to your point, I haven't touched or moved anything. With the exception of some of the chicken bones. I kicked a few of them into the canal so that Herc didn't eat them. Do you think I'll get in trouble for that?'

'From the swan sanctuary people, maybe. From the cops? I don't know, but you should tell them.' I pointed at Herc, who was squatting beside the canal, and handed her a poo bag. 'Your boy is about to add one more thing that you're going to want to remove from the scene.'

The Incident Response team arrived first, motioning us to wait away from the body. Two men moved to set up a perimeter, closing off the canal path from both directions, while the third responder just looked at the body and shook her head.

'You're the ones who found him?'

I pointed at Yaz, who nodded.

'Touch anything?'

'I kicked a few chicken bones into the canal so that my dog wouldn't eat them. There are still a few closer to the ... man ... I couldn't get close enough without Herc ...'

It was unusual to see Yaz at a loss for words, but finding a dead body would do that.

'You see anyone else?'

'Dead or alive?' Yaz asked.

'Either.'

'There were a few joggers on the path. They were alive,' she added helpfully. 'I didn't see any other dead people. I thought he was just sleeping. Or maybe a tramp, like the guys across the canal. The ones who are always drunk.' She pointed over her shoulder. 'Oh yeah, I saw them too. They're on the bench just before the bridge. They're always there. And alive. Just about.'

Yaz was babbling. I met the responder's eyes and could see the effort she was making not to roll them. 'Anyone you recognise?'

'The guys over there are regulars, I guess. But if you're asking if I recognised anyone else along the path, the answer's "No". But I didn't really take a good look.'

'Great,' the officer said, deadpan. 'Stay over there.'

A couple of uniformed PCs arrived with a roll of blue-and-white striped police tape. They nodded to the response team, who left the canal only to reappear moments later carrying poles and white canvas.

'There's no traffic on the road,' Yaz whispered.

'I imagine the cops will have stopped it. And pedestrians. Maybe especially the pedestrians. At least until the body is under the tent.'

'That's what happened last time?'

'I think that's what happens on the telly, but don't quote me on it.'

The female responder moved through the long weeds that edged the path, checking to see if there was anyone else there. Maybe someone alive. Maybe dead. Either way, I felt sick again.

'Thanks for calling me,' I said, feeling the cold October air permeate my sweatshirt.

Yaz ignored the sarcasm. 'Thanks for coming. I'd hate to be here by myself. And it's not like Herc's great moral support in these moments.' Meanwhile, Klaus was fidgeting, trying to join his friend on the path.

'Oh jeez. I'm sorry,' I said, and put him down. He didn't waste time, but instead of going to Herc, he circled a few times to find the right place, which was as close to the canal as he could get without falling in. I grabbed a bag and scooped it up. The water was relatively clear today, and I could see the chicken bones that Yaz had kicked in, along with a rusted Boris bike and what looked to be a shopping trolley further out.

'Here comes the cavalry,' Yaz said, pointing at a small cadre of men in white paper bunny suits, with masks, gloves and booties over their shoes. 'You think they're the CSIs?'

'SOCOs,' I corrected automatically. 'Scene of crime officers. CSIs are American, but I think they're the Murder Investigation Team.'

'How do you know?'

'Because I'm pretty sure the tall bunny man is Andy Thompson, and the stocky one in the back is Scott Williams.'

'Andy Thompson, as in DC Andy, the Tsarina's ... ah ... special friend?' She used her fingers to air quote the last words.

It'd be pointless to ask Yaz to stop calling Irina 'Tsarina'. To be honest, the nickname wasn't entirely unjustified: it wasn't always easy to be Irina's friend. What Irina lacked in self-awareness, she made up for in arrogance and entitlement. Added to that, her on-off relationship with local Lothario Tim Aziz wasn't quite as discreet as she thought, and put the Pack in an awkward position, as we genuinely liked Tim's girlfriend, Sophie. Still, Irina always had my back when I needed her. I felt the need to stick up for her.

'Former special friend. I don't think they've seen each other recently.' I hoped Yaz wouldn't ask how I knew that.

'Why? She back on with Loki's dad? Sophie will love that.'

I shrugged.

'He's cute – the detective that is, not Tim. It's pretty convenient having a cop that'll listen to you around here. Why'd she dump him?'

That was the million-dollar question. 'Gotta ask *her* that.'

Yaz made a *pffft* sound. 'Like she'd tell me.'

'If it makes you feel better, she hasn't told me either.'

Yaz lowered her sunglasses and peered over the top at me. 'Right. Which means she did something crack-brained and was too embarrassed to admit it. Then managed to reframe it in her own mind so that she was some sort of victim?'

Anything was possible, but that assessment felt pretty spot on. Irina's relationship with the truth was pretty fluid; a convenient trait, I supposed, for someone who worked in law.

'I suppose we could always ask Detective Andy,' Yaz mused, mischief peppering her voice.

'Somehow I don't see him ringing us up to spill the deets on a relationship that never really got off the ground,' I said. 'I mean, I got along with him reasonably well when we were looking into Phil's death last June, but it wasn't like we became friends.'

'No? Well, here's your second chance.' She jerked her head towards the bunny men, who'd paused to speak to the response team. The female responder pointed at us, and I could distinctly hear Williams's groan. 'Jesus Christ, not them again.'

Partridge Bark

Fiona (Nala's Mum)

> Looks like the cops closed off the canal path. Anyone know what's going on?

Paul (Bark Vader and Jimmy Chew's Dad)

> Oh, really? I might wander down and have a look.

Two of the bunny men moved off in either direction along the canal. 'I'm guessing they want to check ways in and out?' Any vestiges of Yaz's shell shock had given way to her natural curiosity.

'I guess so.'

Another produced a small jar of aluminium powder and set to dusting the handrails along the entrance to the towpath. 'Anything he gets from there will be a more accurate reflection of who lives around here than the last census,' I noted to Yaz.

The tall bunny man stood next to the body, looking in either direction along the path, and across it, noting the block of flats on the other side of the canal. A photographer was already at work, capturing the scene.

'Wonder what they're waiting for,' Yaz said, tapping her foot.

The detective caught my eye and held up a single finger, asking for a few moments to do, well, whatever he was doing. Finally, he approached us.

'Morning, Detective Thompson,' I said.

'Ms Mallory.' He nodded to me, then to Yaz. 'Ms Dogan. Why am I not surprised to see you?'

I cleared my throat while Yaz jumped straight in with, 'If your mates are going to wander up and down the canal to see if someone dropped anything in a rubbish bin, they'll have a long way to go. Tower Hamlets Council – in their infinite wisdom – got rid of the bins on the canals years ago. Though based on the trash thrown about, even where it is near a rare bin, people round here seem happy enough to throw their litter on the ground for the rats and dogs to find.'

Andy sighed.

'But there *is* a dog poo bin when you get closer to Partridge Park,' she continued, waving the bag in her hand. 'It's not too hard to find – someone labelled it "Poo Tin" with a picture of Mad Vlad. You think it was your friend Irina?'

Andy produced a small notebook. 'We'll check that out, thank you, Ms Dogan.'

'Who's that with Williams?' I couldn't resist asking.

'Harriman, the CCTV officer.'

'There's CCTV around here?' Yaz asked.

It was a good point; CCTV on the street was rare enough in this part of town and – as far as I knew – non-existent along the waterways. 'Hopefully they'll be able to find something.'

'My money's on death by greasy chicken bone.' A sanctimonious expression settled across Yaz's face. 'Someone should have told him that fried food could kill him.'

3

ANDY

Bright October sunlight sparkled off the canal. Standing beside the dead man, Andy Thompson squinted, surveying the scene. As far as he could tell, there were three logical entry points: the canal towpath stretching in either direction, and a nearby staircase. One of the other officers would dust any handrails for prints, as well as the bench the man was sitting on, just in case it turned out that the situation wasn't what it initially appeared to be. The last thing the Met needed was to be caught short if things took a turn.

The dachshund barked and, with one last look at the scene, he approached the two women waiting for him on the path. No point trying to put it off any longer. Not to be left out, the brown-and-black boxer gave a woof as he arrived that, compared with the sausage dog, sounded somehow half-hearted. Andy allowed a few moments for the women to get their dogs under control, and to give Yaz a chance to finish her poo bin/'Poo Tin' spiel, before he got down to business. 'So. You've found another body, Ms Mallory? Take me through it.'

'You can call me Louise,' she said. Her hair was in a messy plait, and she wore a heavy black sweatshirt over what looked like teal pyjamas. Printed with sausage dogs, trophies and the words 'The Wiener Takes It All'. As far as he could tell, there was something particular about sausage dog owners; they seemed to have everything branded with their dog's breed.

He nodded, although he was sure she knew that he had to keep everything official. 'Tell me what happened.'

She gestured to the shorter, smart-mouthed woman with the boxer. 'Yaz was the one to find him.' Her voice held a wry tone when she added. 'She called me for moral support.'

'Ms Dogan?'

'Actually, Hercules found him.' Yaz pointed to the boxer. 'Wasn't me. We were out for a morning run. We reached the brick area under the bridge when he saw something that interested him. He sped up and I tripped. Came damn close to falling face first onto a couple of used condoms.'

Andy swallowed, not sure whether to laugh or not. Used condoms under bridges were common enough, but falling on them wasn't high on his to-do list. 'We'll bag them.' He looked at her raw hands and knees. 'We'll need a blood sample, too. To exclude you, if we find your blood there.'

Her canny eyes narrowed; she knew that they were treating this death as suspicious.

'Who did you see?' he continued.

'Stars, mate. I saw stars.'

Louise elbowed her friend, and Yaz sobered. 'As I told the

woman responder, I saw a few joggers, and the drunks on the other side of the canal, before the bridge. They're always there. I thought the dead guy was one of them. You know, had a bit too much lager and was sleeping it off. He had nice clothes though, didn't he, Lou? Except for that ratty cap.'

Andy jotted her observation down. 'Did you recognise him?'

'Nooo,' Yaz said, but there was an uncertain tone in her voice. 'Can I see him again?'

'I'd rather you didn't contaminate the scene, Ms Dogan.' *Any more than it must already be contaminated.* 'Hold on a sec.' He retreated under the tent that had been set up to protect the body, coming back a few minutes later to show her a photo on his phone. Yaz handed the green poo bag she was holding to Louise so that she could take the device. 'Don't worry, it's not evidence this time.'

Andy was grateful for the mask he wore; it hid his smile. The first time he'd met Yaz Dogan, she'd handed him a poo bag containing a mobile phone she'd found in the dog park near their crime scene. It had been a lucky break in the case.

'Is his mobile phone on him?'

'You know I can't—'

Yaz didn't look up from the image on Andy's phone. 'I didn't see one beside him. Didn't look like there was a bulge in his front pockets, but I guess some people keep their phones in their back pockets still. Just to make it easy for the pickpockets.'

Andy didn't respond, allowing her to fill the pause. She didn't let him down, using her fingers to zoom in a little more and tilting her head. 'If it were me, I'd have chucked it as far into the canal as I could. Ejiro dropped a phone into the ... ah ... sink. We chucked it into a bag of rice, 'cos that's what you're supposed to do, right? But it was deader than dead. Anyway, it's the ratty cap, isn't it?'

'What about it?'

'It's wrong. He's got nice trousers, nice shoes. The jacket is casual, but I'd bet it's Reiss.' She slanted a glance at Andy. 'Ejiro has one like it. But not the ratty cap.'

'Yes,' he said, only partly in response. He remembered Yaz's partner, a tall Black man who worked in the City. Andy got the sense that Ejiro, like his dog, was a gentle giant. With a sensible head on his shoulders and the dress sense of a GQ model. The last word anyone would use to describe Ejiro was 'ratty'.

Keeping the sausage dog on a short lead, Louise peered over Yaz's shoulder at the phone. 'Zoom in.'

Yaz complied, and then grunted to herself.

'You know him?' Andy asked.

The women exchanged a look. 'Well, yes and no ... I think.' Yaz hesitated.

'Ms Dogan?' Andy asked, feeling a rush of optimism. It couldn't be that easy, could it?

'I know the face. Seen him around, although I don't think I've ever spoken to him.'

'Not with the cap,' Louise agreed. They exchanged a bemused look. 'It can't be him, can it? Fedora never struck me as the sort who'd eat Cluckin' Good anything with his fingers on a park bench.'

'Secret life?' Yaz offered.

'Fedora?' Andy asked.

Louise answered, 'He doesn't wear a cap, even in the summer. Come autumn, he's got a grey fedora that he wears. At least during the week when he's going to work. Kind of retro. Bogart-like.'

Andy understood. 'Hence the nickname.'

'I struggle to remember most humans' names,' she admitted.

'You remember the dogs' though,' Yaz said.

'Yeah, them I remember, but he didn't have a dog.' Louise turned back to Andy. 'I don't know his real name, sorry.' She offered a half shrug. 'Can't even tell you where he lives, although I'm pretty sure he's local.'

'Where have you seen him?'

'The café in the park, The Nest, maybe? Maybe just on the street. I don't know.'

'That's fine. We'll identify him. Thanks for your time, ladies. We'll need you to come to Lambeth to give your official statement, Ms Dogan. And to provide a blood sample so we can rule you out.'

He looked at Louise, whose face had gone pale. 'Are you all right?'

'Just a bit of déjà vu, Detective.'

'Yeah, well ... Please don't take this the wrong way, but leave it to us, we know what we're doing.' The words seemed hollow even to his ears, and from their expressions, he could tell that Louise and Yaz didn't believe him either.

'Ms Mallory – Louise. Trust me, we'll do whatever we can to find out what happened to your ... ah ... Fedora.'

'Before it happens to someone else,' Yaz muttered as he walked away.

4

LOUISE

Barbara Lane

> Hey Babs, running a little late for our 9am catch up. Had a bit of a local situation here this morning.

> Dare I ask?

Yaz headed home in the opposite direction, so I was alone with Klaus when he let out a loud warning bark ... about half a second before I crashed into an impossibly wide and solid chest.

'Morning, Lou.'

I looked up into dark blue eyes and a face that looked like a forty-ish Hugh Jackman. My mouth went dry, and my brain, blank.

'Hey, Jake.' I took a step back and gathered my thoughts.

Wrong move: my neighbour Jake Hathaway was wearing a black leather jacket over a pair of jeans. He had a rucksack slung over one shoulder and looked like the textbook description of 'rugged'.

'You're looking pale – you okay?'

I wasn't, but I was still trying to process the morning's events and wasn't yet ready to talk about it. Even to Jake.

Klaus emitted a bark that this time sounded more like a disgruntled *whoof*. I looked down, realising that there was no sign of Jake's grey-and-white Staffordshire terrier, Luther. Klaus must have been disappointed not to see his friend.

In the few months since moving to the neighbourhood, Jake had rarely been out and about without Luther, which meant that this time 'out and about' was more likely to be 'out of town'.

'Off anywhere interesting?' I asked.

'I wish.' He leaned down and ruffled Klaus's ears. 'Just heading out of town for the day, but should be back later. Got a dog walker to stop by and see to Luther at lunchtime.' He'd headed my next question off at the pass. He was good at that; in the four or so months since I'd met him, the extent of what I knew of the man could fit on the back of a postcard.

Which is part of the fascination, isn't it? a sly part of my brain asked.
Is it more than that?
Do I want it to be more than that?
'What about you? Guessing you're not heading to the office today?' Jake said, with an amused look. I followed his gaze and felt a furious blush march up my cheeks. He looked like Wolverine, while in my sausage dog PJs I looked like a brunette Bridget Jones. With a dog.

And while I could have spun my leggings into 'Dog Park Chic', the 'Wiener Takes It All' jammies were a step too far.

'Mutt-wear Mondays,' I said, issuing a silent apology to Klaus. 'It's the new work-from-home fashion trend on TikTok. Trying to lighten the start of the working week.'

As far as I knew – and my cyber-sleuth friend Irina had checked – Jake had no social media presence. In fact, no online presence at all. In theory, I could have probably gotten away with worse, had I wanted to.

His half smile bordered on a smirk. Clearly there was some way to go between 'in theory' and 'in reality'. At least he wasn't going to call out my lie. 'Looks comfy.'

'It is. Good luck with the trip. See you tomorrow?'

'The usual Tuesday movie night? Yeah. You're hosting this week.' He took a few steps away, only to pause and look at me over his shoulder. 'The jim-jams are cute, but don't expect me to follow that fad.'

'Right.' I stared after him, not sure whether to picture him in PJs with Staffies on them.

Or not.

'And try not to get yourself into any mischief,' he added.

I felt my shoulders deflate, realising that warning had come about two hours too late.

5

ANDY

The afternoon was an exercise in futility. While Williams was walking the streets with Harriman, Andy joined a team of uniforms knocking on doors with scant luck. Strictly speaking, it wasn't his job, and he brushed aside the niggling inner voice that asked him what – or who – he thought he'd find.

While some people were working from home, far more weren't in. Or weren't opening their door to a couple of cops.

Those that did displayed a cursory curiosity. *What did I hear last night? Does this have anything to do with what's going on at the canal? What was it? Murder?*

The conversations digressed from there. After a general tirade about crime in the neighbourhood, there were the usual complaints. The loud music blaring from flat 501, partying until two in the morning. Again. Didn't they know people had to work the next day?

The young men smoking weed and sucking on nitrous oxide balloons who couldn't be bothered to clean up after themselves. There was a sea of those canisters around the door this morning.

That couple the next building over who were always rowing; he'd banged her head against the door to the building. Broken the glass – the brute should be arrested!

But no one had seen or heard a thing from across the canal. He glanced at his watch; the team would be regrouping to share what they had learned soon. Another team would continue with the door-to-doors later, after people had come home.

Andy decided he'd come back afterwards, on his own. Get a better idea of what the scene looked like after dark. Where the lights were. What sort of people congregated where.

This was a strange neighbourhood. You had the old school East Enders, with an innate disdain for the police. They preferred to sort things out themselves. In their own way.

Then there were the professionals, people like Louise and Yaz, who moved to the area due to its proximity to Canary Wharf and good links to the City.

The third distinct group, as Andy saw it, was the large Southeast Asian population, who had as little to do with the other two as possible.

On a good day there was an uneasy détente between the groups. On a bad day there were clashes, either within a group, or between them.

Andy took a deep breath, stepping out onto the street. A spicy smell tickled his nose, and his stomach rumbled, reminded him that he hadn't eaten since the sausage roll he'd grabbed on the way to the scene.

He headed towards the high street and the DLR. He'd have to switch to the Tube to get to Lambeth in time for the update. He couldn't help a quick glance at the old upholstery factory that had been converted into flats, in equal parts hoping and not hoping that he'd see her.

That batshit crazy Russian lunatic.

Irina.

6

LOUISE

Partridge Bark

Yaz (Hercules's Mum)

Happy morning. Guess what I found this morning?

Paul (Bark Vader and Jimmy Chew's Dad)

A replacement for @Ejiro? I mean, the cat is away, no?

Fiona (Nala's Mum)

Uh oh. Did someone leave more raw meat out for the foxes and rats?

> Wait for it ...

Fiona (Nala's Mum)

Oh nooo ... Not another dead body?

Paul (Bark Vader and Jimmy Chew's Dad)

I saw the police along the canal this morning. Do we know who it is?

Yaz (Hercules's Mum)

I think it's the cat-in-the-hat. The Asian (maybe Chinese?) guy who wears a fedora in the winter? Does anyone know his name?

Fiona (Nala's Mum)

> OMG – is that who died? The hat was weird but he seemed nice. What happened?

Yaz (Hercules's Mum)

> I don't know. Yet.

Paul (Bark Vader and Jimmy Chew's Dad)

> They moved the body about an hour ago, but the tent's still there. And it looks like there are divers checking the canal.

Irina (Hamish's Mum)

> I hope they've had their tetanus shots.

'Hello, lovely,' Barbara Lane, my second-in-command, office manager and friend said, placing a coffee in front of me. I looked up, startled, and put my phone face down on the table.

'Hey, Babs,' I said, my calm voice masking my surprise. 'Klaus is losing his touch; he usually lets me know when someone comes close.' I looked down at the black-and-tan ball of fur curled on my lap. Big brown eyes blinked at me, as if to say, *I will always let you know if a stranger comes close. Babs isn't a stranger. Hence no danger.*

'Maybe he was asleep?'

Klaus offered Babs a belated bark of greeting, tail wagging.

'Sure.' I pushed a chair out with my foot. 'What brings you to East London?' *What's important enough to hike all the way over here when a phone chat would do?*

'Saw an article online about a dead body found by a couple of dog walkers this morning. You okay?'

I blinked. *That was fast.* 'The *Chronicle*?'

'Yes, but not with Claire's byline. I figured, dog walkers.' She shrugged and sat down opposite me. 'They didn't mention names, but I knew you'd be involved somehow. Was it you again?'

'Not this time. You could have called instead of hunting me down at The Nest.'

She shrugged again. 'Figured you'd be here or at home. This was on the way.'

'From Wimbledon?' I made a point of closing the laptop that was open in front of me and pushed it an inch or two towards her. 'Please don't take this the wrong way, but why are you really here?'

Babs stared at a point over my shoulder. Her dark hair was perfectly styled in loose curls around her face and shoulders, her make-up done, her blazer-and-jeans combo carefully constructed. On anyone else that wouldn't have been worth noting, but Babs was more a jeans-and-jumper sort of woman, her casual look hiding a razor-sharp mind. She'd become a valued friend as well as my right hand at work. Whatever was bothering her, she'd put thought into her appearance before trekking east to track me down at my local dog park café.

When she hesitated, I went on, 'If you're still worried about how Mandy's dealing with the death of her boyfriend, she's seeing a therapist.'

'I know. And I know you're paying for it yourself, not out of the company funds.'

'So?' Klaus readjusted himself and I began to feel like some sort of modern Goldfinger, only I was female, Klaus wasn't a cat, I had a full head of hair and I did my best not to be evil.

Okay, so maybe not Goldfinger, after all.

'Don't make me ask a third time, Babs.'

'Right. I need to know something, and I didn't feel comfortable talking about this on a call, so . . .' She offered an awkward shrug.

Need to know, rather than, *I need to tell you something.* I breathed out, feeling at least a little confident that she wasn't about to quit. 'Go ahead.'

'There are two different investors eyeing up the company. You've been stepping back for a while. I need to know if you're thinking of selling up.'

And there it was.

'Babs, I started the company with two friends and a good methodology. We built a solid model around it and

I'm glad I was able to buy them out when I did. I'm stepping back because you're capable and this is part of your professional development. That doesn't mean I'm putting myself out to pasture.'

'You haven't answered my question, Lou.'

'I've already turned both down, Babs. Turned down others as well. I'm not going to sell the company off only to have a bigger one run it, and my people, into the ground.' I softened my tone. 'I can't say I won't ever sell, but right now it's doing well as it is.'

Babs leaned forward, her elbows on the table. 'I'm not just speaking for me, Lou. No one wants to be sucked into a Deloitte or IBM Borg. That's not what we're about.'

I tilted my head to the side, my hands once again stroking Klaus's soft fur. 'Talk to me, Babs.'

'We're about change. With a capital "C". We're about making a difference. You can't do that in the big firms – you need to buck the system to get anything done there. But you've brought together a bunch of people, most of whom didn't know their arse from a hole in the wall at the beginning. You've taught them what to do, how to act. You've devised a good methodology, sure, but also the right structures to train everyone on it. On how to get things done. Not by a book, but in the real world. And you've stood by us, building bridges and removing obstacles in your own crazy-arse way.'

As the founder and chief exec of my boutique business change and transformation consultancy, that was my job, as far as I was concerned. We weren't big, but we were effective, mostly because we practised what we preached.

After all, it'd be hard to pitch 'being about people' if we didn't take care of our own. 'Okay ...?'

'I don't want to lose that, Lou. The team doesn't want to.'

I felt choked up, and nodded my head. 'I can't promise not to sell the company,' I repeated. 'But I will promise you this, Babs: if and when I do, you will be involved, and you will have your say.' I leaned back. 'And you'll be able to say no if you don't think the culture fit is right.'

Babs stared into my eyes, as if looking for any hint of duplicity, but there was none. I meant what I said. I'd worked too hard to build my company and my team to sell them down the river.

'Good,' she finally replied, her expression softening, relief evident in her voice. 'Thank you, Lou, I appreciate that. We all do.'

Joe the barista approached, placing a steaming cup of coffee in front of Babs. She waited until he left before leaning forward. 'But while I have you in front of me, we've been approached by one of the NHS's integrated care partnerships. How do you feel about wading in to help our beloved National Health Service avert disaster?'

'Which one and why?'

'Let's hold off on the "who" for now. But I can say we've got a section of the NHS whose area is struggling with winter pressures all year long.'

'That's pretty much every section, as far as I can tell, Babs.'

She nodded. 'It's in all the papers – the long waits for ambulances because most of them are parked outside the hospitals, waiting to get people admitted. Why? No beds. Why? Problems with discharging people who are "medically fit for discharge".'

'I suspect that's rather a simplistic summary. There are staffing issues – training and recruitment, as well as retention, strikes and far too many years of insufficient funding.'

'True enough. But here we have one area whose commissioning group is willing to prise open the door for us and let us help them crack the discharge nut.'

'We do change and transformation, not so much business process reengineering,' I mused. 'But, we do have people who can handle it.'

'We do.'

'So, here's the big question: the NHS well is perpetually dry. Has been for years. Can they afford us? Our rates?'

'Well, they didn't flinch. They're looking at a try-and-buy sort of thing, though. Initial phase is analysis, followed by a proposal for what to do next. We have the option of moving out after the analysis if it doesn't feel like a good fit. What do you think?'

New business was a good thing, but she didn't need to come to me for the decision. How much longer would she be willing to be a CEO-in-waiting?

'If you're happy, I'm happy.'

'Good, because, if I remember correctly, you did some work with the NHS a few years ago. If you have the time, can you share oversight of the project?' Babs offered a wry smile. 'If you're not too busy solving crimes, that is?'

7

ANDY

'To summarise: Mr Atty, after popping a couple of MDMA pills at an illegal rave, detoured to the water fountain in the Poplar Recreation Park,' Detective Chief Superintendent Grieves said. Unlike the incident rooms shown on TV, there was no murder-board mind map taking up a wall. With ten or more ongoing cases at any time, there just wasn't enough space. Instead, there was a temperamental digital whiteboard hooked up to a printer so decrepit that only when the right stars were aligned would it deign to spit out a copy of whatever was written on the board. Modern technology at its finest.

'Coordination inhibited, or maybe because he thought it was funny, Mr Atty drank from the dog water bowl. Unhygienic for sure, but someone had spiked the water bowl with antifreeze. Presumably to poison the dogs. Not the first time that bowl's been poisoned, so unlikely he was the target.'

'Give me ten minutes with that wee shite in a dark alley,' Nicole Saren muttered.

'Something to say, Flo Jo?'

'Yeah, Sir,' Nic said, ignoring the nickname. Grieves called every family liaison officer 'Flo Jo', regardless of their name or gender, and to the despair of Human Resources. 'What sort of person does that? Poison a dog's water bowl? That's just sick.'

Andy knew that Irina, Louise, Yaz and their dog community would have stronger words to describe that person and made a mental note to warn them to keep their dogs away from the bowl.

Grieves frowned, making his fleshy cleft chin waggle in a way that couldn't be unseen. He leaned a shoulder against the whiteboard, confident that the half-dead markers wouldn't transfer to his dark jumper. 'Won't disagree with you there. But the poisoner is part of someone else's investigation. We have enough of our own. Right. We can close the file on Mr Atty. What do we have on the man found this morning on the canal bench? Let's go through the 5WH.' He banged the whiteboard with his free hand, picking up a battered touch-sensitive marker with the other.

Grieves was the sort who thought better with a marker in his hand, though it was a pity his handwriting was so bad that the scribbles looked like chicken scratches.

Sitting beside Andy, Nic had already written the 5WH questions on her tablet: Who, What, Why, When, Where and How. Taking notes just in case the digital whiteboard let them down. Again.

Andy had loaded paper into the printer half of the contraption this morning, but he'd take a photo of the board once they were done with the update. Just in case Nic missed anything. Beside the whiteboard was another screen, upon which Williams, in charge of evidence, and the only one who had any luck with the tech in the room, beamed up a picture of the man taken by the photography officer.

'Who,' Grieves said, writing the word with two branches coming out of it. 'Thompson, what do we have? Victim's name? Suspects?'

'Neither, guv, but we're still working on that. Door-to-doors are ongoing. We do know he's a local, found on the bench by a couple of dog walkers.' Andy ignored the groans about more dogs, following Mr Atty's death by poisoned dog bowl. 'We estimate he's approximately thirty-five years of age, of Asian descent. We don't have a name yet – there was no ID and no phone on him, and his fingerprints aren't in the system, although he is recognised in the area by sight. We're checking with Missing Persons to see if anyone's logged him as AWOL. The coroner's scheduled to do the autopsy tomorrow. Then we can narrow the search a bit.'

Grieves put question marks against the 'Who' and wrote 'What' below it on the board. 'Evidence Officer?'

Williams cleared his throat. 'The victim was posed on a bench beside the canal. Estimated time of death between 10 p.m. and 1 a.m. last night. There was an empty box of chicken wings from a new place, Cluckin' Good Chicken, at his feet. Bones discarded all around him.'

'Death by chicken?'

'More complicated than that, guv. There were three sets of prints on the box. His were there, but I don't think he was the one who brought the chicken.'

'Why?'

'The prints weren't where they would logically be if you bought a box of wings, carried them to the park, then ate them. I mean, they were for the second set – we're still running those. My guess is that the second set would be the person who brought and ate the chicken. The vic's prints . . . no.'

Grieves tilted his head. He was pretty senior to be standing at the front of this particular room, but there were some investigations, or rather some areas, that he preferred to run hands-on, and 'interesting' cases on or near certain stretches of the canal, like Mr Atty and the man on the bench, met the criteria. There was plenty of speculation as to why Grieves was so keen, but so far no one had cracked the code. While it could be irritating, on balance, it was good for the team. You knew where you stood with Grieves. Could tell his mood from the complexion of his skin and act accordingly. And you knew he'd have your back. Mostly.

'What aren't you sharing?' Nic asked.

Williams smiled and moved to the front of the room, looking like a rugby prop masquerading as a professor. 'You eat chicken, you get greasy fingers, right?'

'Unless you eat it with a knife and fork,' Nic said. At the raucous laughter, she grinned. 'Dated a posh boy once or twice.'

'What were you, the bit o' rough, Nic?' There were a few wolf whistles.

'Enough of that.' Grieves pointed at the offenders, then at Williams. 'Go on.'

Williams waggled his fingers. 'Greasy mitts. Even if you've got a pile of serviettes. Those greasy fingers give you nice finger marks. Your hands are dry – even for Nic's posh boys that moisturise – those prints aren't as clean. The vic's prints are there, but not as distinct. He didn't eat the wings.'

'And the third set?'

'My money is on whoever served the chicken. Should wear gloves if you're serving food, but ...' His big shoulders rose and fell. 'Some places, even new ones, aren't so interested in food hygiene. Might want to get someone to go visit this Cluckin' Good Chicken, guv.'

'What? You hungry already? Up for a second lunch?' Nic teased.

Grieves stepped in before the banter sank any lower. 'Continue.'

'Blood was found about four metres from the body, but the blood test indicates female, consistent with the story of the woman who found him. Seems she tripped and fell on the bricks.'

Andy smiled, certain that Yaz Dogan would have a smart comeback to that.

'The woman will be coming in tomorrow to give us a sample.'

'Is she a suspect?'

'Doubt it, guv,' Williams said. 'Met her on the Phil Creasy case last year. I don't get a sense that she'd have done it, but we'll check her alibi, regardless.'

Andy hoped that was a task for Williams. Yaz had said

that she'd been sexting her partner in New York and he had no desire to see those messages.

'We'll check with the concierge in her building, confirm that Ms Dogan finished her dog's evening walk by nine and didn't leave until seven-ish the next morning. Also . . .' Williams cleared his throat. 'We found two condoms at the scene.'

Nic made a face. 'With a dead body a few feet away? How romantic.'

'Not sure when they were, ah, left there.'

'DNA? Was our man out there for a bit of horizo— . . . vertical Hokey Cokey? Then a bit of post-coital, post-murder chicken?'

'Throw the dog a bone?' someone muttered.

Williams continued as if he hadn't heard. 'Anything's possible, guv. We put a rush on the DNA testing, but it'll take a couple of days for any details. Forensics, caveating that this is only their initial results, tell me that the first condom was a bit of man-on-man action. The second condom – brace yourselves – is man on two different women.'

'At the same time?' Nic made a gagging sound. 'Nice neighbourhood.'

'Mobile phone?' Grieves asked.

'Not sure if it's his or not, but one was found midway across the canal. Waterlogged. The techs are seeing what they can do.'

'Anything else?'

'Nearest rubbish bins are about half a mile away in one direction, quarter mile in the other, near Partridge Park. We've searched them, but so far no weapon, though we did recover a fair amount of Molly and E,' Williams said, confirming Yaz's theory about how the drug dealers used the rubbish bins. 'We've also cleaned out the dog poo bin in Partridge. The good news is that it looks like everything was bagged.'

'The bad news?'

'The bad news is that the poor sods in Forensics still have to go through all of it.'

Better them than me, Andy thought.

'Finger marks?'

'Half the neighbourhood, if I had to guess. Running what we have, but you're looking at a very public place.'

'Footprints?'

'Hasn't rained in four days. The towpath is mostly packed dirt, with some bits of brickwork. We got nothing there.'

'CCTV?' Grieves asked, his tone making his frustration clear.

'Some. More coming in. Not had the time to go through anything yet.'

'Anything else, Williams?'

Williams took a deep breath. 'Locals – and by that, I mean the women who found him – recognised him by face as someone in the neighbourhood. Thompson's following that up, but they claim that the cap he was wearing wasn't his style. That if he wore a hat, he went old school and wore a fedora.' Williams mimed a snap-brimmed hat. 'À la Sinatra. So we're looking at that cap and why it was left on him. It's been dusted for prints and sent down to Forensics to see where the good Doctor Locard will lead us.' He assumed the posture of a university professor again. 'Wherein the perpetrator of a crime will bring something into the crime scene and leave with something from it,' he explained, although everyone in the room was familiar with Locard's Exchange Principle.

'Good. Anything else?'

'You'll be the first to know.'

'Right. So, the when. You said between ten and one last night. How about the why?'

Grieves looked out at a room of blank faces.

'It's still day one, guv,' Andy said, even though he knew that the clock was ticking and the first twenty-four hours were critically important.

Grieves didn't need to remind him, and just nodded. 'All right. And the how?'

'None of the victim's blood's at the scene, but bruising at the neck suggests manual strangulation,' Williams said.

'So, someone murdered our well-dressed man and posed him with chicken bones all around him, maybe swapping out his smart hat for a cap. Why? Do we know what happened to the fedora?'

'Hasn't been found yet, guv. Although, a well-dressed man. That's your type, isn't it, Nic?'

Nic crossed her arms and leaned back in her seat. 'If I was going to kill someone, they'd never be found, Williams. Even if that someone was you.' She uncrossed her arms and nodded to herself. 'But someone wanted us to find him. Wanted us to connect him to the chicken shop. Correct me if I'm wrong, guv, but the question we need to focus on is who gains from this. That'll lead us in a straight line to why they went through all this crap in the first place.'

8

LOUISE

Partridge Bark

Fiona (Nala's Mum)

The cops are back.

> Last I checked the uniformed guys hadn't left. The canal path is still closed.

Fiona (Nala's Mum)

Yep, they're still there. But the detective is back on the scene. @**Irina's** friend

> from last time, by the looks of it. And someone said they're going door to door, asking questions. Anyone know who or what they're after?

Paul (Bark Vader and Jimmy Chew's Dad)

> I imagine whoever killed the man on the bench …

'Paul's insights are as useful as always,' I said, putting down the phone. 'I'll bet he spent the day sitting at one of The Bells's picnic tables with a cup of coffee and a pair of binoculars pointed at the crime scene. Pity that it gets dark so early these days.' Klaus appeared to be ignoring me, sitting on the end of the sofa, his attention on the door to my flat.

The lift bell dinged and he trotted down the ramp, his deep bark warning the building of stranger danger. He doubled back from hallway to kitchen, scoffed down the last couple of kibbles in his bowl, and returned to the hall.

It was the bowl thing that told me who was at the door.

It opened to reveal Hamish, Irina's Scottish terrier, who joined in Klaus's bark-pocalypse while Irina tried to unhook his lead, his nails scratching on the floors and providing an accompanying staccato melody. Within moments, two small black furballs were tussling their way into my living room, before Hamish extricated himself from Klaus to investigate the bowl situation, in case his best furry friend had been foolish enough to leave any food lying around.

Unlikely. Klaus had learned his lesson years ago. As a pup he'd hidden any nice treats in his crate, where they'd stayed until the first time Hamish had visited. Hamish had jumped in and helped himself. Pooped on the floor to make more room, then pretty much cleaned out Klaus's crate. Since then, the only edible thing that Klaus left lying around was a yak milk chew or a bit of horn. He loved Hammy, but not enough to give up his dinner. Or his treats.

'Some guy standing outside of CGC called Hammy "Satan" just now.'

At the sound of his name, Hamish looked up, one ear standing straight, the other curled over. His pink tongue lolled out the side of his mouth. It was hard to think of anyone considering this sweet little thing evil. A canine trash compactor, yes. A shaggy furball that could pass for a bear cub? Maybe. But Satan?

'Are you sure they weren't talking about you?' I asked.

Irina raised one shoulder in a disinterested half shrug and moved to the wine rack in my kitchen, uncorking a bottle of Malbec and pouring herself a glass. Her fair hair was swept up in its usual messy bun, but her clothing – dark teal Alo running tights with a matching top – was a far cry from her sharp office suits. She must have gone home to change clothes and pick up Hammy before coming over.

She glanced at me, and poured a second glass. 'Anything's possible.'

My phone buzzed and I snuck a glance at it.

Yaz (Hercules's Mum)

> I took another look at the pics I took of Fedora this morning. Lou, I didn't see it then, but it looks like there's a bit of blue around his neck.

> Blue? Like the camera filter?

> Blue, like the camera filter saw bruising when I didn't. Do you think I should tell the police?

> Probably. But my money is that they'll already know or that it'll come up as part of the postmortem exam. But I'm serious, Yaz. Let's leave this with them. It's their job, not ours.

Face taut under her still-perfect make-up, Irina gently pushed Hammy away to sit beside me, facing out onto the balcony.

'Your neighbour isn't home yet?'

'Which one?'

'The fit one that friend-zoned you.'

'Jake hasn't friend-zoned me.'

'Are you shagging?'

'No.'

'Snogging?'

I wasn't enjoying this game. 'No.'

'There you go. You're friend-zoned.'

There was no point in defending myself by telling her that he'd seen me in my pyjamas. Given that they were the wiener ones instead of a pretty pair from Victoria's Secret, she'd have her case in point. 'I saw him earlier,' I said instead.

'Saw him earlier, or *saw* him earlier?'

It was my turn to shrug; we both knew that she had zero interest in Jake Hathaway's comings and goings. I picked up my glass and took a small sip, waiting for the interrogation to end.

'I heard you and Yaz found a body this morning.'

'Yes, councillor.'

'Any idea who it is?'

There was no sign that she heard the sarcasm in my voice so I tried again. 'No, councillor.' *Come on, Irina. Give me the chance to shout* 'objection!'

She wasn't playing along. 'And I guess Andy was there?'

Which she knew from the Partridge Bark chat. She

didn't want confirmation; she wanted details. Which made this game more fun. 'Yes.'

'Yes, no, yes, no. What's with you today, Louise?'

'Remind me,' I drawled, watching her over the rim of my glass. 'Weren't you the one who told him to take a hike? After the "big betrayal" of him adding his number to the group chat. Using your phone. After you were stupid enough to give it to him.'

'There was more to it than that, Lou.'

'He was there for you after Hamish got ill. And he was there for us, arresting the man who killed Phil Creasy. Who *poisoned* Hammy.'

'He wasn't the one who found the killer, Lou. We did.' Irina touched her wine glass to her chest. 'We, the Pack. Not Andy. Not the Met Police.'

'They'd have got there in the end,' I said, resisting the urge to smile. 'We just got there faster.'

'And he's on this case, too.' Irina took a large gulp of Malbec. Her face remained neutral, but her fingers, holding the glass's stem, were white. I hoped she wouldn't shatter it.

'So it would seem.'

'Does he expect us to solve it for him again?'

'Is that what you think of him?'

She stared back out the window, although it was her own flat she now watched, not Jake's. 'Did you speak with him?'

'Yes, of course. He questioned both Yaz and me this morning.'

A muscle jumped in Irina's arm. Wine sloshed in the

glass, but didn't spill onto my cream-coloured sofa. 'Did he ask about me?'

I set my own glass down on a coaster, hoping she'd do the same. 'No, Irina. We only talked about the man we found this morning.'

'Did he find his way back into the chat, do you think?'

'You took him out?' *Of course she did.* And it would be easy enough to find out if he'd somehow rejoined, even without Irina's legendary Internet stalking skills. 'Want me to check?'

'No,' she said glumly. 'If he's in, it's on another number.'

I was on the verge of asking why he'd bother when she'd made her disinterest in him pretty clear, but stopped myself. *There be dragons.*

It was a pity that it hadn't worked out. I liked Andy, and had hoped (as had most of the Pack) that he'd be able to smooth out a few of Irina's rough edges. But while he had been keen enough to return the interest Irina had initially shown in him, he didn't strike me as a glutton for punishment.

'Fiona said they're going from door to door,' Irina said. 'Asking questions.'

'So? You didn't see anything, did you?'

'No. I was home last night. But my flat doesn't face the right way.'

'Okay. Then what are you scared of?'

'What makes you think I'm scared of anything?' she growled, before waving her phone, changing the subject. 'What do you say about ordering in a pizza?' Typical Irina methodology: divert attention away rather than admit to any vulnerability. My notoriously tight friend must have been desperate not to discuss Andy if she was willing to pay for the pizzas.

Knowing that with him on the case, there would likely be more opportunities to press her, I smiled and said, 'Go ahead. I'll have the pizza tartufo.'

9

ANDY

Scott Williams

> Got some news, mate. The coroner's girl gave me a quick heads-up. Looks like the vic had a chicken bone stuffed down his throat when he died.

> So he choked to death after all? Case closed?

> Didn't say that. Said he had a chicken bone shoved down his throat.

> The whole damn thing. She wasn't sure if it was peri or post mortem, but if post, then it was just after he died. Coz, you know, it's hard to force-feed a man when you're strangling him.

Why would anyone force-feed a dead – or dying – man a chicken bone? Maybe he was strangled when they were trying to force it down him?

> Jolly good question, mate. Let me know if you find out why. Oh, and we found the owner of the red cap.

Yeah? Who?

> Steve Danners. Chap's got an alibi, of sorts, for the night – out drinking with friends. And witnesses

> that say it'd blown off a couple of days ago.

> Shit. Any idea where?

> Not far from where you're standing. Smile for the camera, Andy!

Andy looked up and across the river, spotting Williams and a uniform talking to the vagrants. Presumably Steve Danners was one of them, and Andy wasn't about to ask how reliable the friends giving him an alibi were. Or whether they'd also claim to have seen nothing untoward that night.

He raised his hand in greeting towards Williams and flashed his warrant card at the uniform guarding the crime scene on his side of the bridge.

The PC raised the police tape, allowing Andy to slip under it and walk down to the canal. The body had long since been taken away, and Forensics were pretty much done, but there would be uniforms keeping the public out for another day or two.

He stood where the man had been found and took in what he could.

The canal was still, almost silvered in the moonlight. From this angle, you couldn't see the discarded shopping trolleys, Santander bikes and other crap that people threw into it. Couldn't see most of the rubbish left on the path either – the beer bottles, cans, crisp bags. The sea of discarded nitrous oxide canisters. The dog poo, some of it already bagged, some not.

Andy held himself still, taking in the way the streetlights reflected on the water. Hearing how the sound carried through the tunnels. Smelling ... well, weed. But this was East London; in this part of town the smell clung to the walls like a miasma long after any smokers had left the area.

Unless someone had been brave enough to swim the canal, the only way to get to and from this bench was by foot, along the towpath, although an attacker could have left the path in moments. There were no rubbish bins nearby, which meant that any relevant evidence would likely have been discarded in the canal, along with the victim's mobile, or carried away to be disposed of later. At least it looked like strangulation, which meant they didn't have to check for weapons as well.

A laugh carried on the wind, hoarse and harsh. The vagrants on the other side of the canal, still talking to Williams. Andy guessed that he'd asked if they'd seen anything on Sunday night. He knew that even if they'd had front row seats to the murder, Williams wouldn't get it out of them. In part because of the amount of alcohol consumed, but even more so because the first rule of East London seemed to be that no one ever saw or heard anything.

What had the chicken man seen, before he died? Had he simply been here to eat his tea and fallen foul of one of the groups of teens that hung out down here? Or was there some other reason he'd been killed?

Why had he been here so late? Why did he die here? Was the bench part of the message – chosen specifically by the killer or killers – or was it just convenient?

Why had someone shoved a chicken bone down his throat? The murderer couldn't possibly believe the Met would write that off as an accidental death.

Andy's gut told him it was a message. But to whom? Why? And what was the bloody message?

He closed his eyes, trying to stop his mind from questioning and instead open it up to the scene. The canal was still now; he could check with the lock masters to see if it had been last night as well. Fireworks were going off somewhere near the ExCel centre – they might have been last night too, and if the murderer had timed it right, the bangs might have covered some of the sounds.

From what the door-to-doors had produced, there'd been a house party, loud enough that most of the people the PCs had talked to complained about it. Again, it could have covered sounds of an attack. But was that a coincidence? The murderer being opportunistic? Andy didn't know.

Lights winked at him from across the canal. The vagrants were huddled close together, Williams no longer with them.

The buildings on that side were flats, mostly, with businesses on the ground level. Mostly small businesses that would have been closed by the time it had happened. He looked up again, his eyes straying further along the canal.

The old upholstery factory wasn't far, but far enough that no one there would have heard anything from their flats. Could they have seen something? Someone coming home late at night? Maybe someone walking their dog?

'Stop it,' he muttered to himself. 'She was clear then; you misread the signals. Maybe you overstepped, but Jesus, she'd have been hard work, blowing hot and cold. She did you a favour. No complication with prosecuting the killer in the Creasy case. No complication in your life.'

There was no point in asking Irina anything, and maybe that was just as well. He could just as easily speak to Yaz and Louise tomorrow when they came in to give witness statements, maybe ask them then if the dog people knew anything.

Or he could see for himself.

He slipped his phone out of his pocket, scrolled to the Partridge Bark chat, only to realise that someone (Irina) had removed him from the group.

He shook his head, unsurprised. He rubbed at a crick in his neck and realised he had learned as much as he could today. He'd return again after the cordons came down, see what it was like with the usual canal traffic of an evening. Maybe talk to the locals.

Who knew? Maybe someone had seen something that could help.

Another message flashed on his screen.

BONE OF CONTENTION

Scott Williams

> You might want to get back here, mate. CCTV found something you're gonna want to see.

> What?

> Looks like the vic went for a stroll with a woman last night.

> Do we have a good enough image to identify her?

> Better than that. One of the techs recognised her. Uniforms are going around to collect her and bring her in for questioning. I'll text you the post code, but brace yourself. This is going to get ugly.

10

LOUISE

Partridge Bark

Fiona (Nala's Mum)

Hey guys, I just walked past The Bells. Looks like the cops have someone.

Paul (Bark Vader and Jimmy Chew's Dad)

Can you see who?

BONE OF CONTENTION

Fiona (Nala's Mum)

No. Someone short. Looks like a woman. She's in the middle of a small platoon of ... omg.

Meg (Tyrion's Mum)

What? Is it someone we know?

Fiona (Nala's Mum)

Yeah, but I don't understand. They have Claire with them.

Ella (Bark Vader and Jimmy Chew's Mum)

Our Claire? Tank's mum?

Paul (Bark Vader and Jimmy Chew's Dad)

WTF?

> There's got to be some mistake. Stay there, I'm on my way.

'We've got to go,' I told Irina.

She looked at me as if she'd rather go have her toenails pulled out, and I relented. 'Fine. Stay here and watch the boys. I'll be back as soon as I can.'

'Where are you going?'

I was already shrugging on my coat. 'It looks like the cops have Claire. I'm going to see what's happening. Someone will need to pick up Tank.'

Ignoring the wounded look Klaus gave me for leaving him, I closed the door behind me and then stabbed the lift's call button, cursing when it first stopped on the fifth floor. When it reached eight, the doors opened on an empty lift, but the pungent aroma of skunk told me which neighbours had gotten off downstairs. Holding my breath, I counted the seconds until it arrived on the ground floor, then sprinted through the door and out the ornate wrought iron gates. I passed Jake's side of the complex and trotted down the street. It couldn't have been more than a couple of minutes, but the scene when I arrived was chaos, with lights flashing, people shouting, dogs barking and CGC's clientele watching from the queue outside the shop.

'ARE YOU BLOODY MAD?' A redheaded woman leaned forward into a PC's face, shouting in a broad Australian accent. She was tall, maybe five foot nine or ten. About an inch taller than him, and holding a snarling cocker spaniel behind her, but the PC held his ground.

Beside him another woman – shorter, stocky with curly hair – held up her hands. 'It's okay, it's okay. It's a misunderstanding. Just someone make sure Tank's okay. He can't be left too long by himself.'

I slid between the PC and the redhead, murmuring, 'I've got this, Fi.'

'What's going on here, officer?' I asked. I kept my eyes on his while my fingers ranged through my pockets, hunting for a treat to pacify the cocker. Nala was fairly chilled by nature, but she'd been set off by the lights and shouting. In particular, Fiona's shouting.

'Excuse me, ma'am,' he said, not answering my question, but being gentle as he brushed past me.

'Look, my friend has a dog upstairs,' I said, trotting backwards to remain in front of him. Claire didn't appear to be in handcuffs, but the PCs held her arms in a grip that appeared no less firm.

'Please let her take him,' Claire asked. Her face was pale, her eyes wide. She was terrified.

'It'll make it easier for you to search her flat,' I said, casting about for something logical.

'WHAT?' Fiona howled. 'Search it for what? Dog treats? Notes on some exclusive scoop she's working on?'

Another dog started barking. A deep-chested bark, which in my experience could have meant either a big dog or a dachshund.

The PC looked around. Someone must have given him the okay, because he looked back and nodded at me. I sprinted across the street as a van arrived, the words 'Dog Warden' emblazoned on it.

Fiona must have seen it too as her temper erupted. Two people were leaving the building and I pushed in past them, skidding into the lift and holding my breath as the numbers flicked through to five. As I got out, I slipped out of my jacket and left it straddling the lift and the fifth floor, half in, half out, so that the door wouldn't close. Hopefully that would buy me a bit of time before the dog warden made it upstairs. I took a quick left, then another left. A PC stood outside Claire's door.

'I'm here for the dog,' I said, hearing Tank's bark from the other side.

'No, ma'am. Dog warden's on his way. That dog might be dangerous. He's a bulldog.'

'Officer, Tank's a small French bulldog. He's got the usual Frenchie breathing issues, and wheezes after the slightest exertion. Vomits when he's excited. He's only dangerous to treats ... and I guess if he thought Claire was in danger.' I leaned closer. 'She isn't, is she? Have you arrested her, or just brought her in under caution?'

The PC's face was stony.

Andy is on the case.

I pulled out my phone and dialled Andy's number. 'I need your help,' I began, as soon as he picked up.

'I know.' He sounded out of breath.

'Your men have Claire. I'm at her flat, and I want to take Tank home with me. He'll be scared – the PC here's talking about waiting on the dog warden, but Tank'll be a wreck if he's taken away. They won't let me in to get him. Can you authorise it?' I held my breath, then let it out with a small *whoosh*. 'Please?'

'What's the PC's name?'

I read the man's name off the plate pinned to his chest. 'Can I hand you over to him?' I didn't wait for an answer, just handed the officer my phone. 'Detective Andrew Thompson,' I explained.

The PC scowled, but took the phone. 'Yeah?'

I couldn't hear what Andy said, but the PC nodded.

'I'll sign whatever you need to confirm that I have custody of the dog. Tank. One male French bulldog, four years old.'

The PC didn't answer, but opened the door behind him a few inches. Just enough for me to squeeze through, without letting Tank out.

Only Tank wasn't at the door. His barks erupted again, with the distinct sound of nails on wood; Claire must have secured him in the bedroom before leaving.

I was familiar enough with the flat to know where Claire kept Tank's collar, harness and lead. 'I'll open the door and keep it open while I put him on the lead,' I said, so that the PC wouldn't think I'd do something dodgy while he was supposed to have secured the flat.

He nodded. I fished a few treats out of my pocket and led with those, but Tank wasn't interested in the treats, and for a foodie dog like him, this showed just how upset he was. I cracked open the bedroom door just enough for me to slide through, and stroked his champagne-coloured fur. He snorted while I snapped on his collar and straddled him to guide him into his harness. With

Tank secured, I opened the front door further. 'I need to get some of his food. If you come with me, you can see what I'm taking.'

The PC looked reluctant to get close to a dog that, while small, was muscular and clearly angry. I shortened the lead and marched Tank with me into the kitchen.

I poured kibble from the plastic container on the counter into a canvas bag. Tossed in a few tins of the pâté Tank loved. 'I'd have used my dog's food,' I explained. 'But Tank is allergic to chicken.'

The PC shook his head.

'My name is Louise Mallory. Detective Thompson has my contact details and can vouch for me, but do you want me to sign anything to confirm what I've taken from the flat?'

'No, it's fine.'

'Good.' I didn't wait for him to change his mind. Tank was shaking. Keeping him close to my side, I led the way through the flat and back out the door. Picked up my jacket from the lift that was still trying to close on it, and slipped it on before getting in. 'Right then, Tank. Just the two of us going for a walk. Everything will be fine, and your mum will be back before you know it.' I wasn't sure if my words were more intended to calm him or me.

And I hoped I hadn't lied. I hated lying to the dogs; it seemed wrong when they were always a hundred per cent honest with us.

Bloody hell. Claire. Of all people, the cops thought *Claire* had something to do with it? They'd realise their mistake soon enough and let her go, surely.

'Ready to go, sweetheart?' I asked, looking at Tank's frightened face.

The door slid open at ground floor, and the dog warden, a balding middle-aged man holding a pole with a loop at the end, stood back to let me pass. I offered him a smile, and did my best to assume a regular-girl-walking-her-dog vibe, hoping I didn't look as sick as I felt. If I'd been even a couple of minutes late getting here, Tank would have been in the warden's vehicle, terrified and alone. It didn't bear thinking about, and I didn't look back. Just kept walking through the doors onto the street.

Someone in the crowd further down the block, maybe from the CGC queue, crowed, 'Look at that bee-atch with the pugly dog – geddit?'

As much as I felt my ire rise, I resisted engaging, keeping my face blank, my eyes straight ahead. Tank was neither a pug, nor ugly. But he was unsettled, and I wanted to get him away from the area before he reacted to the stress. He wasn't a big dog, but he was strong, and if he lunged, I'd have to work to keep him under control.

Glancing back, I saw the police car was gone, and there was no sign of Claire. Fiona, however, was still there, now with Yaz and Hercules, and Paul with his two black Labrador retrievers, Bark Vader and Jimmy Chew. They weren't the cleverest dogs, but if there was another dog barking, they wanted in on the action. Not unlike their dad. In the centre of the maelstrom was Andy Thompson.

Figuring he could take care of himself, and someone

in the Pack would post an update, I raised an arm to the detective in silent thanks and continued back to my flat. I'd see him tomorrow, when I was scheduled to go to Lambeth to give my witness statement. Maybe I'd find out what was going on and what they thought Claire had to do with things.

Tank might not be any happier than we were with the situation, but at least having Klaus and Hammy to play with would help until Claire came home.

And with any luck, Irina hadn't finished the bottle of wine.

Or the rest of the wine in the rack.

Tuesday

11

LOUISE

Meg (Tyrion's Mum)

How's Tank? Did he settle last night?

Not really. Every sound and he'd run to the door, expecting Claire to be there to take him home. Klaus of course just had to keep him company.

He misses her, and he's worried about her. Dogs are sentient beings, you know. With their own strengths and weaknesses, thoughts and desires. We're supposed to celebrate that in children, but people don't always know to celebrate that in dogs too. Right, lecture over — not sure what came over me. I know you know all this. How are you doing?

Me? I'm fine. Haven't really had much time to process what's happening. Have you heard anything about Claire yet?

Nope. As far as I know, Fi hasn't either. But I'm sure she'll text as soon as she can. I can't believe it. Of all people, they think CLAIRE would kill a man?! I mean, on paper, with her writing, sure. But not in real life!

> I just don't understand. But if you hear from her before I do, let me know that she's OK.

> Of course. I'm sure it won't be much longer.

Or at least, I hoped it wouldn't be much longer. Tank wasn't settling, and to be honest, neither was I. From Meg's message, I understood that the stress was getting to us all. The logical part of my mind told me that if Claire was still at the police station, it had less to do with how many questions they needed to ask her, and more to do with how many other people they had to question first.

But there was a deeper, darker fear: what if they arrested her anyway? Meg was right. Claire was a journalist: she was more than happy to roast someone in *The Chronicle*'s pages, but physical violence? Murder? No. Not Claire.

Still, it wasn't unheard of for the police to arrest innocent people. And Claire had a nasty habit of mouthing off at the wrong times. They might not arrest her for being snarky, but would they arrest her for being in the wrong place at the wrong time? Or because they didn't – yet – have whoever killed the chap in the hat?

'"Chap in the hat." Even the name is demeaning. Who

was he, Klaus?' I asked. 'I mean, I saw him around. Kind of sad that I didn't even know his name. I really need to make more of an effort with humans.'

Klaus, sitting on a fluffy donut-type bed by the window, yawned, his long tongue curling. Tank was back at the door. I'd stopped trying to lure him away and just left one of Klaus's spare beds by it, so he could at least be comfortable.

'Who are the people who know everyone around here?'

That was easy: most of us who lived here recognised each other on sight. The Tesco workers might recognise our faces, but probably wouldn't know our names.

So who would? Maybe he was on a first name basis with a server in one of the greasy spoons? Someone in the light fixtures place? Or maybe he was a regular in the charity shop?

Not likely, but it didn't hurt to ask around.

I looked at my watch. 10:26. The shops would all be open by now, maybe with the exception of the hair salon, and that would be a stretch anyway. Not because they did a bad job – they didn't – but I just couldn't see the chap in the hat listening to heavy metal music while he was having a trim.

I checked my diary, feeling my pulse begin to race. No one would notice if I went off the grid for an hour, and I'd feel better doing *something*.

'You're in luck, boys. We're going for another walk.' I was already heading to the door, hearing Klaus's nails clicking on the hardwood floors behind me. 'I know,

I know. His name will be released as soon as the cops inform his next of kin, but this isn't about that.'

Tank was sitting on the mat by the door, a gag gift from Paul and Ella that read 'Don't step on my wiener'. He allowed me to put on his harness, but Klaus was less accommodating, pointing his snout into the corner when I tried to get him into a jumper. 'Come on, you know the deal: if it's under ten degrees, you're wearing the jumper. It's cold outside. You don't like the cold.'

He also didn't like the jumper. I had a bad feeling his friends made fun of him, but that was better than watching him shiver.

By contrast, Tank didn't feel the weather. Sun, rain, wind, even snow, it didn't matter. Claire only put a fleece on him if the temperature dove below freezing.

I slipped my own jacket on and guided the boys to the lift, then out of the complex and onto the street. We crossed the bridge over the canal and headed towards the high street, but we hadn't even passed News-N-Booze when Tank pulled me towards the entrance to the tall brick new build beside it. At least there wasn't a police presence outside anymore.

'Sorry, sweetheart,' I said. 'You're not going home just yet.'

He wasn't having it, digging in his paws.

'I'm sorry. As soon as your mum is back, you can go home. I promise.'

I gently led him past the teenagers milling on the corner and into News-N-Booze. The spotty kid behind the till, Zed, winked at me and leaned forward to grin at Klaus. 'Yo, mate. You brought a friend?'

'My friend Claire's dog,' I said, picking up a Diet Coke and putting it on the counter.

'Oh yeah. The one what got arrested yesterday? Good you're keepin' her dog.'

'She wasn't arrested, she's just being questioned,' I said, hoping it was true. I watched him from under my eyelashes and, keeping my voice light, asked the question I'd come in for. 'The guy that died ... the one that always wore the fedora? Did you know him?'

'Like you, mostly,' he said, scanning my drink. 'The odd bottle of Sauvignon Blanc. Maybe a pint of milk. Guess he shopped at Tesco or online.'

I paid for the Diet Coke and lingered a bit. 'Did you know him though? Maybe his name?'

'You back in the crime-solvin' business?' He winked again.

After telling Yaz to leave the detecting to the detectives, why on Earth was I getting involved again?

Claire. Because the cops went after Claire.

I didn't say anything, just held his gaze until he looked away.

'Yeah, no. Soz, mate. Knew him well enough to say awright to but y'know, not like I'm gonna join him for a drink at the pub.'

'You saw him at the pub? Which one?'

He shook his head. 'No chance. Naw. Never saw him out, just sayin'. Lives around here though, don't he? The big brick building, I think.'

The same one as Claire? Which might have been why the cops thought she knew him.

'Did you ever see them together? Him and Claire?'

Zed shrugged, his skinny shoulders rising almost to his ears. 'Sure. But not much since the summer.'

Since the summer? What had changed? I took a guess. 'Walking together, like a couple?'

He tilted his head back and forth. 'I dunno. Maybe. Kind of got the feeling he wanted it, but she didn't.'

Sensing that Zed had told me all he could, I picked up my drink. Unscrewed the top and toasted him before taking a sip. 'Thanks. Here's to finding out what happened.'

'Yeah, sure,' he said, with less interest. It was as if he was saying what we all knew: this was East London. Crime was a regular occurrence.

But at least I had learned two things: Claire knew Fedora, and something about their relationship had changed during the summer.

'Wait,' I said aloud, standing at the crossroads in front of News-N-Booze, while I tried to make sense of it. I looked at Tank. 'Was Claire actually *seeing* him? Because if she was dating *anyone*, she kept it damned quiet!'

'Maybe 'cos she didn't want you to know she were banging *your* man,' one of the teenagers behind me said, as the rest of them giggled. A couple of nitrous oxide canisters were propped next to the wall; the kids were high as kites. I shook my head and kept walking, not least because I'd been single even longer than Claire. The only man I regularly spent time with was ...

Jake?

The lizard voice in my head brought me up short. Was she banging *Jake*?

'It's not my business if she is,' I muttered to myself. 'We're just friends. He can see whoever he wants.'

My voice sounded plaintive, even to me. Hoping no one had heard, I peered into the dry cleaners. There were no customers in there and the woman behind the counter was reading a paperback. No surprise: they were famously bad at cleaning. One of my neighbours had complained to me once that his shirts came back dirtier than when he dropped them off, and with hairs on them that weren't his – or his boyfriend's.

Local scuttlebutt was that the dry cleaners was a money laundering operation, as was the lighting shop next to it. I continued past them both, and paused in front of the charity shop. Tanzima, the petite Bangladeshi woman who ran it, was terrified of dogs. I'd have to come back later without them.

Feeling like this was more of a fool's errand than I'd expected, I continued past the Tesco, skirted the stained flagstones outside the closed Cluckin' Good Chicken and stopped at the Hands-On hair salon. Heavy metal blared from inside the shop. There were no customers, but the stylist and colourist seemed to be having a good time. At first glance, they looked like a forty-something version of Bill and Ted, having a most excellent adventure in hair styling. That is, if Bill had let himself go and had a thing for drag, while Ted had given up air guitar for air drums.

Today the proprietress – Caren – wore her fringe slicked down on her forehead like a grey-and-white barcode, throwing the rest of her teased monochrome hair around to the loud bass beat. The colourist sitting in one of the cutting chairs, wearing his usual oversized black jumper and jeans, seemed in the zone, eyes closed and head nodding as his arms flailed around, hitting the imaginary drums and cymbals in perfect time.

While Caren was uniformly grumpy, Benny seemed to have three settings: confidence on the air drums, competence with a bowl of dye in one hand and a brush in the other (at least according to Meg) and a nervous soul at all other times. By and large, I liked them both, although there was no way I'd have my hair done at their salon.

'This was a waste of time,' I confessed to the dogs.

As if they understood, Tank raised a hind leg and urinated on the corner. Not to be outdone, Klaus strode over and weed in the same place. Tank looked inclined to wee over Klaus's patch, starting a never-ending cycle, so I fished a pack of treats out of my pocket, ensuring two instantly compliant dogs for the short walk home.

Fiona (Nala's Mum)

> Do you know if Claire is seeing anyone?

> Not as far as I know. Why? What have you heard?

> Nothing. I just realised how quiet she was in the chat this week. And wondered if there's someone we can call to give her an alibi. If she needs one.

> Oh. OK. Sorry. Not as far as I know, but good luck.

'Those kids are spouting bollocks just to wind me up,' I said to the dogs, jamming my key in my door and letting the boys run into the flat. Logically, I knew Claire preferred the pale, reedy, academic types. She'd be more interested in someone like my ex-husband, who worked out like mad but never seemed to bulk out, than she would be Jake. I was ashamed of my own overreaction.

I opened my laptop to see what I'd missed in the last half hour.

A whopping nothing.

My job was turning into a PR role in which I took prospective clients out to lunch or dinner, reviewed financial figures and resolved staffing issues. And now, kept an eye on the work being done for the NHS, of which there was nothing. Yet.

I brewed a pot of coffee, but before I could pour myself a cup, my phone buzzed, informing me that someone wanted to come in. 'Hello?'

'It's me,' a tired voice slurred.

Heart pounding, I almost fumbled the phone as I hit the button to grant access. Taking a deep breath, I tried to keep my voice as even as possible as I lifted it back to my ear and spoke again. 'Come on up.'

12

LOUISE

Irina (Hamish's Mum)

> All right, I'll ask. Have you seen Andy?

I saw the message pop up and put the phone face down on the countertop. I'd deal with Irina's ego later. I braced myself for the knock on the door, unsure what to expect.

Tank, who rarely barked, seemed to know Claire was on her way, and began howling and scratching at the front door.

'Give it a moment, sweetheart. She'll be right up.'

The lift dinged, and Klaus joined in the barking. My smartwatch buzzed, warning me that I was in a loud environment. Something that I'd already figured out on my own.

'Brace yourself,' I warned through the door as I opened it.

The dogs pushed through, tails wagging, barking with happiness. Claire got down on her knees, pulling Tank and Klaus to her, burying her face in their soft fur as they knocked her onto her back.

'When the boys are done greeting you, come on in,' I told her. 'I just made a pot of coffee.'

She nodded, lying flat on her back and hugging the squirming bodies. She tugged Tank onto her chest, allowing him to lick the tears from her face. I picked Klaus up, giving them a little time together, and retreated to the kitchen to take a second mug from the cupboard and pour the coffee.

The door opened, and I could hear Claire's footsteps. 'You don't need to . . .'

'I already made it.' I offered her a smile. 'I even poured it, so it'd be rude to say no.'

She nodded. Tank was still in her arms, licking her face. She settled him onto the sofa and sat down beside him. It was too far away, as far as he was concerned, and he crawled back into her lap.

Klaus, not to be outdone, pawed her leg for attention.

'Don't take this the wrong way, but you look like shit,' I said, putting the mugs on my coffee table and sitting down. It was true. Claire's curly blonde hair was wilder than usual, her eyes were red and glassy and she smelled like . . .

'Have you been drinking?'

She blinked. 'What? Why?'

'Because you smell like Irina after a bender. Not sure you look that much better, either,' I pointed out, settling on the other end of the sofa and turning to look at her.

'Nice.' She pulled an elastic hair tie from around her wrist and captured her hair in a high ponytail, the curls spiralling out like a springy pineapple. 'Better?'

'Marginally. How did it go?'

'Well, on the plus side, they didn't arrest me.'

My hand, about to spoon sugar into my coffee, froze. 'Did you expect them to?'

'For a while, although heaven knows I had nothing to do with it.' Claire looked down at her lap, then out through the window. 'They finished with the questions a few hours ago but I wasn't ready to go home. Fi texted that you had Tank, so I wasn't worried about him. I just needed some time.'

'Okay.'

'It's amazing how many bars are still open, if you know where to look.'

Still? When did she start?

'After the questions ... maybe after hearing that Jonny was dead, I just needed a drink.'

'Jonny? That was his name?'

She blinked at me. 'Jonny? Jonathan Tang. Didn't you know?'

'No.'

She shrugged. 'You seem to know everyone. I thought you might.'

'Did you ... I mean, well ...'

'Did I kill him?' Her voice was more tired than sardonic. 'No, Lou. I didn't. He was my friend.'

'That wasn't what I was going to ask,' I said.

'Do I know what happened?'

'That's a good start.'

'Then, no. I don't. When I came home, the usual yobs were out and giving it large, but no worse than usual. I could have handled it; I do every day, several times a day. But this time Jonny came out and walked me back to my door.'

'What happened after that?'

'I went into my flat, and Jonny left.'

'Do you know where he was going?'

'Out, I guess,' she said, sounding slightly offended. 'I don't know, I didn't ask.'

'Any ideas where he might have gone?'

'No. The cops asked that too. I'm sorry, I don't know.'

Something occurred to me. 'How was he dressed?'

Claire's hand was raised. She paused for a few seconds, before tucking a stray blonde lock that had escaped the ponytail behind her ear. She stared into the distance, her other hand distractedly stroking Tank. 'I don't know. It was cold. Leather jacket, maybe. The fedora?'

The fedora. Not a baseball cap. So, where was the hat? And whose baseball cap was he wearing? Would there be DNA on it to confirm anyone specific – or rule them out?

'Okay.'

'You're doing it again, aren't you, Lou?'

'What?'

'You're trying to solve the crime.'

I shook my head. 'I found him yesterday, Claire. Jonny. Well, actually, Yaz and Herc did, but then she called me. This is the second dead body I've seen in less than six months. What do you expect me to do? Ignore it?'

'It can't be related to Village Vets. They've closed.'

'I know that. And I know the people who killed Phil Creasy are in prison. I know it's not connected to them, but it's connected to the area. And because I was one of the first to see him, I want to know what happened, because I think he deserves justice. It's not right that he's dead and his murderer is running around scot-free. And I'm going to be selfish here. I don't like the idea of another murder happening around our neighbourhood.'

'You can't solve every crime, Lou. This is London. There's a lot of crime going round.'

'I know.' Now I was beginning to feel offended. 'I don't intend to.'

Claire nodded, and I realised that with all the messages flying around, one name had been missing. The journalist had no questions to ask? That didn't make sense.

I didn't know how to phrase my next question. 'But you knew already, didn't you? About Yaz and Herc finding him? About them calling me?'

She hung her head. 'Sorry I didn't text to check up on you, Lou. Yesterday I was kind of ... well ... busy.'

'Huh.' Being busy had never stopped her before. She was a journo. I'd heard that she'd run out on dates – with men she actually liked – for a good story.

'Yeah. Deadlines – you know how it is.'

I nodded, even though every fibre of my being insisted that she was lying to me.

But about what?

Her eyes wouldn't meet mine.

Maybe she was ashamed of showing up here pissed to pick up Tank?

No, she would know that I wouldn't judge. Not after the night she must have had.

'So, what next?' I asked.

'For what?'

I wasn't sure of the question either. 'For Jonny, I guess. For the police investigation. If they released you, they must know that you had nothing to do with it. Did you get the feeling that they had other avenues of inquiry?'

'"Avenues of inquiry"? You've been reading up on this?'

Claire was angling for an argument. Maybe she wanted to blow off some steam, but I wasn't about to wade in. I decided to make light of it. And maybe test the waters.

'Nah. Must have picked it up from the telly.' I watched her closely and added, 'Occasionally I hang out with Jake. He's into crime flicks.'

Her expression didn't change. 'Yeah, he seems the sort.'

Which told me absolutely nothing.

Other than the fact that she didn't want to answer my questions.

Claire didn't linger much longer. I let Fi know that she was back, and that she hadn't been arrested, then looked at the messages from Irina. There were six of them, all with the same gist: had I spoken to Andy, and had he asked about her.

Irina (Hamish's Mum)

> Remind me again: weren't you the one to cut him loose?

> It was better for the case. I was a witness, it wouldn't have looked good.

> Technically, we didn't witness anything. We found Phil's body. And the time stamps on the pics from Fi's party the night before showed that we couldn't have been involved when he was killed. A 'rock solid alibi', as they say on TV.

> It's a fine line, Louise. And you're not answering my question. Did you see him, and did he ask about me?

> Why do you suddenly care?

> I don't. I'm just curious.

'Curious' didn't lead to six messages. She'd been keen on him back then, despite the case, and I'd hoped romance would blossom. Only it hadn't, and I'd put money on that being down to the actions of one very temperamental Russian.

'How long do you think I can keep her guessing before she storms over here?' I asked Klaus. He'd returned to his bed by the balcony door. He raised his head and then lowered it, still looking at me from under his tan eyebrows. He was sulking, unhappy that Tank had gone home.

I stared at my laptop screen for a while, my eyes skimming over the same paragraphs without registering the content.

'Fine,' I sighed, and brought up a browser. I typed in 'Jonathan Tang' and came up with a massive list of possibilities: chemists, researchers, entrepreneurs. None of the pictures seemed to fit the chap in the hat.

I checked *The Chronicle* and the BBC's websites to see if either had posted anything about his death.

There was nothing on *The Chronicle*'s site, but the BBC had the usual vacuous text:

> **DEAD MAN FOUND IN TOWER HAMLETS**
>
> The body of a man in his late thirties was found along a canal in Tower Hamlets, in the vicinity of Partridge Park, yesterday morning at approximately 7 a.m. by a woman walking her dog.
>
> The police have yet to release the name of the man, pending notification of his next of kin, or any further details. However, they are treating his death as suspicious, and urging anyone with any information to contact the Metropolitan Police.
>
> Crime is on the rise in Tower Hamlets, and following a recent spate of stabbings in the area, the borough's mayor has indicated that he is working closely with both the Mayor of London and the Met Police to tackle violent crimes and gang activities, although local action groups claim that his promises are too little, too late.
>
> This June, the body of local entrepreneur Philip Creasy was found in nearby Partridge Park and two people were subsequently arrested for his murder. The police are treating this case as unrelated.

At the bottom of the article was a series of related links that included a borough-by-borough breakdown of crime statistics, an opinion piece on knife crime (although as far as I could tell, Jonny Tang's body had shown no sign of a stab wound), a biography of a guy who had made it his life's work to rehabilitate people who'd been involved in gangs (likewise, Jonny didn't appear to fit any gang member stereotypes) and several articles covering Phil Creasy's murder back in June.

Although just because Jonny Tang had dressed well and seemed a decent sort, that didn't mean he hadn't been involved in something dodgy. The same way looks had been deceiving in Phil's case. His murderer hadn't been in a gang or anything. He'd been a bloody veterinarian.

Frustrated, I pushed the laptop away. 'It's going to be a long day.'

From his bed, Klaus sighed.

13

IRINA

Partridge Bark

Fiona (Nala's Mum)

> I hear the police are knocking on the doors of any flats facing the canal and asking anyone else who might have been out and about if they saw anything suspicious on Sunday night.

Yaz (Hercules's Mum)

> They should try talking to the people who sit across

> from that bench every day, getting wasted.

Fiona (Nala's Mum)

> I'm sure they will, if they haven't already. Whether they can get any coherent answers from them ...

Louise (Klaus's Mum)

> I took a walk around earlier to see if I could find anyone who knew anything, but no luck.

>> You're a cop now?

Louise (Klaus's Mum)

> Haha, nope. But this is East London. A lot of people would rather talk to me than a cop.

Irina lay on her sofa, pulling Hamish to her chest. 'And then what would she do if she learned anything, Mischka?' The little Scottie snuggled closer, tucking his soft black head under her chin. 'I'll tell you what she'd do. She'd call Andy.'

Hamish moved his head at Andy's name but she held him in place.

'Would that be so bad?' she answered aloud, as if her internal voice was Hammy's.

'Look, I know she's trying to help. She's like that. She'll want to help get Claire off the hook. Maybe even find justice for this dead guy, like last time. And probably next time. And you know, she likes feeling like she's making a difference.'

What's so bad about that?

Irina frowned, wishing she could slap that internal voice.

Maybe because it isn't Louise you're angry with?

She glared at Hammy. 'Don't judge. There was an investigation. Any involvement I had with Andy would have complicated things. I made the right decision to walk away. I saved both of us a lot of problems.'

She picked Hammy up, placed him gently on the ground and went to the window. The clocks were about to go back at the end of the month – it was already dark out, the courtyard half-heartedly lit by a lamp in each corner. They were barely enough to see by and did little to deter the teenagers getting stoned by the canal.

Same canal, but different view. Irina couldn't see the bench where Yaz had found the body from here, but would that stop the police from asking her what she knew? What she might have seen? She might have been out that night ... Maybe walking the dog. Maybe walking home from an evening out. Any detail was important, she knew.

Irina began to pace. She peered into her bedroom, where it looked like her closet had exploded onto her bed in the search for her favourite black top. Closed the door. Went to the bathroom and brushed her hair. Twisted it into the usual topknot. Picked up a lip gloss, only to put it back down.

He wouldn't come to interview her. She knew that. He'd send someone else. One hundred per cent. Maybe it'd be his partner, Williams. Maybe it'd be one of the uniforms.

And that was how it should be: uncomplicated.

She checked the WhatsApp group again, scrolling through the participants list. There were almost a hundred names in the group. Most she knew – they usually had at least a first name plus their dog's name. Some she didn't. Maybe they'd moved away but used the group to stay connected to the area. Maybe they were people who visited infrequently. Maybe she just hadn't been bothered enough to put their names into her phone.

'The Great Clean Up', as she called it, was something she'd done fairly regularly since June, when Andy and Williams had arrested Dr Cooper for killing Phil Creasy. Not to mention poisoning Hamish. What person in their right mind – what *vet* in their right mind – would poison a dog?

Then again, what person in their right mind would kill someone and lob them over a fence into a park?

Then *again*, what cop in his right mind would sneak his number into a group chat when her back was turned?

After she'd *entrusted* her phone to him. She'd given it to him and trusted him to use it to pay for a damned coffee, not to stalk her from within a WhatsApp group!

For the first month or two, she'd noticed his name still in there. The group knew about their flirtation, and probably had a few theories about how she'd messed it up. They probably thought that it served the 'Tsarina' – she hated that nickname – right, although no one had been there, no one understood the situation and it wasn't like it was any of their business anyway.

And what had happened when she'd talked to Lou? Lou had drawled that it was good to have the cops aware of some of the local issues. Right, well it wasn't like he'd used *Lou's* phone to get into the group.

And it wasn't like he'd even been active in it. He'd never posted. Or responded to posts.

And he'd never messaged her. No calls. No texts. No bloody thumbs-up emojis. Not even a chance encounter, when he knew perfectly well that she was at Partridge Park most mornings and evenings.

So one day, fuelled by wine and fury, she'd deleted his name, removed him from the group. He shouldn't have been in there in the first place; he didn't have a dog.

He had a child up north somewhere.

Not that she cared about that. It wasn't like she'd met the kid. Wasn't like their friendship had even gotten much beyond hanging out together a time or two.

And why was that, exactly?

The phone buzzed again, and she picked it up, hoping it would silence that damned internal voice. Give her something else to focus on instead of waiting – *hoping?* – for the doorbell to ring.

Needing to release a bit of tension, she swiped open the new message.

As Is

> Fancy a late evening dog walk?

From experience, she knew that a walk was not quite what Tim had in mind. She'd heard he was on the outs with his girlfriend Sophie again, although that's what he usually said to people who seemed to care, or wanted to believe him. Irina figured that keeping him faithful to another woman wasn't her job. She didn't want a relationship with him; what they had was simple and uncomplicated. The way she liked it.

A distraction was just what she needed. She responded with a thumbs-up emoji, and scanned the other chats.

The unread count in the pack chat was ramping up and she dipped in.

Partridge Bark

Meg (Tyrion's Mum)

> I'm having my hair done next week – usually

there's hot goss at the salon. I can stop by earlier – kind of talk through what I'm after – and see if they know anything?

Yaz (Hercules's Mum)

You have your hair done at that salon by the new chicken place? You actually trust Angry Karen to cut your hair?

Meg (Tyrion's Mum)

Actually, her name is Caren. With a C. Pronounced Cah-ren – and don't make the mistake of mispronouncing it! But no. I have the cut done near my mum's but Benny – the guy that works with Caren – does my colour.

BONE OF CONTENTION

Yaz (Hercules's Mum)

Cah-ren, huh. With a C. Remind me, someone... that orange veg that bunnies eat... how do you pronounce that? 😉

Meg (Tyrion's Mum)

You're a braver person than I am if you point that out to her.

Louise (Klaus's Mum)

Especially if she's holding a pair of scissors! Thanks, @**Meg**.

Irina sighed and went to stand at the window again, this time waiting for one man and his dog to cross the courtyard.

14

LOUISE

Partridge Bark

> @**Irina**, can you get in touch with your doggie daycare lady? She's not in this group – I checked – but she usually seems up on the goss when I run into her at the park.

Irina (Hamish's Mum)

Angela? Probably because she starts most of the gossip.

> Excellent, so let's see what she's come up with.

Irina (Hamish's Mum)

Yeah, sure.

She was usually abrupt – that was just Irina – but I'd expected some sort of sarcasm from her. That it was missing made me wonder what was going on. Maybe I'd DM her . . .

There was a knock at the door. Klaus was already there, on guard dog duty, and I peered through the peephole, mostly for show as I was getting tired of Jake telling me to be careful. The man on the other side was older, slim instead of muscular, with thinning grey hair. It wasn't Jake, but someone that Klaus was always happy to see. I opened the door. 'Hey, Geoff. What's up?'

Dr Geoffrey Baggott was a retired entomologist, and my next-door neighbour. For years we'd passed each other with polite courtesy, but during the Covid years, we'd got to know each other from balcony to balcony. He'd even doggie-sat for Klaus before I'd discovered the dog community.

'Did you see the police outside yesterday?' he asked.

'Yeah, there was a dead man found on a canal bench. They were going door to door questioning everyone.' I gestured for him to follow me into the living room. 'Cup of tea?'

'No thanks,' he said, slipping Klaus a treat. 'I can't stay.

But no, I meant here. The police were on the third floor. Seems old Mrs Latenby was burgled.'

'Seriously?'

'Broad daylight, Lou. While she was home.'

Klaus, seeing that he wasn't going to get any more treats from Geoff, padded to his bed by the window and flopped back onto it, watching us with serious eyes.

'Oh shit.'

'Quite. Just wanted to make sure you knew to be careful.' He gave me a rueful smile. 'As if any of us need another reason. This neighbourhood...'

The door was pushed open again, and Klaus sprang up, barking and racing towards it. Luther entered the kitchen ahead of Jake, ignoring Klaus's bark-fest.

'Hey, Geoff,' Jake said over the din. Then to me, 'Still on for movie night, Marple?' He unclipped Luther from his lead, slipped a rucksack off his shoulder and shrugged out of his black puffer jacket. He hadn't shaved and his usual five o'clock shadow had lengthened to about an eight o'clock. Which complemented his usual edgy look of jeans and black T-shirt.

Marple? Geoff mouthed. He winked, raised a hand in farewell and let himself out of the flat. Normally, Klaus would have followed him, but he was too preoccupied sniffing Luther's butt. Jake's Staffie was more interested in scoring prime bed space by the window.

I turned to Jake. 'And why wouldn't I be?'

'I don't know.' He pulled a bottle of Sauvignon Blanc from his rucksack, placing it on the glass coffee table. 'New case to solve?'

I moved the bottle to a coaster and went to fetch some glasses. 'Not my job, Jake,' I said, knowing he wouldn't believe me. Hell, *I* didn't believe me.

He flopped into the spot on the sofa I'd recently vacated. 'And yet, I'd bet you're already in the thick of it.'

He made it sound like I was some sort of ghoul, on the hunt for murder and mayhem. Which, in this neighbourhood, didn't seem that hard to find.

'Well, I found the body again, didn't I? Or at least, Yaz found it,' I hedged, pausing with a glass in each hand. I knew I sounded defensive, but I couldn't seem to stop myself. Even though I knew he was teasing me. 'But she called me and told me she needed me. Of course I went. I mean, how was I supposed to know that she'd found a dead body and called me as well as the cops?' I returned to the table, unscrewed the bottle and poured the wine.

'You were wondering what to do once you handed over the running of your company to Babs?' He raised a glass in a mock salute. 'Here's to the newest superhero, fighting crime in her daxie jammies.'

'And you managed to say that without even a smile. Impressive,' I retorted, fighting a reluctant grin. 'Pretty ridiculous, isn't it? Local entrepreneur turned amateur sleuth? Who am I kidding?'

'Cute jammies though.' He toed off his shoes and held up the TV remote. 'Your turn to choose. Remember the rules?'

'No chick flicks. No cartoons. No weird stuff that we can't follow. Yeah, yeah, I get it.' The list was actually longer, but there was no point in reciting it. I took a sip of lukewarm wine and debated adding an ice cube. 'What do you say about adding "No true crime" to the list?'

'Good for me if that works for you? I wouldn't want to curtail your research.'

'Funny.'

He grinned and my belly flip-flopped. I looked at the glass in my hand. How many times would I need to refill it before I'd have the nerve to make a move?

Did it matter? Jake was good company, and I wasn't inclined to lose that. He looked down at his hands, and for a heartbeat I wondered if he was thinking the same thing.

Or worse, if he understood what I was thinking and didn't fancy reciprocating...

'Your friend's okay?' he asked, and the tension broke. 'The one who was arrested?'

'Claire? Yeah. I kept Tank here while she was being questioned.'

'Any suspects?'

I tried to make a joke. 'I thought we decided against true crime tonight?'

'We did. And you don't have to answer the question.' I stared at him until his shoulders shifted. 'You and your friend had a bad day. I'd be a shit if I didn't ask how you all were.'

'All of us?'

He shrugged again, and this time glanced away. 'Look, Louise. A man was murdered. You and one of your friends found him. Another friend was questioned. That's got to hurt. And if it doesn't, it should at least scare you. This is the second murder you've put yourself in the middle of in less than six months. I'm not going to tell you what to do, but I do hope you're being careful.'

'Sure, I've got the sausage security with me whenever I go outside.'

His handsome face was stony. 'It's not a laughing matter. I'd rather not hear that it's you that's found dead on a park bench next.'

I nodded, even though I didn't know what I was agreeing to. Fumbling for the remote, I chose the first film that Netflix recommended – a spy flick with amazing cinematography but a predictable plot.

Which was just as well. My mind was still thinking about Jonny Tang, the fastidious man in the hat, dead on a canal bench, surrounded by chicken bones.

15

ANDY

Scott Williams

> Just heard from the mort. Autopsy is done on Canal Man. I'm heading back to hear the results. You in?

> On my way.

Andy closed his laptop. From the start, he'd sensed that this case wouldn't be straightforward. For starters, the dead man didn't look like someone who would sit on a bench in the middle of the night with a box of wings.

But what if he'd been depressed? Suicidal?

Death by chicken bone? Unlikely. Especially if – to

use Williams's words – it had been shoved down his throat.

Andy shrugged into a wool coat and tucked his warrant card into the breast pocket. He walked the short way to the overground line that would take him under the Thames to the south side of the river, something that made his son shake his head every time he visited. He'd giggle and say, 'I thought it was the *overground*, Dad. Not the *underwater*.' Andy knew he hadn't gotten it right with his ex, but they had somehow managed to raise a good kid.

Williams was waiting for him outside the mortuary. 'I hate this place,' he said by way of greeting. 'Especially at night.'

'The dead are dead, Scott. They're not going to come back, claw their way out of the freezers and eat your brains.'

'It's not that, mate. It's the feel of the place. The smell. And I guess what happens here. Getting carved up after you die. Like some extra insult, as if being dead wasn't bad enough.'

'But if it helps the dead find justice?'

Williams held up a finger. 'A conundrum.' He pushed through the door and led the way to the pathologist's office.

Andy knew Dr Stephanie White was every bit as much of a conundrum. She was in her late fifties, with well-kept silver-grey hair falling thick and straight around her shoulders, but her face was unlined, as if she was so comfortable in her own skin that Nature had no reason to mar it. Her eyes were the colour of gunmetal, reflecting the strength of her character. Station gossip speculated as to whether she was on the spectrum, but Andy had never cared one way or the other. Dr White was thorough and straight-talking, which he appreciated.

As he knocked on the half-open door, he could see that today she was wearing a clean pair of scrubs, which meant her job wasn't yet done for the evening.

'Dr White.'

She looked at him over the top of her glasses and nodded him into a chair on the other side of her desk, before opening a folder at her elbow and beginning without preamble to list off the characteristics of a clean-living, healthy man.

An otherwise healthy man, who was dead.

'Stomach contents,' she began, 'indicated that he ate a salad shortly before his death. With a cup of dandelion tea.'

'No fried chicken? Chicken wings?' Andy asked.

'No.'

'Anything chicken-related?'

'No chicken, Detective. And from the state of his body, I'd be surprised if he ate much fried food at all.'

'But the chicken bone?' Williams prompted from where he stood behind Andy. His tense body was making it clear how eager he was to leave. 'Was that the cause of death?'

She shook her head. 'Inserted after his death. There were wool fibres under his fingernails—'

'Any skin? Any indication of who did it?'

'I sent the samples to the Forensics team. They'll be able to answer that question.'

'Defensive wounds?' Andy pressed.

Dr White shook her head again. 'No.'

'He could have been taken by surprise,' Williams suggested.

Dr White continued as if he hadn't spoken. 'There was bruising around his neck. Broken hyoid bone. Petechiae in the eyes.'

'Strangulation,' Andy said. 'Manually? With his hands?'

'Yes, Detective. Although the bruising at the base of the neck and shoulders could indicate that someone was standing behind him.'

'Two people? Or one person who moved around him?'

She shrugged. 'Inconclusive.'

'Any sign of prints? Distinguishing marks?'

The pathologist tucked a lock of hair behind her ear. 'No, but I'll give you the measurements so that you can potentially rule a suspect in or out based on size.' She waited for him to nod before continuing. 'The assailant wore neoprene gloves, but relatively thick ones. Not like the one doctors wear during a routine examination, or that were discarded everywhere during the pandemic.'

'Who would have access to these gloves?'

'I can't help you there, Detective. I'm afraid they're readily available.'

'Right. Were there any fibres left behind other than those under his fingernails?'

'Nothing that I could find.'

Which meant there wasn't anything there. And that the attacker had been very careful. Or very lucky.

Williams spoke up again. 'And from the angle of

insertion, was the attacker shoving the bone in from in front or behind?'

'Good question, Detective.' Dr White gave him a hint of a smile. 'From the front, moments after he died.'

'Which means that it was done by the killer, not some random kid that happened on the body and thought he'd have a bit of fun.'

'Very likely.'

'Anything else you can share, Doctor? Bruises? Anything?'

She took off her glasses and pinched the bridge of her nose between thumb and forefinger. Replaced the glasses and leaned forward. 'As a matter of fact, there is. And I think you'll find them quite curious.'

16

MEG

'Brace yourself,' Meg shouted, barely audible over hell-hound barking.

'Good thing Tyrion likes me,' Ethan called back from the other side of the door as she eased it open. 'Jesus, he sounds like he wants to kill me.'

'T's fine, but you'll need to make friends with Phoebe.' Meg lifted her leg slightly, using it as a barrier to keep the dogs in the flat. 'Her mum only dropped her off earlier this afternoon. I think T might be showing off to her.'

She pointed to the thick cream-coloured fur of a smaller but much louder dachshund. The tiny dog's snout wrinkled as she bared her teeth and growled at Ethan.

'Jesus, Meg!'

'That's Phoebe,' Meg said, certain she'd told him that she'd be dog-sitting as a favour for her new neighbour, Frances. Hadn't she?

Phoebe continued to growl and snap at Ethan with her long white fangs.

'I don't think she likes me.' Was that a quiver in his voice?

'Don't be ridiculous,' Meg said, but she scooped Phoebe up, just in case. She trusted Tyrion with her life, but hadn't yet built a bond with Phoebe. 'She likes everyone.'

Phoebe lunged at Ethan and he jumped back. Meg held out her hand. 'Here. Give her a treat.'

His fingers closed around the little piece of meat, his already pale complexion going a ghostly white.

'She's not tall enough to bite your face off,' Meg joked.

'Uhm . . .'

'She's fine, Ethan. Really.' Meg wasn't worried, although Phoebe's barking was reaching a fever pitch. Tyrion, on the other hand, trotted out and bounced his little legs off Ethan's shin, expecting his usual pats.

Phoebe was what, four point five kilograms? Maybe five, tops? But it wasn't as if Meg was entirely unsympathetic. She knew her boyfriend was more of a cat person than a dog person. Though she also knew that if their relationship had any chance of success, he'd have to meet her partway. And Tyrion and the Pack were helping.

Even if half of them still referred to him as Cat Boy.

Slowly, Ethan unfurled his fingers, offering Phoebe the treat. It was gone before he could blink, but the dachshund was quieting down. Meg slipped him a second treat for Tyrion.

'Thanks.' His hair – groomed by nature to look like something out of an anime cartoon – looked crazier than normal.

'We're watching her this week.'

For a moment, a series of emotions flitted across Ethan's face, until he realised that the 'we' was Meg and Tyrion, not Meg and him. 'Oh. Okay.'

He followed her back inside and held up a black rucksack as a peace offering. 'I brought a takeaway. I was going to go get chicken from that place on the high street, but I remembered that you're not into wings, so I went with that Chinese place that you like.'

'I used to like wings fine,' Meg said, slipping on her jacket. 'Until I got a dog and saw how many people leave the bones lying around. I stopped eating them when Tyrion started hunting them.'

'Fair enough.'

'I need to walk the dogs. You can start eating if you like or come with me?'

'Cold Chinese with the hot girlfriend, or hot Chinese by myself? No choice there.'

Ethan had kept his voice light, but she knew that underneath his smile was the fact that he wasn't comfortable with her being out after dark by herself. Even less so when a murderer was on the loose. He knew she could take care of herself – and Tyrion – but he still worried about her; that was one of the many things she really liked about him.

He looked away and slipped Phoebe a second treat from his pocket – when had he started carrying treats? Something inside her melted, realising that he'd make every effort to bond with the dogs to please her.

She clipped Tyrion into his harness and handed his lead to Ethan. Then she slipped a spare harness (Phoebe's owner Frances had only given her a collar) onto the bonkers blonde daxie.

'Pity you can't teach them to use a litter box,' Ethan joked.

'For sure. Especially when it's raining outside. T won't leave the house.' Which is why Meg still had a Piddle Patch on the balcony. It was either that or have to clean up an 'accident' later.

She zipped up her oversized black puffer coat and locked the door behind them. Waiting for the lift, she stood on tiptoes and nudged Ethan's shoulder with hers. 'Thank you for coming over.'

As far as she was concerned, Ethan was the one good thing that had come out of that awful incident in June. They'd both been in the vet's office when the Pack had realised who had killed Phil Creasy. While she'd chased the vet, Ethan, who'd been there to have some of his cat's teeth removed, had sprinted after the accomplice.

The lift opened, and they rode it down, exiting the building and entering the park.

It would be incorrect to say that Partridge Park was unlit, but like most municipal things in East London, the lighting was half-hearted. Several of the bulbs in the streetlamps were broken or missing, and the result was a watery light, made eerie by the wispy fog that had formed over the green.

Tyrion bounced his paws against Ethan's leg until Ethan ruffled his ears and scratched the side of his neck, making his rear foot twitch. 'Got your spot, huh?'

Tyrion walked well on the lead, stopping regularly to

wee, like most male dogs, but Phoebe's nose was constantly moving, scanning the area with forensic precision. 'What's she looking for?'

'Chicken bones, mostly,' Meg said. 'Sometimes tissues. At lunchtime, she scored half a sandwich, so don't be surprised if she drags us to the picnic tables.'

'You let her eat it?'

'Hell no. I wrestled it out of her mouth. But she's smart. She'll remember where she found it, and where I threw it.'

Ethan nodded and changed the subject. 'Any news on the dead guy your friend found yesterday?'

'Nope.'

'Thoughts? Theories?'

Meg paused. 'Why would you think we had theories about this?'

Ethan shrugged, and Meg didn't have to be a genius to know that he'd been discussing things with Paul. It was her own fault; she'd added him into the Pack WhatsApp chat once they'd started seeing each other. 'Isn't that what happened last time? You – well, your friends – found a dead body and solved the crime before the police could.'

'You helped, too.' Meg cleared her throat, and brought herself up to her full height of five-foot-almost-nothing. 'But I'll have you know that we don't make a habit of solving crimes. That's why we have a police force. Arrgh! Put that down, Phoebe! Drop it!'

'Unless the crime is committed by the dogs?' Ethan smiled.

Meg knew he was trying to keep things light, but she looked away. Dogs hadn't killed that man and posed him on a bench. And while she wasn't keen to get involved in hunting down another murderer, she wasn't about to let her neighbourhood friends live in fear. Not again.

Not without a fight.

17

ANDY

'The murderer kicked him in the 'nads before strangling him? Kind of adds insult to injury, doesn't it?' Williams breathed as soon as they left the mortuary.

'And then shoved the chicken bone down his throat,' Andy added. 'But to me the first thing, kicking his nuts, seems personal. Female.'

It wasn't a firm rule. There was technically nothing that would stop a man from going for the nuts, but it went against the bro code. It was far more likely that a woman would aim there, one kick delivering maximum pain.

'Drink?' Williams suggested. 'I could really use one.'

Andy kept walking. He could murder a beer, but his fridge was pretty well stocked...

'We can go to your side of the river. The Prospect? City of Ramsgate?' Williams wheedled, hiding a smile when he saw Andy relent.

'Just one.'

'Sure, sure,' Williams said, trotting alongside him down the steps to the Underground. They remained companionably silent until Wapping, where they came out of the station and turned right.

In the dark, the streetlamps cast a yellow glow on the cobbled street. 'Someone with half an imagination could almost see how it must have looked a hundred years ago,' Williams said, surprising Andy.

'You know, Scott, you might have the face of a rugby prop, but you've got the soul of a poet.'

'Soul of a lover, or at least that's what the missus says.' He held up one thick finger. 'And she'd know.'

It was a standing joke between them, albeit a dark one. Andy knew that Williams was single. Had been since Rosie had died. Twenty-three and pregnant, his wife had been going to the corner shop when a drunk driver had jumped the kerb. Theirs weren't the only lives lost that day. Scott had joined the force then, first out of anger and a burning desire to put every drunk driver behind bars, but as the anger had subsided, he'd taken comfort in the sense of purpose. In the ten years that Rosie had been gone, there'd been women, sure, but none that had lasted more than a handful of months.

The Prospect of Whitby was a short walk away. They ordered a couple of Peronis from the bartender and headed around the corner to the tables between the main bar and the beer garden. 'You know this place dates back to Henry VIII's time? Used to be Execution Wharf,' Williams said, lowering himself into a chair.

'Too dark to see it now, but they have a hangman's gallows outside.'

Andy was aware of the history; this pub was one of his locals. He liked the dark wood interior, the exposed beams on the ceiling, the stone floors, the nautical theme. And the beer was good. 'The gallows are just for show now, Scott. The pirates are long gone.'

Williams sighed. 'I don't believe in the death penalty, but sometimes I do think that the threat of it might keep people in check.' He took a gulp of beer and looked around. No one was near enough to hear but he leaned in anyway. 'Dr White thinks there might have been two people who killed Tang?'

'Not much hard evidence to support that theory yet, but I wouldn't bet against her. Think of it this way: Tang wasn't massively tall – five foot nine – and kneeing him would have weakened him, distracted him. He'd have doubled over.'

A group of giggling young women came in. Their faces were flushed from the cold, and maybe a couple of Proseccos, quaffed in another pub.

'Wonder what they'll do with those big tattooed eyebrows when the fashion changes?' Williams mused aloud. 'I mean, whatever happened to the natural look?'

Andy shrugged.

Williams leaned forward again, lowering his voice, even though the girls didn't seem to be paying any attention to them. 'As Dr White said, the bruising tells us he was strangled. But if it was a woman, she'd have had to be strong enough to get him on the ground, even after kneeing him, then maybe strangle him there? I don't think many women would have the size or strength any other way. Not without help.'

'Unless when she disabled him, he'd already fallen to the ground. She knees him, and the poor bastard's on his knees gasping for air. Then she goes for his throat.'

'He'd have had to know her to let her get that close, man.'

'And she'd have had to be fast. Tang would have known he was in danger. He'd have fought back. He wasn't tall, but he wasn't unfit either.'

Williams nodded. 'Okay, hold that thought and let's look at a two-person scenario. Woman lures him in. Gets close enough to knee him. Person Two – either male or female – wrestles him to the ground. One or the other gets on top, finishes the job. They get him back onto the bench and stuff the bone down his throat.'

'But no defensive wounds? Nothing under his nails but a bit of neoprene? Unless there's something Forensics can see that Dr White couldn't.'

'Depending on how fast the attack was, Tang might not have put up enough resistance to need to be restrained, hence no bruising around the wrists.'

'Shit.'

They both closed their eyes.

'I'll check to see if anyone found a pair of discarded gloves, neoprene or not. Something might have a print. And if the doc was right and there were two people, the other person might have left something somewhere,' Andy mused aloud.

'Too many murder shows on TV. They never get the procedures right, but now every yob knows to wear gloves,' Williams muttered.

'Yeah. And we need to see what sort of romantic partners Tang had. This murder still feels very personal.'

'Ex lover?'

Andy nodded.

Williams put his phone down, took another gulp of beer and watched Andy from under his lashes. 'Speaking of which ... the dog community.'

'How is that ... Funny, Scott.' Andy knew Williams had been waiting for his moment, but he drew it out. 'Think there's a connection?'

'We questioned one of the Pack who knew Tang. The journalist, Claire Dougherty. Said they were friends but not romantically involved, and I believe her. She seemed genuinely cut up over his death. All I'm saying is that it's funny that group keeps cropping up when there's trouble.'

'Look, you know how many bodies are found by dog walkers each year,' Andy said, his voice wry. 'And this is Tower Hamlets – plenty of crime to go around.'

'I believe your friends would point out that it's the dog that finds the body, not the walker.' Williams was barely able to suppress a grin, glad to get one over on Andy.

'My friends?'

'We can use the "lover" word again, if you'd rather?'

Andy sighed and tilted his head to the side. 'She's not my lover,' he said. 'Not my ex-lover. Not my ex-girlfriend. Not even my ex-friend.'

'Not ex, then?' Williams winked.

'Never made it out of the gates, Scott.'

'Really? She didn't bin you because you were ...'

'No. Snogged her once or twice, but we never slept together.'

Williams nodded. They'd been the first detectives on the scene when Irina Ivanova and Louise Mallory had found Philip Creasy's body in Partridge Park, and from the get-go, Irina had seemed keen. When Andy had gone silent Williams had thought he was just keeping any relationship with her quiet so as not to not rile the boss.

'Sorry about that, mate,' he offered. 'Lucky escape though. She seemed mad as a box of frogs.'

Andy looked away and Williams fumbled for something nice to say. He couldn't think of anything, but he had to ask, 'You know, with two of her friends finding Tang, chances are she'll find some crazy-ass way of getting involved. You'll probably run into her again. If you want to.'

He watched the expressions flit across Andy's face, almost too fast to put names to. The one that remained at the end was a sort of resignation. 'Best I don't.'

'Good,' Williams said, picking up his beer and draining it. 'Couldn't agree more.'

'You never liked her, did you?' Andy's voice was curious rather than harsh, so Williams thought about his answer.

'It wasn't that I didn't *like* her. She was cute. As a person, she was trying *really hard* to be fun. But there was something ... well ... *off* about her from the start.'

'The trying too hard?'

'That, yeah. But I didn't like the way she treated you,

mate. The way she dropped your arse the first time.' He paused. 'But that second time? After we closed the Creasy case? That was on you. Shouldn't have given her another chance when she already had her crazy on.' He softened his voice. 'You go for the crazies, Andy. At least this time you dodged that bullet before you got to the altar.'

Andy gave him a dark look.

'Look, I like the dog park pack. They're royal pains in the arse, but they're clever. Maybe even fun. If you've got to fish in that water, though, next time avoid the mad one. Right, lecture over.' Williams held up his empty beer glass. 'One for the road?'

18

CLAIRE

Fiona (Nala's Mum)

> Just checking in ... Again.
> How are you doing?

It was the sixth message from Fiona. The others had checked in too, then expressed some sort of relief that she'd been released after questioning, as if they believed the police might actually have some reason to arrest her for killing Jonny.

'As if,' Claire huffed aloud, and refilled her glass.

Only Fi knew about Claire's friendship with Jonny. And that she had been crushing hard on him. It wasn't something she'd been ready to share with the others – not yet. But Fi was her closest friend, and there was little one was doing that the other didn't know about.

She stared out from her balcony overlooking The Bells, towards the canal. The water was silvered by the moonlight, masking the litter along the towpath and the bored teens who congregated under the bridges to smoke weed. From here, right now, it almost looked pretty.

Tank sighed, resting his head on his front paws. He wasn't overly fond of the cold, but was even less in favour of staying indoors when she was outside. She knew he thought his job was to protect her, and he'd done his best, barking and growling when the police had come.

Only, her job was to protect him, so she'd shut him in the bedroom, hoping that someone would see what was happening and come to pick him up, in case they kept her in for a while.

Her eyes wandered down, towards the bench Yaz had found Jonny on. She was grateful that it had been Yaz and not her. She didn't want to see him dead. Hell, she didn't want to think of him dead. That quiet man from upstairs with the silly hat, like he was someone out of the Forties. A Dick Tracy, Bogarty sort of person.

At least from the outside.

It'd taken a couple of years of polite chit-chat in the lift before Claire had suggested a walk, maybe a drink. Jonny had looked over his shoulder at The Bells, aghast.

'No, not there,' she'd laughed, knowing that she didn't need to add, 'And properly chaperoned by Tank, of course.'

'Anywhere but there,' he'd responded with a shy smile. 'But I'd like that.'

They didn't meet often, and Jonny didn't share much,

introvert that he was. But she'd gleaned bits and pieces over the years. He had no family nearby, but was close to them nonetheless. He was more comfortable behind a screen than with people. While he worked in finance, he was not one of the men – most of them were still men – shouting on the floor of the stock market. Instead, Jonny quietly grew his customers' wealth from behind a computer.

And his own? Was that what this was about? A mugging?

Or had someone lost money based on Jonny's advice? Found him and killed him for it?

Claire's imagination provided the details, and she closed her eyes, willing the images away. Willing herself to remember Jonny's shy smile instead. His determination when he was riled. He didn't scream and shout. No. He was a keyboard warrior, and his emails and messages could be ruthless. He didn't stop with the building's WhatsApp group, often escalating issues to the estate managers. Or the council. Or the local MP.

He was very good at using those messages to try to rally people around whatever was bothering him, whether it was recycling (*Why don't we have another bin for food waste?*), the thugs roaming the streets (she knew they'd targeted him more than once) or the policy the building had banning fairy lights on the balconies.

More than once, one of his pet peeves had made it into one of her articles for *The Chronicle*.

She rested her head against the wall, her mind returning to the police's lines of questioning.

Where were you Sunday night?

She'd been out for dinner. When she and Tank had come back and were running the gauntlet of the Cluckin' Grim Creeps outside the chicken shop, Jonny had appeared, dressed to go out.

'Out on a Sunday night?' she'd teased. 'Hot date? Meeting a lady friend?'

'Something like that,' he'd said. His voice was polite, but it was clear that he didn't want to answer any questions.

And Claire hadn't wanted to ask them, feeling a stab in the region of her heart. She'd opened her mouth to wish him a good evening, but the words that had come out were bitter, tinged with hurt. 'Yeah, good luck with that.'

She didn't know why she'd said that. It wasn't as if they were in a relationship. Or even that they'd once had one. But it'd felt like it might have been moving in that direction.

What was it to her, if he was choosing someone else over her?

Nothing.

Or it would have been nothing, if he hadn't been found on Monday morning.

Dead.

Wednesday

19

CLAIRE

Chron Tom

> Hey Claire, I know you were away for the weekend, and heard you got arrested the moment you got back. I was thinking, instead of the feature you've been working on, how about something like 'Innocent Until Proven Guilty? My 24 Hours in Police Custody, Banged Up for Something I Didn't Do?'

> Assuming you didn't kill that man, LOL.

> Since when did *The Chronicle* become a tabloid? And no. I didn't kill him.

There was no point in educating him on the difference between being arrested and being questioned simply because she knew the victim.

> But thank you for your condolences on the death of my friend. I've got another story I'm pursuing. I'll let you know when I'm ready to file it.

Claire muted the conversation. She knew sarcasm would be lost on Tom. He had the nose of a hyena when it came to a story – the more festering, the better – and she wasn't about to allow him to throw her and her byline under a bus for one.

Jonny Tang was dead. She knew she should be starting to come to terms with it, but she was still struggling to believe it was true.

Mild as he had been in person, being a keyboard warrior from the safety of his flat meant he had probably pissed off a fair few people for a shedload of reasons, some big, some small. But the question was who? Who had been angry enough to kill him?

Assuming of course that he had been the actual target, and wasn't just in the wrong place at the wrong time.

Claire threw back a couple of paracetamols with a Berocca and headed out.

As she and Tank exited the complex, she continued to turn things over in her mind. The problem wasn't just that the cops had her on video walking with Jonny. The problem was that the CCTV had caught their last interaction. The police hadn't needed to hear the words to understand that they hadn't parted amicably. And it had caught her going back out ten minutes after she'd gone home.

Why? they'd asked.

She'd needed air. She'd needed space.

And, if she was being honest with herself, she'd needed to see Jonny. Although she wasn't sure if it was to apologise, or to see who he was with.

Someone bumped into her and Claire looked up. Angry Caren's usual scowl eased when she saw her. 'Sorry mate. How are you doing?'

'Fine,' Claire lied, shortening Tank's lead to bring him closer.

The hairdresser held two takeaway coffees in her hands. Despite her hard exterior, her eyes were surprisingly sympathetic. 'I mean, how are you *really*? I heard you were arrested for killing that guy.'

'Questioned, not arrested,' Claire corrected. 'They asked, I answered, they let me go.'

'Good. You hear about too many people getting banged up for crap they didn't do.'

'Thanks for the vote of confidence,' Claire said, feeling a prickling behind her eyes. It wasn't that she was close with the hairdresser, but she knew what people must be thinking of her.

'Nah, no chance it were you, mate.' Caren winked at her. 'You don't got it in you. Anyone can see that.'

Claire realised she meant it as a gentle compliment and took it as such. 'Thank you.'

'Or at least anyone what knows you. You were his friend, right?'

'Yes, I am. I mean, I was.'

'You know anything about why he was killed?'

'No.' Claire shook her head. 'I wish I did. Might make it easier.'

'Or not. Just be careful, right? Assuming it wasn't a case of wrong place, wrong time, whoever killed him might know you was his friend. Might make you a target.'

'But I don't know anything!'

Caren smiled. 'Oh, I believe you. Just watch your back, okay? You're a good egg. Don't want to see you hurt, right?'

'Right,' Claire echoed miserably.

'I hadn't thought of that. Good point,' came a familiar voice. Claire hadn't heard Ella come up behind her – and because Ella didn't have either Jimmy Chew or Bark Vader with her, Tank hadn't given any warning bark. 'You need to be careful, Claire.'

Angry Caren nodded and opened the door to her salon. Ella was pale and her hands were shaking. She looked like she wanted to linger and chat, something that Claire usually would have been up for. A cup of tea, a chat, find out what was bothering her friend.

But she already knew the answer. And she didn't want to talk about it. Didn't actually want to talk at all.

You're a target.

For something she didn't do? Something she didn't know?

Claire wasn't the victim type; she didn't like the way it felt. She mumbled an excuse and led Tank to the half-dead plant on the verge that he liked to poop on. She scooped it up in a yellow poo bag and tossed it into a bin overflowing with CGC branded carrier bags, then turned around and went home.

She pulled the drapes, turned off her phone, crawled into bed and, with one arm around Tank, cried.

20

LOUISE

Partridge Bark

Ethan (Cat Boy)

If anyone heard mad yowling in Partridge Park last night, don't worry – it was @**Meg**.

Paul (Bark Vader and Jimmy Chew's Dad)

That's ma boy!

BONE OF CONTENTION

Meg (Tyrion's Mum)

Not this time. I was watching Phoebe – my new neighbour's dog – and her mum Frances hadn't warned me that Phoebe likes to eat poop.

Fiona (Nala's Mum)

I know that's a thing with some dogs ... but still gross.

Ethan (Cat Boy)

It's way worse than you think. Meg saw Phoebe chewing something and thought it was a chicken bone. Told Phoebe to drop it, but the Phoebs wouldn't.

Meg (Tyrion's Mum)

So I tried to fish it out of her mouth. I do that to T all the time.

> Oh no ...

Meg (Tyrion's Mum)

It was gooey, so I threw it. What else was I supposed to do?

Ethan (Cat Boy)

Cue the howling, and demands for sanitizer and wipes. Only I forgot to bring the wipes ...

Meg (Tyrion's Mum)

I had the antibac and tissues in my pocket but didn't want to touch anything, especially my coat. And someone (@Ethan) was almost wetting himself laughing.

Ethan (Cat Boy)

> Phoebe was barking her head off. Offended that Meg robbed her of her treat.

Meg (Tyrion's Mum)

> Honestly, there wasn't enough antibac or soap in the world last night.

I was giggling to myself, knowing how lucky I was that Klaus wasn't a scavenger. He'd wee on litter, but it'd have to be something really good for him to risk taking a bite. Chicken bones and poop didn't make the list – thank heavens.

Irina (Hamish's Mum)

> A PC. Can you imagine, that chickenshit detective sent a PC to ask me questions!

> You mean Andy? I wouldn't take it personally. I think most of the questions were being asked by the uniforms. Might just be a manpower thing. Did you actually want him to knock on your door?

> NO! Of course not!

I didn't believe her, but wasn't about to call her out on it. That said, the way things were in our neighbourhood, it would only be a matter of time before they came face to face with each other again.

And *that*, I would pay money to watch.

My phone buzzed again, but this time it wasn't Irina. Or an update on Meg's poogate, although it was good to see that her relationship with Ethan was going well.

Sophie (Loki's Mum)

> Morning, lovely. Any chance you're free for a coffee this morning?

That was strange. While I got along well with Sophie, we weren't close. She was a pretty girl in her twenties but had pumped more Botox and beauty treatments into her body than any three of my friends put together. Maybe it was typical for girls her age, but I suspected that having a cheating boyfriend might also factor in.

Tim Aziz wasn't even subtle in carrying out his infidelities. Everyone knew about it. Hell, I'd bet even Sophie knew about it, based on the way she and Irina tended to avoid each other. Sophie could do a lot better than him, but that was a 'her' problem, not a 'me' problem.

What was a 'me' problem was that I turned a blind eye when Tim was carrying out those extracurricular activities with Irina. But if Sophie was asking me for coffee, it must mean that she wasn't judging me for that, right?

I responded that I was working from the café in Partridge Park, and that she was welcome to join me.

A group of older women were getting up from the table in the corner. 'Come here, Klaus.' I scooped up my hound, settling him over my shoulder, and tucked my laptop under my arm as I relocated to my favourite table.

Sophie arrived shortly after, wearing a fuchsia puffer jacket and black leggings. Her dark hair was straight today, pulled back from her face by a pair of fluffy pink earmuffs. Her eyes were serious, but she gestured for me to wait until the barista, trailing behind her, put two coffees on the table between us.

Klaus barked at her and sniffed, before giving a soft *whoof* of disgust that she'd dared arrive here without his friend Loki.

'Sorry, gorgeous,' she said, slipping him a treat. Klaus was a simple soul, which he'd probably sell for a handful of chicken nuggets, and a piece of doggie sausage from Sophie went a fair way. He wolfed it down and licked her hand for more.

'As if I don't feed him,' I sighed.

'They're all like that,' she replied with a laugh, then met my eyes and sobered. She poured a spoonful of brown sugar into her coffee and stared at it for a few moments.

'Sophie?' I asked. 'Are you okay?'

'Me?' She blinked, surprised. 'I'm fine. Look, Lou. I heard something . . . I mean, if I heard something, would you want me to tell you?'

Oh shit. I haven't told her something about her relationship, and she's here, worried about telling me something about mine?

I mean, I'm not in a relationship, but if I were, would I want to know?

'Yes, of course.'

'I heard that you and Yaz found that dead man the other day.'

'Jonny Tang. Yaz and Herc found him,' I clarified.

'Right. So what if I heard something about it . . .'

I didn't think twice about that answer. 'Then you go to the police.'

'But what if it's something I heard from the police? Something they already know. Would you want to know what it is?'

Klaus pawed at my leg while I considered the answer. I

picked him up and settled him onto my lap before speaking. 'What did you hear, Sophie? And how?'

'It wasn't as if I meant to hear anything, Lou.'

'But?'

'But, me and the girls were walking home from the Tube last night. I knew you found the body ... ah ... Jonny. And I'd heard that the same detectives were on the case as last time.'

'Williams and Thompson?'

'Yeah. Like, I remember meeting Andy Thompson once and I recognised him.'

She would have met both men at the Hound, if it was the time I was thinking about, but I could understand why she only remembered Andy. 'You followed them?'

She nodded, then looked away. Her expression was guilty enough to make me wonder just why she had followed them. I had a feeling it was less curiosity about the case, and more the possibility of flirting with a man that Irina had once fancied. A bit of *quid pro quo* for Irina messing around with Sophie's boyfriend.

'Yeah, to The Prospect of Whitby, over in Wapping,' she said. 'He and the other guy, I guess Williams – big guy?' She broadened her shoulders to imply wide, but not fat. 'With a smashed-up face? Like a boxer might have?'

'That's him.'

'Right. Like, the girls didn't care where we went for another drink, so we followed them in. I didn't tell them anything. I mean, Stacey would have screamed it at the top of her lungs or something.'

'Right?' I prompted.

'They were loud. The girls, I mean. The detectives, not so much. They sat in the sort of way that didn't really invite company. Kept their voices down. I couldn't really hear, but their table was on the way to the loos . . .'

'So, you did a bit of eavesdropping on the way?'

'Eh?'

'Listening in on their conversation.'

'Yeah. A bit. I didn't hear much, but it sounded like Jonny was strangled, and there was something about a chicken wing caught down his throat.'

'Like he choked on a bone?' Although Yaz thought there'd been bruising. Maybe the police hadn't noticed, or hadn't thought it was related?

'No. Like it was stuffed down his throat.'

Shit. It was whole?

So, Yaz was right.

'I guess it's different if you're a dog,' Sophie said. 'Then it's kind of like "Oooh, someone left a goodie for me on the street!" I used to have to keep pulling them out of Loki's mouth. The little hoover would chew faster when he realised I saw what he had.'

Used to? Are she and Tim on the outs again?

I didn't want to break the train of the conversation and filed that away for later. 'They don't think it was an accident?'

'No.' She shrugged. 'At least, I don't think so. I definitely heard the word "strangled". Can you be strangled accidentally? And I'm not talking doing it for kicks.'

'I don't know,' I said, trying not to think about that.

'But I didn't hear anything about the why. Just that

they were guessing about the how. I mean, how he was murdered. Not how he got a wing stuffed down his throat. Even Loki chews them before swallowing.'

'Are you sure you didn't hear anything else?'

'Sorry, Lou. That was it. When I came back they'd moved on.'

'They'd left?'

'No, they were talking about someone being mad as a box of frogs. I guess they might have been talking about the killer, but they didn't seem to know who it was before, so I think the conversation just changed direction. To be honest, what I heard could have been about another case, but I thought I should tell you.'

'Why?'

Sophie pursed her lips, accentuating her trout pout. 'Thought you'd want to know.'

I'd tried to stay out of this, not wanting to get sucked into another murder, another investigation. Last time, I'd accidentally made myself a target and almost got killed for it.

And yet, what was happening here, again, wasn't just impacting the wider neighbourhood, it was impacting my friends. Claire had been brought in as a suspect just because she'd been friendly with the deceased. Who would be next?

This was *my* community.

And that was where I drew the line. If I could do something, however small, to protect it – maybe make it a little bit better, a little bit safer – then wasn't it my responsibility to do so?

21

LOUISE

Partridge Bark

> It's a bit early in the week, but does anyone fancy a drink tonight at The Hound?

Paul (Bark Vader and Jimmy Chew's Dad)

> Is this about the dead man? Johnny Tang?

Claire (Tank's Mum)

> Jonny. Have you heard anything or is this a brainstorming session?

> Does that mean you guys are in?

The 'Ayes' had it over the 'Nays', and I booked the back room of our local pub.

Sophie peering over my shoulder, I brought up a browser on my laptop and began to search. 'You know, I've never actually heard of a case where a bone splinters in a dog's stomach,' she said. 'Loki eats them pretty regularly. Not sure why people don't throw their trash into a bin. There are bones *everywhere*.'

'Don't get me started,' I muttered. 'But I wonder, is this maybe part of someone's MO? Like some sort of gang ritual when they've killed someone?'

'Huh,' Sophie watched. 'Google says "No".' She finished her coffee and stood up. 'I'd love to stay but I need to get to the office.'

'Sure. Thanks for, you know, sharing what you heard. See you at The Hound later, right?'

She gave me a thumbs-up and shrugged into the pink puffer.

'Sophie?'

She paused and, while her face was frozen in place,

her eyes widened a fraction. Darting from one side to the other. 'Yes?'

'You don't have to answer the question, but you said that you *used to* take the chicken bones out of Loki's mouth.'

One side of her mouth twitched. 'I thought you might have caught that. Yeah, me and Tim had a row. I'm staying with some mates in Wapping at the moment.'

'Which is how you managed to overhear the detectives.'

'Yeah.'

There was no point in asking what the row was about, or if 'row' equated to 'breakup'. Chances were pretty good that Sophie had caught Tim cheating on her – again – and just had enough. I couldn't blame her.

'Well, as grateful as I am for what you heard about Jonny Tang, I'm sorry about how it came about. I hope you can work it out.'

She looked like she would have raised an eyebrow if she could have. 'Do you?'

Because she knew Irina was one of the women Tim was bonking on the side? There was no use pretending I didn't know. Hell, half the neighbourhood knew. And the other half were probably on Tim's to-do list.

But if he was still cheating after the 'quiet word' Sophie's brothers had that landed him in A&E last spring, then he was a lost cause.

'Honestly?' I said before I could stop myself. *I think you should have kicked him to the kerb years ago.*

'Yeah.'

I made a mental note to text Tim, asking him not to

show up tonight, and tried to craft my response in a way that wouldn't offend her. 'You need to do whatever's best for you. But I think you deserve better.'

'Yeah,' she said, looking away from me. 'Me too.'

I'd moved to the area from West London, leaving genteel for 'up and coming' without really understanding what some of the factors were. On the plus side, I had a lovely, large flat and had found a great community. On the downside, the number of East End boozers still outranked the sort of gastropub that I preferred.

The King's Hound was a little further away than The Bells, but it was worth the walk, even on a cold October night. Situated in a pre-war building that had become foreshortened due to the Luftwaffe's urban planning, it was a mishmash of a place, but that was part of its charm.

As soon as we got close, Klaus began to pull on his lead, knowing where we were headed. If he was lucky, he'd see friends there. On the other hand, if he was lucky, no one else would be there and he could curl up on my lap. Either way, he won.

A few of the potted plants retained their leaves, but others now sported naked branches or were decorated with fake spider webs. A plastic skeleton was propped up by the door, an empty beer glass in its hand.

We pushed through the entrance and paused so I could remove Klaus's jumper.

'The rest of your Pack are in the back room, Lou,' Sheri

the bartender said, waving me past. 'There's enough wine in there even for Irina.'

'That's saying a lot,' I laughed.

I waved to a few friends as I crossed the main room. Some had dogs and would have been welcome to join us, but for whatever reasons preferred to stay on the Pack's periphery.

As we got closer to the back room, Klaus's confident walk turned into even more of a strut. Even though I loved everyone inside, I braced myself before opening the door to The Hound's function room.

The teal wallpaper was flocked and decorated with Art-Deco-type prints of London's sporting achievements, from a 1920s boat race to the 2012 Olympics – a bit old fashioned, but they made it work. The room was elegant; the dogs inside, less so.

I pushed the door open wider, allowing Klaus to enter first. There were the usual yaps and barks while he greeted the others. I unclipped him from his lead and smiled as he ran over to Hercules. Herc stood up suddenly, toppling a nearby chair, then sank back to the ground, edging forward at Klaus height to greet his friend. Tyrion scrambled from Meg's lap to join the fray.

As usual, the half dozen tables were pushed together to form a single long length, and were almost bowed under the weight of assorted nibbles and buckets of beer, wine and Prosecco. A water jug sat neglected in the centre, on a coaster depicting a Jack O'Lantern with a microphone advertising The Hound's Halloween-themed open mic night on Wednesday.

The usual Pack suspects had gathered around the

table: Ejiro, looking tired but still dapper in his city suit. Well done him; when I got back from the States, I was out cold by 4 p.m. and looked like an extra from *The Walking Dead*. Beside him, Yaz leaned into his side, her feet propped up on a chair with Hercules lying below her. She must have still been feeling the shock of finding Jonny Tang on Monday; both she and Herc looked uncharacteristically subdued.

The rest of the Pack sat in clusters – Paul and Ella, Fi and Claire, Sophie and Meg and Ethan, and, on the end, looking bored, Irina. She was idly watching Hammy, Tank and Tyrion try to hump a cream long-haired dachshund that I'd not seen before. Klaus leaned back, his behind wiggling in the air.

'That's Phoebe?' I guessed.

'Don't trust the butter-wouldn't-melt look,' Ethan warned.

'She's an angel,' Meg disagreed.

There was no sign of Tim or his Jack Russell, Loki. I was glad they'd decided to stay away, although the only person who might miss them was Irina.

She shrugged when I caught her eye. 'What? She'd tell him off if she didn't like the attention. It's not like she's in season.' It took a moment before I realised she was talking about Phoebe.

Meg's head snapped to the corner and sighed as Klaus began his I'm-cute-you-must-love-me dance for Phoebe. 'She's an angel but a floozy. Anyone else notice we have a disproportionate number of boys on the ground?'

Nala bared her teeth at the scene. As the usual

floozy-in-residence, I didn't think she liked sharing the attention with the pretty daxie. Fi rested her hand on her cocker's head.

'It could have been worse,' Ella said. 'We could have brought Jimmy and Bark with us.'

'Fair. You know I love them, but those two bring their own wave of chaos. Are we expecting anyone else or shall we start?' There were some general murmurs of assent as I slipped into an empty seat partway down the table. 'Good. Anyone have any problems with Claire writing about this?'

'Stealing my sandwich on that one, Louise?' Claire joked, but without her usual joviality. 'Despite me getting a first-hand tour of Murder Central on the other side of the river, I still feel like we're in catch-up mode. And I'd rather find who did this before they manage to kill someone else.'

'*Oui.*' Paul leaned forward. 'Is that why we are meeting here instead of using the chat?'

'Also because Irina had to add her cute detective to the chat last spring.' Yaz's voice was bland, but her expression was just on the far side of holier-than-thou.

'I didn't put him in,' Irina began, then seemed to realise that she'd have to explain more and backed out. 'But I did take him out.'

'I kind of liked having him in there,' Meg said. 'Even if he didn't say anything, it was good to know that if we had a problem, he might be able to help.'

'Not sure he would have wanted to stay in . . .' Yaz slid her glance down the table towards Irina, ignoring Irina's two fingered salute.

There was a tentative knock at the door and a woman I didn't know poked her head around it. She was in her late forties, with dark hair pulled back into a sleek ponytail and the sort of toned physique and lineless forehead that said 'I might not be able to stop the aging process, but at least I'm gonna look good.'

'Is this the Partridge Bark group?' the woman asked, then looked at the dogs around the room as the barking began. 'Guessing it is. I'm Kate Marcovici. I've got the two beagles, Percy and Andy.' She grinned unselfconsciously. 'Or Perseus and Andromeda, when I want to be formal with the furkids.'

I liked her already.

'Sorry I'm late, but those asshats over by the new chicken place thought they were being cute.' She looked around the room and frowned. 'But I did think this was a social thing, not a business meeting.'

'You're not late, and it's sort of both, but you're more than welcome. I'm Louise. The short black-and-tan monster trying to chat you up is my little Casanova, Klaus. Keep your mouth closed unless you want to get Frenched by him; he's got the tongue of an aardvark.'

'I'd much rather snog him than the Cluckin' creeps outside the chicken joint.' Kate leaned down and kissed the top of Klaus's head, neatly dodging a snog.

'We're plenty social, when we're not finding dead bodies,' Yaz said.

'Ah.'

'And when we're not being accused of killing them,' Claire added.

'The Met are overstretched,' I began, only to be interrupted by a *harrumph* from Irina. Ignoring it, I continued, 'So we've started sniffing around on our own. Maybe we'll find something, maybe we won't, but at least we're trying to make the neighbourhood a bit safer.'

'I'm in,' Kate said, sitting down between Irina and Paul. 'I've only just moved here. Some parts of the neighbourhood are great – I love Partridge Park – but even though I have two relatively mouthy dogs, it doesn't feel too safe after dark.'

'Or even during daylight,' Fi muttered.

'I'm Yasmin,' Yaz said. 'Herc and I were the ones who found the guy. But funny you mentioned CGC.' She scrolled through her phone to find the pics she'd taken on the day, then passed it down the table. 'When we first saw him, the man had a CGC box of wings at his feet and, it would seem, a bone lodged in his throat.'

'Which is a bit heavy handed, considering the guy wouldn't be caught . . . ah, he didn't eat fast food,' Claire said, correcting herself. 'So, we've got to wonder: why CGC instead of the other fast food places? Is it random, as in, it could have been any place that sold wings, or was it specific to CGC?'

'I don't live in the building,' Meg hedged. 'But my hairdresser is there. When CGC opened, they were seriously pissed off.'

'Isn't that the place that always blasts heavy metal music?' Ella asked.

'Yes, but heavy metal doesn't stink up the salon the way fried chicken does. They've started pumping out all sorts of perfumes to mask the scent.' Meg waited for the awkward giggles to die down. 'It "brings down the area", Caren says, even though The Bells can do that on its own. I meant to stop by earlier to see if there was any good goss but I've been kind of busy.' She gestured towards Phoebe, who seemed to be taking a lot of pleasure in winding up Nala.

'I do live in the building,' Claire said. 'And yeah, since they moved in, the whole place stinks of chicken. Even on the fifth floor. For the first week, I'd be getting hungry all the time and running downstairs. Now it just makes me feel sick.'

'Fifth floor? Are they using the building's ventilation systems for their exhaust?'

Claire shrugged. 'I don't know for sure, but it smells like it. Everyone in our building's chat is upset.'

'When Village Vets closed down, I figured there would be a few people, maybe companies, who'd bid for the space. They were all turned down,' Meg said.

'Maybe CGC just put in a better offer?'

Meg shrugged.

'How did you find this out?' Paul asked.

'My friend Connor works for Tower Hamlets Council.'

'What does he think?'

Meg grimaced. 'Connor thinks that CGC's owner is chums with one of the councillors. Maybe a donor. I get the feeling that happens a lot.'

'That sounds dodgy,' Kate said.

'Yeah, it's dodgy. But that sort of thing happens everywhere. Every newspaper's politics pages are full of it. So, why draw attention to CGC by putting their box by a dead man?' Meg shook her head. 'I don't know. I just don't buy it. Feels like they're being framed.'

I agreed. 'Maybe there's something else? Something the killer wants us to know?'

'Like what?' Kate asked.

I picked up my glass, looking into its depths, but it offered no answers. Yet.

'I guess that's for us to figure out.' I took a sip and put the glass down. 'Let's go back to basics. Irina, can you look into Jonny's background? See what you can find? There has to be some reason he was targeted.'

'But *I* knew him,' Claire protested. She looked like she wanted to say something else, but stopped herself.

'You're too close, Claire. You know whatever he told you, saw how he presented himself to you. Irina doesn't have that connection, and let's face it: her superpower is the Internet stalk.'

'And deadly mixology.' Yaz glanced at Sophie before adding, 'And . . .'

'If you can't handle your booze, Yaz, that's not my fault!'

'*Enough*,' I said. 'Claire, if you want, you can work with Irina, but let's see what she can come up with. Meg, could you see what else Council Connor can dig up on CGC and its owner? I'll check in with my property developer friend, Annabel, and see if she's heard anything.'

Ejiro, who'd been silent for most of the evening, cleared his throat. 'Can I just remind you that whoever is behind this has killed at least one person? Let's not take any chances. We're going to stir up some muddy waters, and whoever murdered Jonny Tang won't hesitate to kill again if they're feeling threatened.'

Yaz slouched down in her seat, knowing what was coming next.

Ejiro avoided his partner's gaze, instead fixing it on Irina, then Meg. Then me. 'Forgive me if I'm being sexist, but please, please, if you're a single woman, especially if you have a small dog, team up with someone else for any early-morning or late-night walks.'

I felt the need to defend Klaus. 'Nothing shouts louder than a dachshund.'

Ejiro's brow lowered. Usually, it was an early warning of his ire, but now, it felt more like concern.

'Except the sound of an ambulance, Louise. Don't put yourself out there, only to become a statistic.'

He had reinforcement from a suddenly and uncharacteristically serious Paul, who added, 'Again.'

22

LOUISE

Jake (Luther's Dad)

> How did it go?

> You could have come and found out for yourself.

> Busy. But be careful. Whoever killed that man won't hesitate to get rid of someone who's threatening him.

> Yeah. Ejiro made that point.

> Good man.

'So, is this a regular thing?' Kate fell into step beside me.

'What?' I asked, slipping my phone into my pocket. 'Drinks at The Hound?'

'That. And getting involved in murder investigations.'

'The drinks, yes, pretty regular. They let us have the function room when we think we'll have a lot of dogs.'

'Or need a bit of privacy,' Claire said from behind me, where she and Tank were walking with Irina and Hammy. 'And as for getting involved with the police, that's my job.'

'Claire's a reporter for *The Chronicle*,' I explained. 'As for the rest of us, we try not to get involved in murders. Or murder investigations.'

'We only did this once before, when Irina and Louise found a dead man in the park last spring,' Claire explained.

'Partridge Park?'

'Yep.'

'That was you? I remember reading about that. The local vet murdered a dog dad?'

'Yeah. He should be coming up for trial soon, isn't that right, Irina?'

'How the devil should I know?' Irina grunted, sucking on a vape stick.

'When did you start smoking?' I asked.

'When I was sixteen,' she snapped. 'Sometimes I start, sometimes I stop.'

'Huh,' I responded. I'd never seen her smoke before, not

even after we'd found Phil Creasy. What was bad enough to make her restart this time?

'So, your dog is called Klaus, right?' Kate asked. 'Good German name for a German-engineered dog?'

'Exactly.'

'Bah,' Irina interjected. 'Ask Louise what box set she was binging when she got him.'

I glared at her while Claire neatly changed the subject. 'When did you move to the area, Kate?'

'A couple of weeks ago. Still getting used to the neighbourhood.'

There was another question on the tip of my tongue when I heard sirens cut through the night. Klaus and Tank started barking, while the rest of us moved out of the way to allow two police cars to scream past. 'What the . . .'

Muttering an expletive, Claire started sprinting after the cars.

'Where's she going?' Kate asked.

'Professional curiosity,' Irina said, nonchalantly.

'No.' I felt the answer come with a slow, cold certainty. 'They're heading towards her building.'

'CGC?'

'Could be anything, but I don't want Claire there by herself. Let's go.'

'Sod that,' Irina called after us. 'Good luck to you, but I'm going home.'

Claire had a head start, but Klaus was up for an evening run. A fair bit of wine and M&S chocolate bites sat in my tummy, preventing any amount of speed, so by the time we caught up to her just in front of The Bells, Kate and I were wheezing.

'Oh shit,' Kate said.

There was a crowd on both sides of the road in front of Claire's building, spanning from the beauty salon almost to News-N-Booze. Traffic was blocked by two police cars parked at either end of the street while the cops tried to establish a cordon.

We weren't close enough to see much, but you couldn't miss the ambulance.

I put a hand on Claire's arm, but she shook it off. Instead of pushing forward to see, she moved back, towards the front door of the pub. She didn't enter, but handed me Tank's lead while she clambered onto one of the rickety tables. 'Looks like another ambulance is coming through.'

'What do you see?'

'One man on the ground. Another talking to the cops.'

Kate stood on the table beside Claire and took a few photographs. When I gaped, she explained, 'I'm not a ghoul, and it's not for social media. The police always want pics of the crowds in case there's someone lurking in there who might be of interest.'

I handed her my phone for a second pic, and when she handed it back, there were faces I recognised: the shocked expression of Tanzima, who worked in the charity shop, even though it'd been closed for hours; angry Caren-not-Karen looking intrigued; Benny the colourist looking pale; the guards at the Tesco door avidly watching while doing their best not to look like it.

And then there was the small phalanx of the usual men

who lurked outside the chicken shop. I didn't know them well enough to know who might be missing, or who might be on the ground with the paramedics.

Partridge Bark

Meg (Tyrion's Mum)

> I hope everyone got home ok. Ethan said he heard police sirens.

> We're here. 2 men on the ground. Paramedics and cops.

Ejiro (Hercules's Dad)

> GO HOME LOUISE!

'Weren't a drunk brawl,' a gravelly voice drawled from behind me. 'But Ejiro's right, best not to linger.'

Klaus started barking, quickly joined by the other dogs. I turned quickly, locking eyes with the older man leaning against the wall of The Bells. He wore a wool jacket with the collar turned up over a button-down shirt and pressed trousers. Despite his clean-cut appearance, Gavin MacAdams had a colourful past that included links to organised crime and a trip to jail for grievous bodily harm. Now he was a retired (maybe semi-retired?) ex-con and dog dad to a little black Affenpinscher called Violet. Rumour had it that he'd wanted a Dobermann pinscher, but his daughter had got it wrong. Or maybe got it right. Violet was small in stature, but gargantuan in personality.

To Klaus's clear dismay, there was no sign of her. Almost in apology, Gav stooped down to pat the dogs' heads.

'Hey, Gav. Did you see what happened?'

'Almost,' he said, disappointed. 'Heard screams an' came out. One car pulled up. Lads had a bull-and-cow with the yobs outside the chicken shop.'

'Bull-and-cow? You mean a row? With knives?' Claire asked from the top of the table, her eyes still on the crowd.

'Is the car still there? I can't see a car parked by the shop,' Kate said.

Gav pointed at her from behind her back and spread his hands, querying who she was.

'Kate,' I mouthed, and gave him a thumbs-up to indicate that she was okay.

I sat on the bench next to Claire's table. Klaus bounced his front paws against my knees until I put him on my lap, grateful for his warm body on the cool night. Tank was content to lie down, his back legs splayed behind him, chomping on the end of a stick that made him look uncannily like Winston Churchill. He'd probably throw the stick up later.

I shifted to the side to make room for Gav. 'We missed you tonight at The Hound.'

'Not my scene.'

'Right. Last I knew, The Bells wasn't either. Don't

you usually drink at the George and Dragon, over by the market square?'

'*Pffft*,' he exhaled. 'Met an old mate.'

That he didn't have Violet meant that he'd been planning on having a pint or three. 'You don't have to stay out here with us if you want to stay with your friend?' I fished.

'It's fine.'

Which, from Gav's easy demeanour, meant that his friend had already left and it wasn't as embarrassing hanging out with the Pack. I liked Gav, and knew he wasn't prone to offer up information until he was ready. And while I could push him, the answers I'd get wouldn't be worth anything. Rubbing my arms to warm them, I gave it a go anyway. 'Anything you can share?'

He glanced at me from under grizzled grey brows.

'About that,' I clarified, pointing at the street. As I expected, he didn't reply.

The wounded were either being released or loaded into the ambulance, the crowds beginning to dissipate.

'Is that blood in the street?' Kate asked, horrified, though neither she nor Claire looked like they were ready to leave.

But I was.

'It's cold. I'm going to take Klaus home,' I said. I pulled him onto my shoulder and stood up to hand Tank's lead back to Claire. The Frenchie looked up, but seemed content enough to stay on the ground with his stick. 'Let me know if anything interesting happens.'

'Sure thing.'

I just hoped it wasn't something explosive.

Thursday

23

CLAIRE

Jennifer Tang

> Sorry for the late reply and thank you for your kind condolences.

> The police were in touch on Monday. My parents are flying to London and will take him home. They don't want him buried in the country that killed him.

> I understand that. Sorry again for your loss.

Claire had found Jonny's sister's number and texted her on Tuesday, though she hadn't really expected a response. Although she would have dearly loved to say a final goodbye – and an apology – to Jonny, and to pay her respects, the best she could offer in return was to do everything she could to find out who had killed him.

Kate (Percy and Andy's Mum)

> Saw the article online – well done!

> It helped that I had a hand getting the quotes – thank you.

> Been out of the game for a while – and when I was in it, I was an investigator, not a journalist, but it was fun.

> Look, not sure how to say this, but you have the little red Kia, right? You parked on the street? Behind News-N-Booze?

> Yeah. Why?

> I think you're going to want to come here.

Claire muttered an oath and stepped Tank into his harness, before calling the lift and trotting down the street, stopping twice to allow Tank to relieve himself. Kate – without her dogs – was leaning against a black Hyundai. She stood up straight as Claire approached and met her in front of the red car.

'Jaysus,' Claire said, keeping Tank back. Someone had carved 'Bitch' deep into the metal down one side.

'The "C" word is etched on the other,' Kate said.

'Ah, Christ.'

'It could be a coincidence.'

'It could,' Claire agreed, but she heard Angry Caren's voice echo in her mind, telling her that Jonny's killer might see her as a target. 'Or maybe it's not. But then how would they know it's my car? I don't leave anything in there.'

'Irish plates. If I could guess right, maybe they did too?'

Maybe they had. Maybe it was a warning that they were coming after her.

'I think you need to call the police,' Kate said.

Claire nodded, feeling the futility of the situation. Vandalism wasn't a new thing for cars left on the street. Maybe some disinterested PC would come and take a statement. Give her a reference number that she could submit as part of her insurance claim.

Would they connect it to the murder of Jonny Tang?

No. Probably not. Assuming it was even connected; as Kate said, it might be a coincidence.

Only Claire knew that it wasn't. Something dark and ugly bubbled into her consciousness; something someone had recently said – was it Kate? – that murderers often try to insert themselves into investigations.

Claire looked at the other woman from under her lashes, a sick feeling spreading out from her belly, and realised that she had a new line of investigation to look into.

24

LOUISE

Annabel

> Hey, long time no chat. Fancy catching up?

Hey, gorgeous. I'm in Limehouse today, but I can do lunch if you're free? Plans tonight, then off for the weekend. 😊

> Anything nice?

I'll let you know later. Shall we do 13:00? That Italian

> place with the spicy name that you like.

> La Figa?

> That's the one. See you then! xx

I did like La Figa. Good food and atmosphere, great staff and dog-friendly as well. Plus, the portions were generous enough that I didn't have to worry about cooking dinner. It ticked all the right boxes.

I connected my phone to the speakers in my home office, put on a Nineties mix and started trawling though my emails. Then I felt the draw of last night's action. I wasn't surprised to see an article with Claire's byline on *The Chronicle*'s site.

EAST LONDON GANG STABBING

One man in his twenties is dead and another remains in critical condition in an East London hospital's major trauma unit after clashing outside a popular chicken shop in Tower Hamlets last night.

Witnesses saw a dark Kia pull up to the kerb and words being exchanged between two groups of men outside

Cluckin' Good Chicken at approximately 10:20 p.m.. Hostilities escalated and both groups drew knives and shivs – handcrafted bladed weapons common in prisons – one of which was found discarded three streets away, and is thought to be the murder weapon.

Police, including firearms officers, and the London Ambulance Service raced to the scene, where one man was confirmed dead and two others were transported to hospital.

At this point, no arrests have been made and a large cordon remains around the scene, with traffic along the high street diverted.

Local businesswoman Caren Hansen, owner of the Hands-On salon, said, 'We were just closing the shop when we heard the fracas outside. We know there's crime in the area, but we hadn't expected it to escalate to knife fights in the middle of the street on a Wednesday night! It was chaos.'

The police are appealing to the public for any information. Deputy Assistant Commissioner Shahid Armin released a formal statement saying, 'On behalf of the London Borough of Tower Hamlets Council, our thoughts and prayers are with all those affected by last night's violence. Fast-moving enquiries are underway, and we will update the public as things develop. If anyone has any information regarding the incident, including any video footage, please contact us.'

This confrontation happened a short distance from

> where the body of Jonny Tang was found by dog walkers on Monday morning.

From the quotes in there, she'd been busy this morning. I flicked over to the BBC's site, unsurprised to see a version of Claire's article there, almost word for word. Both reports drew a line between this incident and Jonny Tang's murder, although as far as I knew there was no evidence to connect the two, other than a vague proximity.

Unless Claire – and the Beeb – knew something that I didn't?

25

IRINA

Louise (Klaus's Mum)

> Be grateful you went home last night. You missed all the excitement.

> I have enough excitement in my life.

> I'm sure you do. Just a heads-up then. Police are talking to witnesses, but it looks like it's another murder team working on

> it. Just in case you were worrying.

> I wasn't. Now sod off. I have work to do. And before you ask, yes. I'll update you if I find anything interesting.

Irina leaned back in her chair and rubbed her eyes. She had two cases to file, but she was wasting time digging up dirt on a dead man. A dead man that she didn't know, and who meant less than nothing to her.

And yet, she couldn't help herself.

As the BBC article had said, Jonathan Tang was born in Singapore. He'd attended the University of Pennsylvania, majoring in Economics, and continued on to gain his MBA from Wharton.

'Not bad,' Irina muttered. 'UPenn is good, but it's not Harvard. Still, he got into Wharton, and *that* is impressive.'

Social media traced Jonny's path from his time as a fresh-faced fresher – young, eager and pimply, but even then with a determined look in his eyes. The sort of zeal you'd expect from people who take jobs in companies that believe in social justice. And yet, Jonny had returned to the family fold in Singapore, scoring a job with a top consultancy. He'd stayed there for four years, then transferred to New York, living on the Upper East Side.

'Of course.' Nice, genteel area. That made sense.

And then in 2018, he'd moved to London. With a promotion, but no wife.

Three major economic capitals before he was thirty-five. 'What next? Hong Kong? Shanghai? Zurich?' Irina put down the vape she'd been gnawing on and frowned. 'And yet you were living in this neighbourhood? Why here? With that sort of high-flying career, why weren't you in Chelsea, or at least somewhere more high end than Tower Hamlets?'

And what was with the single status? Was he into hookers? Lots of City boys were. Or did he prefer men? Maybe he wanted to hide that from potentially unsupportive parents? Social media was keeping shtum.

She made a note to return to that later; there were still places she could check.

'So, here you have a rich, single man, Mischka. Social media shows him with "friends", but I don't see a steady girlfriend, and no wife. Even if we're close to Canary Wharf here, you'd think he'd be chasing a better lifestyle, well, elsewhere.'

Hammy, sitting on her sofa, didn't answer. Instead he rolled onto his back, raised his little leg and began licking his bits.

'I mean, sure, there are some lovely flats in the Wharf, if he just wanted to be closer to work.' Irina knew; she'd checked them out. She just couldn't afford them. Yet.

Could he?

Maybe he wasn't making the dosh?

Although working for a top consultancy, he probably was.

Unless he had an expensive habit? Clothes? Women? Drugs?
Was he being blackmailed or extorted?

That might explain why he'd ended up dead on a canal path in grotty East London.

Irina replaced the vape in her mouth. Gripping it between her teeth, she began to type furiously. 'Follow the money, Mischka. It'll always lead to the right place.'

26

ANDY

'A *magnet fisherman* found *what?*' DCS Grieves shook his head. His chin, long and loose, waggled in a way that Andy tried hard not to think too much about.

'A magnet fisherman along one of the canals brought up a metal lock box under the Morris Road Bridge,' Williams said, clearly satisfied after getting that reaction from Grieves. 'When he managed to get it open – and I'm not sure how he did that – instead of dosh, he found a gun, and called the cops. No prints, obviously, but Ballistics tested it, and found that it'd been used in a previous crime.'

'Pretty likely considering it'd been wiped and dumped.' Grieves crossed his arms over his chest and leaned back against the wall, his composure slowly returning.

'What's interesting is that it was dumped *in* the box, making it harder to get to. Which also raises the question as to why it was kept safe in the box, maybe until now. 'Coz let's face it, over the years there've been plenty of magnet fishers along the canals.'

'Feels more like it was kept for blackmail,' Andy offered, stifling a yawn. He'd heard about the stabbing outside The Bells last night. Had already checked both the witness and victims lists, and while there were a couple of familiar names, he'd breathed a sigh of relief when the one he was looking for wasn't on either. 'Scott, did Ballistics tell you which crime it was used in?'

Williams pursed his lips and answered, 'Well, yes, Andy. They did.'

'Stop with the double act, you two,' Nic said. 'You got something to say, spill it.'

'It was used in what was considered at the time to be a drive-by shooting. When it happened we thought it was random or, at worst, a case of mistaken identity.'

'It's old? Then why are you bringing it here instead of to the lads on the cold case team, Williams?' Grieves asked.

'They're aware. Thought I'd let you know because it was one of our cases, three years ago. The woman killed, Abby Engels, was an environmental activist of sorts. Not one of the crazies that'll superglue herself to the road or anything. She had a PhD in chemistry, or something like that. The sort that does their homework, fights The Man on his own turf. With cold facts, not hot rage.'

'Abby Engels. I remember the case,' Grieves said. 'Thanks for letting us know, but it's still one for the cold case lads.' He nodded at Nic. 'And Flo Jo. Next. On the subject of canals, tell me about the man on the bench. Jonny Tang.'

Andy nodded. 'We finished with the door-to-doors. I've got a catalogue of parties in the area, on a Sunday night no less—'

'And too early for Halloween,' Williams added.

Andy ignored him. 'But no one saw anything suspicious. In fact, no one seems to have seen anything unusual on the canal path. Usual batch of teenagers with weed or nitrous oxide.'

'Or both.'

'Or both,' Andy agreed. 'A few people on bikes. Thing is, most people know not to walk along the canals at night if they can help it, especially now that it's getting cold.'

Nic nodded. 'Especially if you're walking alone.'

'Right. We've got Tang's wallet, interviewed his neighbours. Most said he was a "nice guy" who "kept himself to himself". Those who seemed to know him said he was frustrated with the neighbourhood, hoping it'd be more up-and-coming. I checked with the council and Tang made regular complaints about boys racing their cars down the high street and also about The Bells pub, from the "dilapidated" state of the building to the "seedy" clientele – those were the actual words used,' Andy said, to explain his air quotes. 'More recently, he raised concerns about the new chicken place, Cluckin' Good Chicken, which opened on the ground floor of his building.'

'So, a Karen. A whinger.'

'A Karen, but one who ended up dead and posed on the canal, with a chicken bone shoved down his throat. There's got to be a reason he was offed, and when we find it, we'll have a big clue who the murderer is.'

27

LOUISE

Claire (Tank's Mum)

> Any more news about that stabbing outside your building?

Just what I uploaded to *The Chron*'s site. And we stayed out until about 1.

> I can't imagine Tank enjoyed that.

Hell no. I took him upstairs and stayed out with Kate.

> She seems to have a nose for news.

> Sounds like you found a kindred spirit, Claire!

Klaus paused in front of the steps. It was common knowledge in the dachshund community that steps were bad for daxies' long backs. He knew that as a rule, I didn't allow him to take them, but if they were long and shallow, as were the steps outside La Figa, I relented. It made him feel like he'd got one over on me, and the look of victory on his face when he reached the top never failed to melt my heart.

He still had an extra bounce in his step as he strutted into the restaurant like he owned it.

La Figa's décor was firmly moored in the last century, but that was part of its charm. The maître d' guided us to where Annabel was waiting at a table on the left side of the big black bar; the side they tended to put people with dogs. A bowl of water waited at her feet for Klaus.

Even though it was October, and cold outside, my property developer friend, Annabel Lindford-Swayne sported the sort of healthy tan that spoke of the Mediterranean rather than the tanning salon. She wore sunglasses on the top of her head, holding her dark blonde highlighted hair back from her face.

'Louise!' She rose out of her seat just enough to kiss

both my cheeks, then leaned down to say hello to Klaus, who was bouncing against her knee with a persistent zeal.

'Klaus, stop that,' I instructed, trying not to cringe at the marks he was leaving on Annabel's immaculate tan trousers.

'It's fine,' she said, moving close enough to allow him a quick sausage snog before righting herself. 'I ordered a bottle of Verdicchio, but held off on food until you got here.'

'Sounds perfect, but we have to stick with only one. I have a client event this evening.'

'Party pooper.' She pushed one menu towards me and opened the other. Her blue eyes squinted at it for a few moments until she sighed and pulled an eyeglass case from a well-worn Hermès bag on the seat beside her. While Irina loved showing off designer names, Annabel wore them with the casual disregard of old money.

'Getting older sucks,' she said, popping the specs on.

Getting old? She was thirty-two. Barely.

'Beats the alternative,' I noted.

'What? Corking it early?' She grinned, flashing perfect white teeth. 'Not gonna happen.'

She glanced at me above the specs' tortoiseshell rims. 'Not that I don't like meeting you for lunch, Lou, but please tell me this isn't a fishing expedition to find out about that stabbing yesterday.'

'The one outside Cluckin' Good Chicken?' I shook my head. 'Nope. No need. I was there.' And Claire was already on the case with that. 'But I do want to pick your brain on the shop.'

'Christ.' Annabel took the glasses off again and

placed them on the table. She looked out of the almost-floor-to-ceiling window and sighed. 'Don't quote me on this, but they're almost as bad as The Bells.'

'What do you know?'

'I'll disappoint you here. I don't know much. The Bells is a shithole that should have been knocked down decades ago, but they won't sell up and let us redevelop. CGC's new, but neither their management nor their clientele are making them a lot of friends. Not unusual to see their punters and The Bells' clash after closing.'

'From what I hear, the contretemps last night was precipitated by someone in a car, not someone coming out of The Bells.'

'That was only one incident, Lou.' She buried her nose in the menu, and when the waiter came, rattled off her order. I hadn't actually opened the menu yet, but I ate here often enough to know what I wanted.

When the waiter retreated, I sipped the crisp wine and asked, 'How did another chicken shop get zoning approval? I mean there's one on almost every block these days.'

Annabel rolled her eyes, a silent answer: *friends in the right places*.

'But you're trying to gentrify the neighbourhood, right? Your company, anyway?'

'Yeah, a safer, nicer neighbourhood commands higher prices.'

'So, why would you lease out that space to a run-of-the-mill fried chicken joint?'

Another shrug. This time accompanied by narrowed blue eyes. Whatever was going on, Annabel didn't want to talk about it. Maybe those friends in the right places putting a bit of pressure on her?

'Who owns it?' I pushed on. 'And did they buy it or are they leasing it? Under what terms?'

'Leave it, Louise.'

'What did they have on the proposal? Was it fried chicken or did they switch that out after ink met paper?'

'*Leave it*, Louise,' Annabel repeated, her voice lowering and her eyes darting around nervously.

'Are the gang of men that hang out outside the shop on the owner's payroll, do you think?'

'How on earth would I know that?' Annabel hissed, but she looked scared now.

'You know something's off there. What is it?'

Face pale under the tan, she stared out the window at the cars going down Narrow Street. Whatever she knew, if she knew anything at all, she wouldn't – or couldn't – tell me.

And I knew enough not to push any more than I already had. Not if I didn't want to damage our friendship. I switched gears. 'Anyway, enough about that. How was your holiday? Where did you go? Mykonos again?'

The rest of the lunch passed amicably, talking about Annabel's holidays and my half-baked exit strategy from my company, and what might come after that.

But as we parted ways in the courtyard in front of La Figa, Annabel leaned forward. 'I can't tell you what to do or not do, Louise. But if you want a bit of advice, stay away from CGC.' She kissed me on one cheek. 'Stay safe.' And then the other. 'And for once, keep your bloody head down.'

28

CLAIRE

Louise (Klaus's Mum)

> I had lunch with Annabel – I asked her about CGC. I think she knows something dodgy is going on but wasn't sharing it with me. Got the feeling that she can't – that she's scared – but she wouldn't say who she was scared of, or why, or anything.

> And she didn't say as much, but I have a hunch

> that she's asking the same questions we are. She has to be, right? As part of her job? Maybe she's been warned off, cos she sure as hell warned me off.

'Kindred spirit, my sweet arse,' Claire muttered, skimming Louise's earlier texts before turning her phone face down, new messages unread, to remove any distractions. She'd parked her work on CGC to have a closer look at the new addition to the Pack.

She'd done a few of the usual searches on Kate Marcovici, although it had taken her a few tries until she'd spelled Kate's surname correctly.

The most recent results were articles about her artwork, mostly sculptures in various galleries, one of them winning an award.

Before then, she had indeed led an investigative team in the Environment Agency, leaving after thirty years. She explained it in one of the artsy interviews: *'Work was always important to me, and the work we were doing was important to the country. I loved it, loved being part of something bigger than I was. Even during the Covid years, when people were working from home, we were out in the field. But it got to a point, you know, where it felt like a losing battle. When one of the people on my team unexpectedly passed away, I re-evaluated my priorities and realised that it might be time to do something for me. So, I quit. Luckily, I found I could make a living from my artwork. Something I'm grateful for every day.'*

'Nice work, if you can get it,' Claire said. She wasn't sure how lucrative things were in the art world, but the term 'starving artist' hadn't come from nowhere.

Was Kate's lifestyle being funded by someone else? Maybe someone connected to Cluckin' Good Chicken?

Someone who might have killed Jonny Tang?

29

IRINA

Angela (Doggie Daycare)

> Hey lady, sorry for the late response – you won't believe how crazy life is!

> You're still ok to have Hamish tomorrow?

> Yes, of course! Hammy's never any problem. But you asked if I'd heard anything about the man found on the canal path? Jon Tang? I haven't, but

> I HAVE heard a rumour about you …

> Probably lies.

> Yeah, maybe. But someone saw the cops knocking on your door and bets are running high that you'll take up again with that handsome detective. Anything you want to share?

'No,' Irina said aloud and put the phone down. She glanced over her shoulder at Hamish. 'Why on earth do you want to go to that place? That woman is mad.'

Hammy's tongue lolled out of his mouth and he tilted his head to the side.

'Fine. You can still go, but no gossiping about me, all right?'

She turned back to her computer. A legal pad was at her elbow, mostly containing doodles around the edges of the pages.

'Cluckin' Good Chicken is owned by one company,' she explained to Hammy, reaching for a bag of crisps. 'Which is owned by another company that also owns a fair few perfume shops scattered around London. The type that tells you that whatever you choose is bespoke just for you, but in truth they're all knock-offs of lesser-known fragrances. You never see a single person in any of those shops.'

She stuffed a handful of crisps into her mouth, not noticing Hammy's surgical strikes on the ones that fell.

'So, why would a company that owns perfume shops branch out to fried chicken? And why choose a neighbourhood that's already reached chicken shop saturation?'

She looked at Hamish, who looked back with wide eyes.

'Yeah, more chicken bones for you to find. You're not complaining, are you?'

She patted his head and returned her attention to the laptop. There was something else, a missing part of the puzzle. And Irina was determined to find it.

30

LOUISE

Partridge Bark

Paul (Bark Vader and Jimmy Chew's Dad)

> El and I just took Vader and Jim out for a walk in the park. We had to chase off a couple of delinquents by the long grass, and found a set of licence plates. Would anyone want to bet they're associated with a stolen car?

> **Yaz (Hercules's Mum)**
>
> Wouldn't it be great to have an easy way of letting the cops know? Oh wait...

> **Irina (Hamish's Mum)**
>
> If you wanted Andy's number so bad, you should have asked for it. Oh wait...

The view from Bōkan 38 was magnificent, with views across lit-up London. 'Rumour had it the C-suite wanted to have the end-of-project celebration at the Shard,' Babs said, handing me a fresh glass of Prosecco. She'd made an effort tonight and wore a navy dress with red poppies printed on it. With a little bit of make-up and, of course, a blue blazer. 'But the staff preferred to keep it here.'

'Regardless of the reason,' I said, putting the glass on a side table. 'It's been a lovely night but I'm going to make my excuses.'

'It's only 10:00 p.m.'

'By which you mean: it's already 10:00 p.m. and I have to pick up Klaus.'

'Fair point.' Babs kissed my cheek. 'Who's he with tonight?'

'Meg.'

'I thought she kickboxed on Thursdays?'

'She usually does, but she's dog-sitting this week and didn't want to leave the other pup alone.'

'Okay, just promise me one thing: don't walk home along the canal. Klaus might think he's a sawn-off Rottweiler, but he's maybe six and a half kilos, soaking wet. And let's face it, you don't kickbox. Watch out for yourself, will you?'

'We'll be fine.' When she didn't look convinced, I added, 'Don't worry.'

It was a short DLR ride, getting off one stop earlier than I usually would, closer to Partridge Park and Meg's. She buzzed me into the building and called, 'Brace yourself', through the door as soon as I knocked. I quickly got to my knees in anticipation of the black-and-tan bullet that would shoot out once it opened. With his behind close to the floor, he did the lowrider lambada, wiggling around me and jumping up to kiss my face as if I hadn't seen him in months, rather than hours.

It was the best greeting a girl could have. I leaned down, trying to hug him, but he was too excited to be contained. The door opened a little wider and two more dachshunds shot through, Tyrion's dappled little body trying to get in on the fun while Phoebe barked at me.

'Klaus knew you were coming and was waiting at the door,' Meg said, handing me his wool coat and lead. She wore a unicorn onesie with the hood pulled back, showing off the mermaid colours in her hair.

'Ethan?' I asked.

'Gaming with Paul. He'll sleep with Marlowe tonight.'

'His cat?'

'Yep. And Marlowe is more nocturnal than I am,' Meg said, winking.

I smiled. 'He's really becoming a part of the Pack, isn't he? Ethan, that is,' I said, buckling Klaus's coat into place. 'I'm not so sure about Marlowe.' I was happy for Meg – she and Ethan seemed to be getting on really well.

'No one is ever sure about Marlowe, that's part of his appeal,' she replied. 'Have you seen the posts, Lou? Stuff going on in the park tonight. Be careful walking home.'

I snapped on Klaus's lead, and switched on the little LED light on his collar. 'There's *always* something going on in the park. But Klaus hates it after dark, so we'll go around. We'll be fine.'

'He isn't afraid of the fireworks, is he?'

'Thank heavens, no. Not unless they're going off directly overhead.'

'Lucky you. Let me know when you get home.'

I gave her a thumbs-up, and let Klaus lead me to the lift, and then out onto the green. The park was dark, and, so far, silent. The few-and-far-between streetlamps barely gave off more light than Klaus's collar lamp, and I lengthened my stride, keen to be home.

A loud BANG shook me out of my reverie. For a second, I wondered if it was a gunshot, but green sparks lit the sky overhead. Klaus, startled, bolted as far as his lead would allow him, ears back.

'Bloody idiots,' I muttered, allowing him to march me down the sidewalk.

Klaus stopped still, his tail straight up, like a flagpole. A low rumble came from his chest. I looked around, expecting to see the idiots with the fireworks, or maybe a bigger dog, but there was no threat in sight. 'It's okay, sweetheart. We're okay. They're just fireworks. Let's go.'

He disagreed, tilting his head. Paws firmly planted, he wasn't going anywhere.

'Okaaay,' I said. 'You actually want to stay out and watch them from the park?'

That was a first. I wasn't keen on the idea, especially if the kids shooting off the fireworks were still inside. I'd seen them before; they were usually high on something, belligerent and unpredictable. Klaus's body language made it seem like he wasn't keen either, but he made for the park entrance anyway. There were metal gates that were supposed to be locked at sunset, but never were, so we entered unchallenged. I scanned the area, looking for the kids and hoping they'd left. Slipped my hand into my pocket, fingers wrapping around a can of defence spray. Just in case.

When I'd graduated university and moved to Manhattan for work, my mum had bought me a can of pepper spray, for self-defence. That can, fifteen years ago, had probably been a heck of a lot stronger than the dinky canister now in my hand, but as pepper spray was a controlled substance in the UK, I'd bought the best I could find online.

More fireworks exploded overhead.

Klaus pulled so hard on his collar that he began to wheeze, making a low, keening sound that, ironically, made me relax. 'It's just fireworks, my love. Let's go home. There're no squirrels in here tonight. They're all sleeping.'

It was a white lie, but not the first time I'd used it. Dachshunds were hunting dogs, bred to hunt badgers and rabbits, and had a high prey drive. Klaus had a thing for squirrels in particular.

He wasn't falling for it. He yanked me towards The Nest, even though the café had been closed for hours.

'No squirrels in there, sweetheart.' I mean, there could be. Not in the café itself, but in the trees behind it. Foxes too. Far too many people tended to leave their leftover food – rice, chips, whatever – there for the animals to eat. I didn't mind the idea of feeding the foxes, but let's see how happy anyone (other than Klaus) would be when a rat colony started to flourish.

What worried me more was the possibility of scarier beings behind the café, not content with causing a ruckus by lighting off fireworks. Klaus seemed less wary of that, and continued to drag me forward.

'Jesus. If you land us in the middle of a rats' nest, or worse, I'm not going to forgive you.'

Klaus didn't care. With a rats' nest, he'd probably think he'd won the lottery.

His keening increased in pitch. I considered scooping him up and leaving; I wasn't comfortable being in the park by myself this late at night, certainly not with stoned kids shooting off fireworks nearby. The wine I'd consumed earlier soured in my belly.

Klaus strained against the lead, dragging me not

towards the entrance of The Nest, but along the side of the building, past long-dead flowers. Suddenly he began to whine.

It wasn't the *I-want* whine of seeing a squirrel; it sounded scared. But he was still pulling me forward, not away from whatever was frightening him.

'What? What do you see?'

And then I saw it. A black ankle boot. Elasticated at the sides, with a high, chunky heel. Disappearing into a tan trouser leg...

'Oh shit.'

I pulled Klaus behind me and dropped to my knees, knowing in my gut what I'd see. The tan trousers would lead to a white top. Dark blonde hair with highlights, and blue eyes that I prayed weren't clouded over.

'Annabel? Oh shit, don't be dead,' I prayed. I fumbled for my phone and turned on the torch.

There was blood. So much blood. On her head, her chest. She was too far into the bushes to see where it was coming from or whether it was still flowing.

I fumbled through the leaves for her wrist. Exhaled loud enough to scare myself. There was a pulse. It was weak, but it was there.

Babs's words played back in my mind. 'Winter pressures... Long ambulance waiting times...'

Hoping that she was wrong, I held my breath and dialled 999.

Partridge Bark

> Do we have any doctors in the group? Pls DM me.

Yaz (Hercules's Mum)

> You didn't stop off for a drink with **@Irina**, did you? 😉

Indy (Banjo's Mum)

> I'm a paediatrician. What's wrong? Are you ok?

Breath left my lungs in a relieved *whoosh*. Indy was a doctor. The dispatcher had said it wouldn't be long, but it was cold out, and Annabel was bleeding, and I didn't know how long 'not long' was.

Indy (Banjo's Mum)

> I found someone in Partridge Park, behind The Nest. She's unconscious and bleeding. I'm waiting for the paramedics to show

> up, but I'd feel better if there was a doctor here. Can you help?

On my way.

I felt my body unclench a little, now understanding why Yaz had been so desperate for me to come when she'd found Jonny's body. I opened another chat, doing what I could before my emotions could overwhelm me.

Detective Andrew Thompson

> Hi Andy, it's Louise Mallory. Sorry to keep bothering you, but I've just found my friend Annabel hurt in Partridge Park, by The Nest. She's still breathing but she's been dumped in the bushes. I'm with her in the park, waiting for the paramedics. It's not a murder, yet, but I'd be grateful for any help and honestly, I'm terrified.

> Stay there. I'll have some uniforms there in about 10. Williams and I are on our way.

The cavalry were on their way – I just had to hold it together until they got here. 'Hang in there, Annabel. Don't you dare die on me.'

Klaus was now barking his head off, and I needed space to work. I tied his lead to a nearby tree and took a few pics to preserve the crime scene. Whoever had dumped Annabel had pushed her in quite deep, but given the nature of the brush, I didn't think it would be that bad to roll her out.

Assuming she had no broken bones.

Crap. What if she had a spine injury and I made it worse? What if she ended up paralysed because I didn't know what I was doing?

Then she'd still be alive, the sensible part of me advised. *But if you're not sure, wait for Indy.*

I crouched by the edge of the bushes, waiting, hoping I was making the right choice. It wasn't too long before lights flashed on the street, and I exhaled again, realising that help was at hand. That her life or death wasn't dependent on me.

Two paramedics entered the park on foot, with two uniformed PCs just behind them. I turned my phone's torch on and waved it over my head. 'Over here!' I screamed.

They trotted over. 'Early response,' the first paramedic – a man about my height but ten years younger – said authoritatively. 'Ambulance is on its way.'

Thank God.

'Have you moved her?'

'Not yet.'

'Good. We got this. Stand back, will you?'

'Stand back,' one of the PCs echoed. I did as I was told, untying Klaus and retreating several metres. Indy arrived, breathless, moments later.

'What's going on?' she gasped.

'The early response team earned their name,' I said. 'But thank you for being here.'

She nodded and approached the responders. 'I'm a doctor, can I help?'

'Ambulance is on its way,' the second one said. 'Please stand back, ma'am.'

The PCs set up a perimeter with police tape, and pointed a couple of battery-powered floodlights into the bushes where the early responders were checking Annabel for signs of life. I turned away, unable to watch. The adrenaline was wearing off now, and I was beginning to shiver. I picked Klaus up and held his warm body in my arms, unsure which one of us was providing more comfort to the other.

Partridge Bark

Paul (Bark Vader and Jimmy Chew's Dad)

> What's going on @**Louise**? Just so you know, I just saw an ambulance stop outside the park.

I ignored his message, not wanting to have the whole Pack here to muddy the scene.

The ambulance arrived and the paramedics worked together to get Annabel out of the bushes and onto the gurney. 'You want to ride with her?' one of them asked me.

Yes, I wanted to say, but I knew that Indy would be better able to navigate the medical situation on the other side. 'You go,' I told her. 'I'll stay here and wait for the detectives.'

'You sure?'

'Positive. Go. I'll text you Annabel's details in case you need them to get her admitted.'

Detective Andrew Thompson

> Williams will be there in 5. I'm a few mins behind him. You OK?

> I'm OK. Or at least as OK as I can be. Indy's riding in the ambulance with Annabel. I feel better that at least now she's in safe hands.

> Right. I'll call ahead and make sure they're expected.

That wasn't entirely true. I wasn't anywhere near okay. My hands were shaking, and I felt physically ill. I couldn't believe this could happen. Not to Annabel, who wore her poshness like a suit of armour.

What if we hadn't come past? What if Klaus hadn't dragged me to her? What if . . .

Klaus struggled to be put down. Once his paws hit the floor, he dragged me to the corner of the café and raised his leg against a post. I tightened the belt on his coat and sagged onto a park bench. I brushed away the tears that I hadn't realised I was shedding and stared out into the dark as I waited for Andy and Williams to arrive.

31

LOUISE

Indy (Banjo's Mum)

> We've arrived. Annabel has just been admitted.

> Thank heavens!

> Can you send through whatever you know of her medical history? Any meds she might be on?

I didn't have a clue. I leaned back on the bench and rested my head against the wall of The Nest. Another couple of PCs arrived and set up more floodlights around the area.

Andy and Williams weren't far behind them. Although I was ignoring it, I knew the Partridge Bark chat would be blowing up with speculation.

Williams went to speak with the uniforms, while Andy sat down beside me. I recounted what had happened to the best of my ability, and then burst into tears. 'This is all my fault,' I whimpered.

'Why do you say that?' Andy asked, not unkindly.

'I met Annabel for lunch today. Asked her about some of the stuff happening in the neighbourhood.' I opened my eyes and blinked at the detective. 'She works for one of the property developers around here. Did I tell you that?'

'Yes, you said. But why do you think this is your fault?'

'Look, less than a week ago, Yaz found a murdered man on the canal path. With a branded box of Cluckin' Good wings at his feet. Last night, Claire saw a stabbing at CGC – right outside her building. I was asking questions, kind of pushing to see if there was a connection between CGC and what else was happening around here.'

Williams arrived and he and Andy exchanged a glance.

'Why do you think the murder is connected to a gang stabbing?'

'Just a hunch.' I fished a slightly used tissue out of my pocket and blew my nose. Put it away before Klaus could take hold of it. I readjusted him on my lap, my fingers stroking his fur, grateful for his reassuring presence. 'But when I asked Annabel, she looked kind of scared. If I hadn't gone to her, maybe she wouldn't have become a target.'

I sniffled, hoping the tears wouldn't start up again.

Williams looked like he wanted to pat my shoulder, but even if he had been going to, a low growl from Klaus warned him about getting too close. 'If she was already scared, then you asking questions might have irritated her, but it wouldn't have made her more scared. I don't think it would have caused anyone to target her,' Williams said, his voice reassuring.

Unspoken were the words, *If she wasn't already a target*.

Also unspoken was the point that by asking questions I might have put a bullseye on my own forehead. I swallowed that thought down.

'Why do you think there's a connection?' Andy repeated.

'I don't know. I suppose it could be a coincidence, but the neighbourhood's just felt less safe since CGC opened.'

'Less safe than a vet who poisons the animals he's supposed to care for?' Williams muttered under his breath.

I ignored him and continued addressing Andy. 'There always seem to be people hanging around outside the chicken shops and kebab shops, but these guys seem, I don't know, older maybe. Harder. They leer at us — at women. I can't usually hear what they say, but it *sounds* suggestive. And there is one thing I've noticed . . .'

'Yes?'

It seemed so ridiculous, I didn't even know whether to mention it. 'They don't seem to like dogs very much.'

'What?'

'I know, right? Even the little ones. I mean, Klaus can

look pretty fierce when he's barking and all, but even Hammy. And he's probably the least scary thing around.'

'Hamish? The little black Scottie?'

'Yeah. Irina said they called him Satan. I mean, I'd understand if it was Violet they were referring to, but Hammy hasn't been groomed in ages. The poor thing looks like a shaggy little bear cub. I can't imagine anything less scary.'

Williams looked like he was struggling to contain his amusement. 'Satan, huh? You sure they weren't . . .'

'Talking about Irina?' I offered with a watery smile. 'I asked.'

He lifted a shoulder in a half shrug as if to say, *Some merit in it.*

'Okay,' Andy said, clearly not willing to go there. 'Williams, you stay here with the uniforms. Get someone to talk to the kids with the fireworks. Maybe they saw something. I'll make sure Ms Mallory gets home and I'll be right back.'

'You don't have to,' I said.

'It's late and you've just seen one of your friends carted off to hospital. Humour me.'

I nodded and placed Klaus on the ground. He shook himself as I stood up. 'Then thank you, I really do appreciate it. It's been a corker of a week.'

32

WILLIAMS

Harriman

> Where you at, mate?

> Scene of crime. Suspected attempted murder in Partridge Park.

> That neighbourhood is a hotbed these days. Speaking of which, we finished with the CCTV footage from last Sunday. Only one sighting of anyone with a fedora – it's

> more a beanie sort of area – and it was on a woman. The quality is pretty crap but I'll send you the clip now.

Williams glanced over at the forensics teams crawling over the bushes Annabel Lindford-Swayne had been found in. They seemed to have it all in hand. He sat down at one of the picnic tables outside the café and played Harriman's video.

The quality was worse than poor, grainy to the point where it looked like the man and woman were walking in snow. He zoomed in. The view was from behind them, so the CCTV hadn't managed to catch their faces. The woman was wearing the hat on the back of her head, differently from the way Williams imagined Tang had worn it: snap-brim down, à la Bogart. She looked about medium height, and it was difficult to tell her body type under a puffer jacket, but from her legs, he guessed that she was on the stockier side. The man beside her had his arm slung around her shoulders. Dark hair slicked down, he strutted rather than walked, with shoulders back and the sort of rolling gait that reminded Williams of sailors he'd seen in movies. The man looked strong enough to kill someone, and the pair were obviously an item, which would negate Williams's theory about the killer being romantically entangled with Tang.

They didn't look like the sort of couple who'd commit murder.

Though, did Bonnie and Clyde? Did the Moors killers, Ian Brady and Myra Hindley?

Williams sighed and shook his head. That sort of thing was rarer than hen's teeth. He sent the clip to Andy, just to cover all bases, then sighed again. 'We don't have crap.'

Friday

33

LOUISE

Partridge Bark

Emma (Flash's Mum)

> The police are crawling around The Nest this morning. Everything's cordoned off, and the café is closed. What did you do, **@Louise**? Find another dead body or something?

Meg (Tyrion's Mum)

> **@Claire's** got the story up on *The Chronicle*'s site. The Nest isn't closed, exactly.

> I just talked to the manager. They're going to brew coffee in urns and take them into the little paved area outside. A bit al fresco, but at least you'll get your caffeine fix. Even though it might not be a latte or a mochaccino.

We'd been past The Nest on our morning walk. Klaus and I had stood well back, but we could still see the police cordon and the people in paper bunny suits moving around. 'As good as the floodlights are, I'll bet they'll be grateful once the sun's out,' I'd said to Klaus.

I hadn't wanted to linger, the image of Annabel broken and bloodied almost transposing itself onto that of the body of Phil Creasy in the long grass on the far side of the park. It was still cold and Klaus hadn't been inclined to dither either, so as soon as he'd done his business, we'd headed home. My coffee wasn't as good as The Nest's, but at least it was safer.

I checked *The Chronicle*'s site and found Claire's article.

**LOCAL WOMAN FOUND BEATEN
IN PARTRIDGE PARK**

The near-lifeless body of a local woman, aged thirty-two, was found by a dog walker late last night in Partridge Park.

> Police raced to the scene at approximately 11:00 p.m. while the woman was rushed to an East London hospital's major trauma unit where she is currently fighting for her life.
>
> The victim's handbag and phone remain missing, and the police are treating this incident as attempted murder. No arrests have yet been made and they ask that anyone with information on the incident come forward as a matter of urgency.
>
> The area in Partridge Park remains cordoned off, with a strong police presence. This comes less than twenty-four hours after the gang-related incident on the High Street on Wednesday.

At the rate Claire was breaking stories, she'd be snapped up by one of the larger news channels in no time.

I'd settled into my home office, Klaus on his bed beside me, looking out the window. My laptop was open, and I should have been working through the company's quarterly figures, but I couldn't look at the numbers. Couldn't face them.

Not because they were bad; on the contrary, I knew this had been one of the best quarters we'd had so far. It wasn't even that I was more of a 'people person' than a 'numbers person', although that was also true enough.

On the 'people' side of things, I could have looked over the draft memorandum of understanding and terms and conditions that Babs had sent across for the NHS work. Or started jotting down the issues I'd remembered from my time working with the service, to form part of the team's briefing.

Instead, my attention kept wandering back to the moment I'd found Annabel in the bushes. And, despite Williams's reassurances, the guilt I felt that my questions might have put her there.

And if they had, what did that mean? That I was next?

I almost spat my coffee onto my laptop.

Klaus looked up as I choked. My hands began to shake and it was almost a relief when my phone dinged.

Almost.

If it wasn't the last message I'd expected to get.

Irina (Hamish's Mum)

> Are you freakin' kidding me? I can't believe you took Andy home last night!

> What are you talking about?

> I saw you two walking together. Saw you hand him a drink in your flat. I was so disgusted I had to pull my curtains closed.

> I thought you were my friend!

> What is WRONG with you?!

My hands were still shaking, but now it was with something close to fury. It would have been easy enough to explain to Irina that Andy had walked me home to keep me safe after what I'd just been through. I could have told her that he'd read me the riot act for getting myself – and my friends – in over our heads. Again. Or that I'd made coffee for him to take back to the scene for him and for Williams.

I would have loved to tell her to stop perving through my window; that if she wanted Andy, and there were clearly some unresolved issues there (possibly on both sides), then she could make a move and try to be less of a muppet this time around.

But none of it would have made a difference, so I didn't waste my time, choosing instead to focus my efforts on where they would actually make a difference.

Indy (Banjo's Mum)

> Thanks for being an absolute ☆ last night. How is she?

> Happy to help. We got her admitted and I stayed until she was out of surgery. Blunt force trauma to the head caused the blood we saw, and she has some bruising to her arms and legs. Some are clearly defensive wounds, but others could be explained by being tossed into the bushes. Samples were taken and sent to the labs. They'll be shared with the police, obvs.

> Thank you. Let me know if you hear anything?

> You'll be the first to know. You OK?

> Yes, but I wasn't the one who was attacked.

Something in Claire's article caught my attention and I opened a new message.

Detective Andrew Thompson

> Hi Andy, thanks again for walking me home yesterday. I was wondering, did anyone find Annabel's handbag? I didn't see it when I found her, but she had a tan Hermès bag, a little beaten up, with her when I met her for lunch. I don't know, but she might have had her phone or a planner in there that might help.

Thx. I'll check. And Louise?

> I know, I know. Leave the detecting to the detectives.

Please. I'd rather not see anything bad happen to you or any more of your friends.

> Will you work on Annabel's case or do you need to hand it over to someone else? It's not murder, but it could have been. And it'd make me feel better if you were on it.

Thanks, yeah, Williams and I have it.

> Great. Can I ask, if you find anything you're able to share ...

NP. If there's something to share, we'll tell you.

My money was on Andy already knowing every item the Forensics team had picked up last night and anything anyone had found this morning, including, maybe, the spent fireworks. Still, now the bag was definitely on his list.

I stared at the accounts on my screen and grimaced, before deciding to print out the agreement and terms and conditions for the NHS work instead. Still the words became squiggles, teasing the edge of my reason and making completely no sense. I hunted around for the reading glasses the optometrist had told me I should be using even when I was on the laptop, but they made little difference.

The problem wasn't my sight, it was my attention span.

I called the Royal London Hospital and asked for an update on Annabel. The receptionist was firm but not unkind when she told me that she could only provide updates to family members. I'd have to trust that Indy could bypass that route.

Still unable to focus, I closed my laptop in disgust. The documents would have to wait.

Gav (Violet's Dad)

> Hi Gav, are you heading to the dog park today?

> Does a bear crap in the woods? Coz Violet won't do hers inside.

> Haha, that's good. Klaus prefers to go outside too. Fancy some company?

> This about what happened last night?

Last night, the night before and pretty much the few nights before that, but Gav would already know that.

With a little luck, he'd also know what was going on in the neighbourhood.

34

LOUISE

Jake (Luther's Dad)

> Hey Marple. Heard you had a bit of excitement last night. Are you ok?

> Yeah, it wasn't me that got hurt.

> I know. It was your friend. But you found her, and I don't know her, so I'm asking about you first. Then I'm going to yell at you for sticking your nose

> into shit that isn't your business. THEN I'm going to ask about her.

> Thanks.

I put my jacket on and went to the door. 'Walkies, Klaus.'

Most dogs would run and go mental at the door. Not Klaus. He sat at the end of the hallway and waited. I reached into a pocket and pulled out a bribe – a little piece of dried meat, which was sufficient to entice him closer. But he backed up again when he saw the daxie jacket.

'You know the drill, Klaus. Under ten degrees, you wear the coat.' Logic didn't work, but still I tried. 'Come on. I don't like wearing winter coats either.'

A second bribe was required before he allowed me to pass the belt under his belly and fasten it over his back. The look on his face said it all: *My friends are gonna kick my ass at the dog park.*

'No, they won't. Violet will be wearing one too. And I'd like to see anyone give her crap for wearing a coat.'

Klaus weed on a discarded CGC bag as soon as we left the building, but was happy enough to strut through the gates and over to the canal path that would lead us to Partridge Park. He only stopped twice: once to do his business, and the other time under duress, while I sent off another message.

Claire (Tank's Mum)

> Hey Claire, quick one. You said you were mates with Jonny Tang. Do you know if he ever had any interactions with Annabel?

> Your property developer friend?

> Yep.

> I don't think so. If he did, he didn't mention it. Want me to see if I can find some sort of connection?

> Please. Both of them, in the same area, within a week? I can't believe it's a coincidence.

> You'd have made a cracking journo, Lou. Don't worry – I'm on it. I don't believe in coincidences either.

The police cordons were still up but the Forensics team were gone, only a lone PC remaining, looking frightfully bored. I kept walking, keeping my head down as I passed him on the way to the dog enclosure at the back of the park.

Gav was sitting on a bench, an open copy of *The Times* on his lap. Violet, at his feet, wore a tiny purple fleece that made her look like a grape. A grape with big eyes, a squished-in snout and spindly legs. The probability of her kicking Klaus's ass for wearing his jacket was slim. More likely, he'd wind her up over her outfit and *that* would cause her to chase him, a game they both loved.

'Awright?' Gav asked as I sat beside him.

'Living the dream, Gav,' I said, deadpan.

'Sure, sure. Nothing going on, eh?' He folded the paper and put it down beside him. While I'd already broken out my puffer jacket, he was wearing a heavy wool blazer over a white button-down shirt, an aging gentleman who was impervious to the cold.

I'd known Gav for years from around the dog park, but had only learned about his ex-con past during the last investigation. On some level I knew it should bother me more than it did. He might prefer to hang out with his old East London clique, but when we needed him, Gav was there for the Pack. For the dogs. And that meant a lot in my book.

He lowered his sunglasses and peered over the rims at me when I didn't immediately reply, his eyes piercing blue. 'Well, nothing more than finding a body. Then finding another body. What're you after? A hat trick?'

'No, no, two in a week is quite enough, thank you.'

'Good.' He replaced his glasses, stretched out his legs and tilted his face towards the sun.

Klaus thundered past us, his little legs making enough noise for a larger dog. His tail was tucked in, less out of fear, and more to prevent Violet from getting hold of it. He looked like he was having the time of his life, and would probably sleep like a log this afternoon.

Violet made less noise but still moved like a demented purple ninja. Klaus was sensible to keep any loose bits out of her reach. Not that she would do anything nasty to him; Klaus was one of the few dogs that Violet genuinely liked.

'So, let me head you off at the pass then,' Gav drawled. 'I've already asked around. No one knew Jonny Tang, much less who killed 'im. The boys are keepin' an ear to the ground, but this might be new blood at play.'

That wasn't good news.

'Any thoughts?'

'Same you've probably had. Owner of the chicken shop, Dave Najafi.'

'Dave?' I echoed the new name, trying not to make my excitement obvious. I'd see what I could find out about Dave Najafi once I got home.

'Not his Christian name, of course, but that's what he goes by. Owns a bunch of perfume and shoe shops. Decided to branch out here.'

'Owns outright or through shell companies?' Gav's flat expression gave me the answer. 'Okay. Shell companies. Why branch out here, of all places?'

'I dunno. Maybe 'cos he got planning permission?'

'How?'

Gav shrugged, 'Probably some money changed hands. Maybe he's got a friend who pulled some strings.' It was said with such sangfroid that I had to remember that this was the way things operated in Gav's world.

Probably not just his, but I didn't want to think about that.

'What do the locals say? I mean the old school locals, not ... er ...'

'Not your lot?' His head slowly turned towards mine. His expression was inscrutable with his eyes hidden behind his dark sunglasses, but his voice held traces of amusement. Then he sobered. 'They think he means business.'

'They think he's dangerous?'

'Dangerous, maybe,' Gav said, his face still stony. 'Definitely savvy enough to bring in his own lads to keep his business safe. But just because he's savvy and wants his business to succeed – and by the looks of it, it is – that doesn't mean he killed that Jon Tang. Or attacked your friend.' He shifted in his seat. 'Think about it, Louise. She's the property developer. It's in her best interests to make sure the property does well. Why would she be a threat to a businessman whose business is on the up?'

'From what I hear, there have been a lot of complaints from residents—'

Gav was laughing before I could finish the sentence. 'They've got no clout against the people who own the building. Or the management company. Even if they own their flats.'

'What about a Residents Association?'

'*Pfft*. Management companies don't give a crap. Yeah, they might concede on small things, but what do you think they'll do? Oust a business that's paying their bills? How often do you turn away an existing client that pays your company, just because you don't like the smell of them?'

I held firm. 'I have turned down work if a client isn't a good fit.' Albeit only after exhausting all diplomatic routes.

'Yeah? Then you're one in a million.' Gav turned his face back towards the sun, effectively ending the conversation.

35

LOUISE

Indy (Banjo's Mum)

Hey Lou, seems Annabel's got swelling in her brain. The doctors put her into a medically induced coma until the swelling recedes and they can see what damage was done. The police stopped by but they were turned away – I think there might be one still lurking around nearby though. Maybe to question her when she wakes up, maybe to

> make sure whoever did it doesn't succeed next time. IDK.

>> Ah, jeez. Thanks for the update.

Why would she be a threat to a businessman whose business is on the up?

She wouldn't be, would she? But what if Annabel was a threat to someone who didn't want that business to succeed, which was pretty much everyone else in the neighbourhood?

Including the Pack, who weren't keen on the increase in the number of chicken bones per square metre in the area.

I shook the thought away. We needed something more concrete. Irina was checking up on Jonny, and now Dave Najafi, after my searches came up blank. Claire was dealing with insurance after some idiots trashed her car. In between that and her day job, she was looking at any connections between Jonny and Annabel. Meanwhile, I was running out of both hope and ideas.

It would have been easier if we had access to the police's avenues of investigation. Who they were talking to, what they were thinking. Bloody hell, what evidence they actually had.

But, thanks to Irina being Irina, we didn't.

So, eat the frog.

The saying came out of nowhere, but it wasn't bad

advice. A former colleague of mine had once run a team building session based on Brian Tracy's theory of dealing with the nasty tasks before completing the ones you'd rather do. Which on the face of it meant that I needed to tackle the accounts and that damned NHS documentation.

Unless there was a second amphibian I needed to nibble?

My mind immediately turned to Irina. She was arrogant and egocentric, but underneath all that, she was painfully insecure. And I knew she still liked Andy. Would it be fundamentally wrong for me to capitalise on that?

Irina (Hamish's Mum)

> FFS, nothing happened last night with Andy. He came to the scene when I found Annabel. Walked me home to make sure Klaus and I got in ok. He did ask about you, though. I guess he didn't want to do that around Williams …

No. No, I was not above that. Feeling neither proud nor relieved, I opened the NHS documents and began reading, knowing that at least I'd now done all that I could right now for Annabel. And Jonny.

36

IRINA

Louise (Klaus's Mum)

> You cannot be serious. If he wanted to find out about me, he could have gotten in touch any time over the last few months.

From what I heard, you made it pretty clear you weren't interested.

> He didn't try that hard to convince me.

> Cut the guy some slack, Irina. He actually LIKED you. Even though you were jerking him all over the shop.

Irina frowned at the screen, uncertain what irked her more: the thought of Louise and Andy walking together and talking about her. Or the idea that Lou, of all people, was offering relationship advice.

It wasn't as though she was a pro. There'd been a man, then a divorce, but that had been years ago. Now she was pining for the guy across the canal. Jake. Although after six months, the chances of them banging were about as close as her being whisked off to Switzerland by Tom Hardy. Seriously, the only successful relationship Irina'd ever seen Louise have was with Klaus.

What could Louise understand about being her? Women rarely liked Irina, and men consistently let her down. Dogs were far easier; they gave unconditionally, no matter what. But humans? She'd been let down so many times that she'd learned to keep things light. Transactional. To date the sort of men that didn't have the ability to get close enough to hurt her. Like Tim.

But now Andy was back on the scene.

She must have said that aloud, because Hammy, on the sofa, gave her a meaningful look. *Maybe the universe wants you to try again?*

Maybe the universe was on drugs. Still, he wasn't unattractive. Wasn't uninteresting. Wasn't ... well ... there wasn't anything wrong with him. Nothing she could find after a few dates, which was exactly the problem.

And Hammy liked him.

And it was Friday.

And she didn't have other plans.

Irina sent Louise an email with the information she had so far, even though there were still more questions than answers.

And before she could think herself out of it, she picked up her mobile.

Andy Thompson

> Hey, it's Irina. Fancy a drink?

37

LOUISE

Barbara Lane

> NHS docs look good. I've made a couple of changes to the terms and conditions and emailed them over. I'll write up notes for the briefing doc over the weekend. How quickly can we get a team on it?

Within a fortnight, which'll give them enough time to work out whatever

> they need to do on their side. And Finance told me you just approved the accounts. Productive day after what must have been a harrowing night.

> You heard about that?

> I'm a news junkie. I won't ask how you are, coz you'll only lie. The same way you'd lie if I asked you to stay away from trouble.

> It's not like I'm going out looking for it.

> Aren't you?

It was six o'clock on a Friday night. I was tired, and frustrated. To make matters worse, I had nothing in the fridge except a few lemons that were growing some sort of green mould, half a lettuce that had turned brown and liquid and a bottle of Gavi that'd been in there since summer. My food delivery was scheduled for the following morning, so it looked like it was going to be a takeaway sort of night.

'Come on, Klaus. You need a walk.'

He lifted his head up from the bed beside my desk. Next to it were a few big treats that he'd been pushing around. It wasn't that he didn't like them; he wanted me to hold them for him. 'Spoiled boy.'

I stood up and headed to the door. Slipping on my jacket, I called out, 'I have treats!' He came running, but wouldn't come close enough to his coat until I'd produced one for him.

Smart boy.

We cleared the gate and before I could let him decide which way he wanted to go, a bark from down the street decided it for him. We crossed the bridge over the canal and headed towards the high street, and whichever hound was calling.

The canal looked placid in the darkness of night, reflecting the lights from the buildings on either side. For a moment, you could almost pretend the neighbourhood was clean, safe.

Klaus and I reached the junction by News-N-Booze, crossing the high street at the zebra lines. Klaus didn't pause, happy to be out and about, enjoying the sniffs.

'Fookin' little rat dog,' someone said as we passed by. Klaus hadn't even barked, but now he began to growl low in his throat.

'Leave it,' I said to him.

'What, the dog's a rat, and I'm an *it*?' The voice became a man's face, dark in the shadows, but moving close to mine. There were others, bobbing behind him, supporting him. My eyes touched on each face, hoping eye contact would make them turn away, knowing that I didn't see myself as a victim. I tried to notice anything that made them stand out. Any distinguishing characteristics. One had eyes too close together. Another had a scar bisecting his thick brow, but there wasn't time to focus on that.

'No,' I said, without thinking. 'You're a shit.' There was no point in explaining that 'leave it' was the phrase our trainer used when teaching Klaus to ignore whatever – or whoever – was triggering him. And now the man was triggering me. 'I'll leave you to figure out your masculinity on your own time.'

Klaus sensed a row brewing and erupted into barks, his lips curled back, his white fangs bared.

Eyes-Too-Close stamped on the sidewalk, his boot landing close to Klaus. Beginning to shake with rage, I scooped up my dog. 'His breed are bred to hunt feral animals more than three times their size. And win.'

The sensible thing would have been to turn around and get both of us away, out of danger, but a ball of red-hot anger threatened to consume me. Anger over the senseless crime in the neighbourhood, the gangs, the violence. The deaths.

Klaus's barking had now reached epic proportions. The man and his friends fanned out around me, out of his immediate striking distance but not far enough. 'You sure you want to call him a rat to his face? Look how much he likes it,' I stupidly goaded. The usual group of kids who loitered outside News-N-Booze moved closer, sensing blood in the water. It would probably be my blood, but I was too far gone to back down. 'But then, you know he's on a lead.' My defence spray was in my pocket. To get it, I had to put Klaus down . . .

The crash of glass breaking was almost lost in the moment, the tinkle of shards falling onto concrete.

'Hate to break up your Friday-night fun,' a deeper voice interjected out of nowhere. 'But I'm pretty sure you can find a better target than a woman and her little dog.'

I froze, ready to turn on the newcomer but unwilling to look away from the men around me. 'I don't need your help.'

'I know.' A soft Scottish burr and a firm hand on my shoulder held me in place. A hand that wasn't bitten by Klaus. 'Just evening the odds.'

I turned my head then, and looked up. A black leather bomber jacket. Higher still, a chiselled jaw with a five o'clock shadow that couldn't conceal the muscle jumping underneath. Eyes that in this light looked black, snapping with anger that wasn't entirely directed at the thugs.

Jake.

And as if he didn't look intimidating enough, Luther stood by his master's side, a formidable mass of muscle and teeth. He snapped at the gang circling us, his lead taut in Jake's hand. Given that the hand in question was also holding a six-pack of Corona, Luther could probably have broken free. If he wanted to.

A fact not lost on the thugs. Eyes-Too-Close stepped back a fraction.

Jake dropped his hand from my shoulder to the small of my back. I allowed him to turn me and guide us away, back the way we came. Klaus scampered to my left shoulder, barking behind us. 'He always needs to get the last word in,' I said, trying to make light of the situation, despite the sick feeling in the pit of my stomach.

'Just like his mam,' Jake said, guiding me across the high street. As we moved over the canal, he took a step away, shifting the Coronas and Luther's lead to his other hand. 'You okay?'

'First question everyone's been asking today,' I said, trying to sound braver than I felt. Now that the danger was in the rear view, I'd begun to shake. Not just my hands, but every muscle, every nerve.

Jake walked us faster, only pausing to allow me to use my fob to get us through the gate into my apartment complex. After that, I think we both breathed a sigh of relief.

As if he understood, Klaus did his business in the nearest bush, paused for me to clean it up, then marched us to the front door.

I didn't ask if Jake wanted to come up; his hand at the small of my back was enough of an answer.

When we made it into my flat, I released the clasp of Klaus's collar and watched him shoot off down the hallway into the living room, probably to claim the bed by the balcony before Luther could get to it. I took off my coat, and sat down heavily on the sofa.

Jake had been in my flat enough times to know his way around. He pulled a red wine glass out of the cabinet and opened the bottle of Gavi. 'That's not a white wine glass,' I said, realising how ridiculous I sounded.

'I know.' He poured a ridiculous amount into it and handed it to me. 'Leave whatever you don't want.' He opened a Corona for himself, leaned against a countertop and called the police to report the incident. When he'd finished, he looked at me.

'You wanna tell your friends what happened, or you want me to?'

Luther padded over to Klaus's bed near the balcony door and waited until Klaus shifted over before flopping down in the middle of it, his hind legs draping out onto the floor behind him. Klaus had never been possessive about his dog beds, and was happy enough to lie beside Luther when he arrived. It was their usual Tuesday-night position, something that looked less ridiculous when they were both curled up in Luther's much bigger boudoir. 'I really need to get a bigger dog bed,' I said aloud.

Jake waited for me to get ahold of myself, and I nodded. 'I'll do it. This neighbourhood is getting worse, and we all need to stay vigilant out there. Before someone else has a problem.'

Partridge Bark

> Bunch of yobs had a go at Klaus and me tonight. We're OK but be careful – I think they're out looking for trouble.

Ella (Bark Vader and Jimmy Chew's Mum)

> What? This early?

Claire (Tank's Mum)

I told you – it's getting bad.

Fiona (Nala's Mum)

Glad you're OK. I think maybe it's time to avoid that area after dark. At least for anyone who can. Soz, @**Claire** …

Jake topped up my glass – I hadn't realised how quickly I'd been drinking it – and picked up his phone again. 'Ordering a couple of pizzas.'

'Don't you need to go somewhere?'

He looked around. 'Got beer. Got Luther. Now got company. And pizza on the way. I'm good.' He held out his hand.

'What?'

'Give me your phone.'

'Why?'

'Because you're a hot mess, Marple. You just faced off against a gang of people who might well have killed one man and put another in hospital. Assuming, of course, that they didn't have anything to do with your friend being attacked in the park. You're shaking like an alcoholic with the DTs, and you still want to sniff around trouble? Give yourself a night off.'

I didn't like to take direction from him, but right now, my body felt like I'd tried to take on a speeding train and lost.

I locked the screen and handed the phone over, feeling oddly exposed. Jake smiled and his shoulders relaxed, making me realise for the first time how tense he'd been since the confrontation.

'Good call, Marple,' he said, leaning back. 'I hope you like extra pepperoni.'

38

WILLIAMS

Williams was standing behind Andy, looking at videos Andy's ex had sent of his son playing football. 'Your kid's got the wingspan of an albatross. He'd make a great goalie.'

'Yeah, but he wants to be a striker. Like every other ten-year-old.'

Another message came in, and Williams reached around his friend and clicked on the notification without looking, assuming it was another video.

Irina Ivanova 🦇💩

> Hey, it's Irina. Fancy a drink?

Williams blinked at the name, then couldn't stop himself from reading the message. 'You have got to be kidding me,' he groaned. 'What does she expect? She treats you like shit and then expects you to sprint over there like a horny teenager?'

Andy was silent, staring at the screen, his face a mixture of horror and fascination.

'I'm surprised you didn't block her after last time. She's nuts.' Williams shook his head. 'And that's my professional opinion. Why aren't you talking? Or deleting that message.' He leaned closer. 'Andy. You're not seriously considering responding, are you?'

Andy put the phone on the desk in front of him, face up. The words seeming to become larger on their own.

'Holy shit, you are.' Williams reached across and turned the phone over. 'Mate, look. It's late on a Friday night. Leave it until you're fresh and rested tomorrow.' *And seeing sense.* 'She's probably had a few sherbets and she's after a booty call. Man, I don't need to tell you this, but you *do not* need to go there.'

Andy looked at him then, his face tired. 'Again.'

'Again,' Williams agreed. 'Look, we had enough on our plates even before that woman was left for dead in Partridge Park. Leave it for now – you can always call her once we get at least a couple of these cases closed.'

Andy still didn't look convinced, and Williams tried to lighten the tone. 'Use the same excuse she gave you: you don't want to muddy the waters while the investigation is ongoing. She can't argue with that, surely.'

Another thought occurred to him and he paused, giving Andy a meaningful look.

'Especially as everything seems to lead back to the Pack.'

Saturday

39

LOUISE

Meg (Tyrion's Mum)

> Morning! Hope you're OK after last night.

> I have an update: I met my friend Connor for drinks — you know, the one who works for the council? He did a bit of research. You know how many residents and small business owners have complained about Cluckin' Good Chicken?

> A lot?

You could say that. And you know how many complaints were acted on? I'll tell you: zero. None. Nil.

> Someone's protecting them? Someone in the council?

Looks that way.

> Any idea who? Why?

I think if we know who the 'who' is, we'll have a better chance at figuring out the 'why'.

> Yeah, me too.

Be careful though – this feels like it could get dangerous really fast.

> It already has.

> Meg, do you think you could set up a meeting for me with Connor?

> I don't see why not. He usually does a long — and I mean really long — brunch at The Parlour in Canary Wharf on Saturdays. Get there anytime from around 11 and you should see him. I'll text you a pic. And let him know you're coming.

Still curled up in a foetal position, I put the phone back on my nightstand. My head felt like it had been used for football practice by the national team. I closed my eyes against the stabbing light and wondered why I hadn't closed the bedroom drapes.

Wine, my memory cheerfully answered. *Too much wine.*

I'd finished most of the bottle of Gavi myself, only to realise that Jake had also ordered a bottle from the pizza delivery place. 'Just in case.'

And at that point, adding a bit of red to the white had sounded like a grand idea. My hands had stopped shaking and I was feeling something close to my normal self.

What wasn't normal was how I felt now.

Or the faint rumble of a snore beside me.

'Oh my god.'

I closed my eyes, trying to catalogue what had happened after the incident on the high street . . .

Jake rescuing me.

I curled up even tighter. God, I hated being the damsel in distress. I didn't need rescuing. I could handle myself. But it did feel good to know that Jake was there for me; that he had my back . . .

What on earth had possessed me to quaff all that wine though? I wanted to say that he should have stopped me, but no. It had been my decision; numbing the fear that crept up long after the real threat was gone.

Random images pulsed behind my closed eyes to the cadence of the soft snore:

An ill-conceived lunge across the sofa.

A misjudged snog that landed on his jaw.

Jake jumping back like a scalded cat.

Rejection and mortification torched my already bruised nerves.

There'd been words, probably nice ones, that explained his reaction, but I couldn't remember what they were exactly.

The warm body on the far side of the bed snorted in its sleep.

Slowly, I turned, terrified. *I don't want to be a one-night stand with Jake!*

Before I could make it halfway, the body moved, a cold nose grazing my shoulder, then my hip, as Klaus burrowed under the duvet.

I exhaled loud enough to hurt. Though fast on the heels of relief came abject humiliation. Of course it was Klaus; Jake had recoiled, hadn't he?

'Oh God,' I groaned, burying my head in the pillow and pulling Klaus's body closer to mine. 'At least you still love me, Klausi.'

Even when I wasn't sure how much I loved myself.

40

ELLA

Ella stood in the bathroom. The tiles beneath her feet were cold; though the door was closed – toilet paper was too much of a lure to Jimmy and Vader – the one leading to the balcony was open.

Paul was sitting outside with his morning coffee and the boys. He might be thirty-seven, but he had the soul of a little old lady who watched life from behind her net curtains. Only he didn't have the subtlety of a little old lady; he'd bought Ella an electric blanket and space heater so she (he) could stay outside when the weather turned cold. And binoculars – which Ella kept hiding.

For him, everything going on was exciting, new. He pitched himself as a suave Parisian, even cultivating the accent, but it was a lie. He was from Bergues, near Dunkirk. And that small-town boy, keen on dogs, football and Star Wars, was electrified by the excitement of living in what was beginning to feel like a war zone.

Ella wasn't. Sure, having front row seats to all the police action in the park had seemed thrilling at first, but more because it'd felt like a one-off. But now there were the gangs. The crime. The deaths. As much as she loved the Partridge Bark Pack, the neighbourhood just wasn't safe.

She looked at the white stick on the faux-marble countertop. A second line was emerging, about as fast as the wave of sickness in her belly.

She lurched to the toilet, vomiting up the few bites of croissant she'd managed to choke down. Retched again, even though there was nothing left.

Exhausted, she sank to the cold tiles, her back against the wall, and rested her forehead against her knees.

This was not how she'd imagined it would be.

And one other thing was clear: this was not the sort of neighbourhood she wanted to raise a child in.

41

IRINA

Partridge Bark

Ejiro (Hercules's Dad)

> Hey, we haven't done the co-ordinated walks in a while, but I really think we need to restart. It's getting dark early and too much going on. It's not safe at the moment.

Yaz (Hercules's Mum)

> Don't kid yourself – it's never safe.

BONE OF CONTENTION

Meg (Tyrion's Mum)

Whoo hoo! The Poop Patrols are back!

> Doesn't @**Ethan** do the last walk of the night with Tyrion these days, @**Meg**?

Meg (Tyrion's Mum)

Well yeah, we walk him together, but the patrols are more fun!

Ejiro (Hercules's Dad)

What do you think? Same as last time? People with smaller dogs team up with someone with a bigger dog? Avoiding CGC and any hot spot after what? 9?

Meg (Tyrion's Mum)

Kind of strange – T isn't a fan of bigger dogs, unless they're the ones he grew up with. Then he'd do anything for them. 🌀

Claire (Tank's Mum)

Same with Tank. But **@Ejiro**, it's kind of hard to avoid CGC when they're downstairs.

Fiona (Nala's Mum)

And didn't **@Louise** have her run-in earlier? Like supper time?

Claire (Tank's Mum)

Yeah – I saw it from my window. Sorry I couldn't get downstairs in time, **@Louise**! Not sure much earlier will be feasible – it's usually not so bad during the commuting time, but yesterday was Friday …

BONE OF CONTENTION

Ella (Bark Vader and Jimmy Chew's Mum)

> If anyone wants a walking buddy, Paul or I can take the boys out and meet you. They're gentle giants, but people tend to leave us alone …

Irina frowned at her phone and the Pack's let's-fix-it attitude. There were lots of messages popping up, just not from Andy. The least he could do was *respond*. Ghosting was just plain rude.

That was fine, she did her best work when she was angry. The problem was, she didn't know where to begin.

'What's the common denominator?' she asked Hammy. He didn't answer, his black eyes fixed on her crisps. She pushed the bag out of his reach. 'Not for you,' she said absently. If she was expecting any answer, it would have been *Gimme those crisps, Mama!*

Picking a starting point, she Googled Cluckin' Good Chicken and had a look at the reviews. The overall rating was three point eight stars; not horrible, considering most reviews were split between one star and five stars. Delving further, the five-star reviews were from names that weren't familiar to her, but quite a lot of the one-star reviews were from her friends around the neighbourhood. And people that she wouldn't have expected to eat there.

Irina squinted at the screen and looked at those reviews. They were full of phrases like 'disgusting' and 'filthy'. The replies from the shop were predictable: 'Sorry you had a bad experience. What did you eat? What specifically was wrong with it?', as if calling out that the reviews were duff.

Only, most people don't usually delve into the review comments, preferring to check just the numbers and the headlines. So, that was what she did.

She looked at the five-star reviews next. 'Worth the journey in from West London.'

WTF? What idiot travels from West London for bog-standard fried chicken? More likely the owner's friends and family had rallied together to up the ratings.

By the time she'd finished, she'd found that there were – unsurprisingly – no duplicate names on the one-star side, but there were plenty on the five-star side, and by the end of the first month, it looked like the one-stars were trailing off, as if the locals had given up hope.

What would I do if I wanted a place closed?

Sure, bad reviews were one good way.

Complaints to the council, maybe?

Irina stuffed a few crisps into her mouth and mused. Then she went back to one of the one-star reviews, the user profile image showing a smiling young man with a pretty cavalier spaniel, whom she recognised. 'So, that's his name.'

He wasn't a regular contributor to the Pack chat, but she'd seen him around. And now she could find his name in the Partridge Bark participants list to DM him.

42

LOUISE

Jake (Luther's Dad)

Hey, Marple. How are you feeling?

> Hungover. Humiliated. Really sorry for being, well, inappropriate. Not sure what was going through my head.

Other than wine? 😉

Look, you had a shitty day after a shitty week. You

> drank a lot – which was partly my fault. It's not a big deal. Take a couple of paracetamols for the hangover and forget about it.

It was bad enough that I had to struggle out of bed just to walk Klaus.

Bad enough that my kitchen looked like it'd been Irina'd.

Bad enough that, instead of at least tidying it up, I could only crawl back under the covers.

Bad enough to admit, even if only to myself, that I'd drunk too much, misread the signals and possibly scuppered my friendship with Jake.

But it was even worse that he was being gracious about it.

Pull yourself together.

My inner voice was right. I'd have to find a way to get past this, simply because I couldn't face the idea of having to avoid Jake, possibly forever, over something that he was clearly willing to let slide.

I replied with a couple of emojis, then showered, dressed and got ready to head down to the Wharf.

BONE OF CONTENTION

Irina (Hamish's Mum)

> When are you going to meet that friend of Meg's?

>> About to head out now.

> Good. I'm going to send you a few names. Can you see if he'll check whether they've raised complaints with the council, and if so, what the result was?

>> What have you found?

> There were quite a lot of people who left 1* reviews online against CGC.

>> Yeah, a good chunk of the Pack included.

> The responses from CGC online sounded fine, but I've spoken to one person – the guy who has Olivia the cavalier – and he says someone found

> him on Facebook and made a few threats. I'm trying to find out if he was a one-off or if this was a pattern.

> What sort of threats? Did he report it to the police? The council?

> Yes to the police, no to the council – although I would have done both – and yes to Facebook, although he didn't hear from them again after blocking the account.

> What sort of threats?

> Shut up or you'll get your arse kicked sort of stuff. He's sent screenshots – I'll forward them to you. The name made no sense, and the profile is gone. The pic was some sort of sketch, not a photo or

anything, so hard to tell if it's anyone we've seen.

> Do we know if Jonny Tang posted one of these reviews?

Yeah, he did.

> OK, I know you're not going to want to hear this, but I think you need to let the detectives know. These people might be the ones who killed him. Do you still have Andy's number?

Yeah. I messaged him yesterday.

> About this? What did he say?

😬

I had a sinking feeling that she'd done what I'd suggested and reached out to him socially. Irina could be charming when she wanted to be, and I'd hoped that she might ratchet up the rizz with Andy.

The problem was that I saw both sides: I knew how hot and cold Irina had blown with Andy, and understood why he'd want to ghost her. But I also knew that she did care for him, even if she hid it well. I felt bad that both had been hurt, but the case was bigger than a pair of egos.

Irina (Hamish's Mum)

> Try again – this feels like a big lead on the case.

> I'll bet they're already on it.

> Then no harm, no foul. Or text Scott Williams if you don't want to go through Andy. Or call the Met's info line, although it'll probably get back to one of them. Lots of options, Irina …

She wouldn't see it that way, but that was fine. As awkward as she could be, I didn't worry that she wouldn't escalate to the cops. She'd work herself up into a righteous fervour and tilt at a couple of windmills first, but she'd get there in the end. Eventually.

I slipped on my jacket and then Klaus's. The sky was blue, one of those clear, cold October days that made me feel homesick. In Connecticut, we'd be at the end of leaf-changing season, when for the better part of September and October everywhere you looked was an explosion of golds and reds. In London, the leaves went from green, to brown, to on the ground in about two seconds.

Regardless, it was a perfect day for a long dog walk; something to tire Klaus out and blow a few cobwebs from my brain. I liked The Parlour, although I usually went there more in the summer, opting for one of the outside tables in Canada Square. This time of year, though, they had blankets so people could still eat and drink al fresco.

Within twenty minutes, I was standing outside. There was an ancillary bar on the green that looked lovely, but Meg had suggested that Connor was more of a beer-in-a-dark-corner sort of guy. I checked outside anyway, worried that the smell of alcohol inside might cause my still delicate system to revolt.

As I'd suspected, the tables were fully occupied, mostly by young women and couples, dashing my hopes of clearing my head in the fresh air . . .

Bracing myself, I pushed through the glass door. At least it didn't smell too boozy inside, and I let out my breath slowly, scanning the tables. I spotted him quickly, a forty-ish Black man sitting in the back, his hair close cropped and dusted with strands of silver. He had a pint of IPA in front of him, and a few empty glasses were pushed to the side of the table.

After all that, I'd expected his eyesight to be blurry,

but his gaze was sharp, assessing me. 'Hi, you're Connor, right?'

'So?'

Meg had said that she'd let him know I was coming, so he shouldn't be surprised. Either he hadn't gotten the message, or was playing dumb, waiting to find out what I wanted. I sat down opposite him. 'I'm Louise. My friend Meg told me you might be here.'

He shrugged. 'I'm here every Saturday.'

He wasn't making this easy. I excused myself, ordered a diet soda for me and another IPA for Connor. And chips, because I couldn't say no to anything with rosemary and truffle oil on it.

The offering seemed to help, and Connor grunted a thanks. 'How do you know Meg?'

'Klaus.' I nodded to my dog. 'He became friends with her daxie, Tyrion, first.'

'Huh,' he said, sounding a little patronising. It didn't put me off; a lot of people without dogs didn't understand that the dog community ran a little like a schoolyard, equalising things like age, race and sexual orientation among the parents. What remained was the important bit: that you were a good person and loved dogs.

But I wasn't here to instruct Connor on dog park dynamics. 'Meg said that you used to work together. And that now you're working for Tower Hamlets Council.'

'Ah, shit.' He drained the last of his beer and started in on the one I'd pushed in front of him. 'It's a job.'

'Oh, I'm not judging. I think anyone who's working to improve the lives of neighbourhood residents is great.'

He guffawed. 'Bloody idealistic, aren't you?'

'Nope. But I've worked with people in local government before. And I'm doing work for the NHS now,' I said. 'I know you don't go into the public sector for the money.'

He eased back a little. 'So, why are you here?'

I took a chance and decided to be honest. 'I live in Tower Hamlets, near Partridge Park. We've had one local – a guy who worked for one of the top consultancies – turn up dead. Now there's a wave of crime that seems to be focused around this new chicken shop. And I'm running into dead ends at every turn.'

'I thought you said you worked for the NHS, not the Met?'

'Yeah. That's true.'

Sort of.

'So, it ain't your job.'

'Nope. But it's my home, and last night I was on the receiving end of a verbal attack.'

Again: *sort of*. Technically, Klaus had been, but I wasn't there to split hairs. 'So, I'm making it my job.'

Connor nodded, as if this made sense. 'What do you want from me?'

Here was the tricky bit.

'I think I might have to ask you to break the law.'

43

IRINA

Claire (Tank's Mum)

> Hey. When CGC opened, were you one of the people who gave them a 1* review?

No. I meant to, but kept being distracted. And I hadn't eaten there, so it didn't seem fair to give them a 1*, no matter how much I hated the idea of them.

> Ten points for integrity. Do you know anyone who did? Besides Jonny Tang?

Yeah, a few people in the building did. I didn't know Jonny had – he didn't mention it. But I'm not surprised. Why? What are you after?

> I checked the reviews. There were a few names I recognised who gave 1*s. Even if they didn't give a last name, most were 'found' on Facebook and warned off.

Shit. Warned off how?

> Threatened by someone called Jack Daws.

'Most were found' but not all? And who's Jack Daws?

> IDK yet. The profile pic is a sketch of a black bird

> with red eyes. Those who weren't contacted either didn't log on with their Google account to leave the review or didn't leave a name. Interestingly, their profile pics weren't of them either – usually a pet or a landscape or something instead.

I think you've stumbled on something important – and I don't know why I haven't heard about this before. Send me the list of names – I might recognise some people you don't. Who else have you told?

> Just Louise. And that was when I'd only found out about it happening to one person, not more than 10.

Check with Gav to see if he knows anything, but I really think you need to

> let the Pack know. And for sure, the police.

Irina put down her phone and looked over at Hamish. His fur was long – something she preferred when it was cold out – and curling a bit in a way that melted her heart. 'So, which crap job do I do first? Let the Pack know what I found, or message that moron detective?'

Hammy tilted his head to the side.

'Or continue looking for this Jack Daws? I mean, I've already searched for that name. Jack Dawson. John Daws. John Dawson . . .'

Hammy remained silent.

'Don't judge me, Mischka. I'm trying.'

Hammy sighed and gave her the sort of side-eye that he had to have learned from Klaus.

'If you're referring to Andy, I messaged him before and he ghosted me. Why should I chase him? I mean, if he doesn't want to know . . .'

Hammy groaned and lay down with his head on his paws, staring up at her. Or maybe at the new bag of crisps on her desk.

'Fine,' she sighed. 'Let me update the Pack and then I'll give him one more chance. After that, if the Pack want to talk to the cops, they can do it themselves. I'm done with being the monkey in the middle of this shitshow.'

44

ANDY

Irina Ivanova 🦇💩

> Hey, it's Irina. Just trying to help. I found out something about Jonny Tang and Cluckin' Good Chicken that might help the case.

'Ah hell.'

Williams looked up from his desk, taking off the wire-framed specs that looked slightly incongruous on the smashed-in face of a former rugby prop. 'What is it?'

Andy didn't answer, but banged his head lightly on his desk.

Williams rolled his chair over to have a look at the phone, and sighed. 'Maybe it's time for you to block her?'

When Andy didn't answer, he looked closer. 'Ah hell,' he echoed. 'They're at it again.'

'Looks that way,' Andy muttered, his forehead still on the desk. Then he straightened up. Ran his fingers through his unruly hair, and sighed in return. 'Give it here, let's see what they've got.'

Williams paused, the phone in his hand. 'Want me to respond?'

'On my phone?' Andy could only imagine what sort of trouble Williams would land him in. 'Hell no.'

Williams looked offended. 'Just trying to help.'

'Then call Louise Mallory. Irina wouldn't be sniffing around any of this if Louise hadn't put her up to it.'

'I thought you liked her?'

'Louise? Sure. She'd make a good cop. But she's not a cop. And she's gonna land herself in trouble – more trouble – one of these days.'

Williams looked away, then pulled out his own phone.

Andy's eyes narrowed. 'What aren't you telling me, Scott?'

Williams cleared his throat and leaned back in his chair with a smirk. 'Nothing,' he said. 'Absolutely nothing.'

Andy didn't believe him. He watched Williams's chunky fingers scrolling through his phone until finally the other detective nodded and turned the screen to face him.

'Remember when you were added to that chat back in spring?'

Andy nodded.

'Well, Irina might have booted you out. But it's a pity she didn't know that you'd put me in too, or she'd have got me as well. I muted it ages ago. Forgot I had it. But it looks like I'm still in.'

'Why'd you mute it?'

''Coz I don't want to hear about dog crap. Who's feeding Fido what, and when there's a good sale on for dog treats. But look at this, it really does look like they might have stumbled across something.'

'Something we should know about?'

'Something we're already working on.' Williams shrugged into his jacket. 'I'd suggest we don't fess up to being in the group, or your girl'll knock me out too. But let's go see them. Listen to what else they have. They might be crazy, but that doesn't mean they're wrong.'

Andy raised an eyebrow. 'You want to see them separately or together?'

'Under normal circumstances, I'd say separately, but this time I think together might give us a more complete picture. If Irina starts acting up, or decides how much she's willing to share, Louise will step in.'

'At least someone knows how to handle her.'

'At least someone does,' Williams echoed. 'And thank God she isn't my problem.'

45

LOUISE

Det. Scott Williams

> Evening, Ms Mallory. Your friend Ms Ivanova got in touch to say that your group might have some information that could help the investigation. We're on our way to meet with her. Guessing you want to be there too?

> Yeah. Thanks for letting me know. I have a bit more information we can share.

I stared at the screen. DC Williams didn't have to include me, but I was glad he had. Irina would be cagey as hell around Andy, and this was too important to mess up.

I shifted Klaus on my lap so I could type more easily, and to keep him away from the truffle fries that sat almost untouched on the pub table in front of me. 'Leave it, sweetheart,' I told him, and answered Connor's querying look with a gesture to indicate that I was talking to Klaus, not to him.

Det. Scott Williams

> I'll let Irina know I'm coming, but it might make sense to meet at my flat instead. It's a bit bigger. I'm at 801 Colourway House.

Bigger, and also neutral territory. Williams either understood that or not, it didn't matter, but he responded with a thumbs-up emoji.

Irina (Hamish's Mum)

> I'm guessing you messaged Andy – the detectives asked to see

> me as well. I suggested meeting at my place.

She also responded with a thumbs-up.

Connor had drawn the line at breaking the law – he wouldn't break confidentiality rules to give me any names, which was fair enough. The last thing I wanted to do was get anyone else in trouble, and after I'd told him what we were dealing with, he wasn't entirely unsympathetic to our cause – although in fairness, that might have been the beer talking.

I made my excuses and arranged to speak to him again on Monday, when I might have better questions to ask, then left The Parlour.

Gav (Violet's Dad)

> Irina messaged me about Jack Daws. I asked around. Mo says he heard the kids outside News-N-Booze talking about a jackdaw, but maybe he got that wrong. He's

> trying to find out who it is, and what they're saying. Already told Irina, but thought you'd want to know.

> A jackdaw? A bird? Thanks, Gav.

> Not a bird, got the feeling it was a man.

> An alias?

> More like a nom de guerre. He got the feeling they were a bit scared of this person, but not sure why. When I know more, I'll let you know.

'Jackdaw', a blackbird, instead of the Jack Daws Irina had mentioned in an earlier message. Not a bad moniker and as good a clue as any.

I was less sure about why Gav had messaged me directly instead of putting it into the Pack chat, but that didn't matter. If it was important, we could update the others easily enough.

As we got off the DLR, Klaus led me towards the stairs, but instead of allowing me to pick him up, he tried to get past me to walk up them himself.

'No chance, sweetheart. Stairs aren't a dachshund's friend. You know the drill.' I patted my left shoulder, waiting for him to leap onto it. Instead he sniffed, and pointedly headed over to the lift, where I cringed as I got a noseful of its usual weed-and-urine reek. 'Not so fresh smelling or eco-friendly, but fine,' I told him, deciding to compromise and allow him some degree of independence. We exited at street level and he shook the trip off, before lifting his leg on a wadded-up copy of the *City AM* paper.

'Any time now,' I said, trying to chivvy him along. 'I'd rather get home before the detectives.' There was no point in trying to get there before Irina. She'd be at the window, waiting for them to arrive before swanning over. Probably dressed up to the nines.

When we arrived, there was no one waiting at the main gate or the door to my building, so we took the lift to the eighth floor alone. I grimaced at the state of my kitchen. Pulled out a bag for life and whacked the empty bottles and pizza boxes into it.

'No time to run to the recycling bin, but at least I don't look like the friendly neighbourhood alcoholic,' I said to Klaus, shoving the bag into the cupboard beneath my sink. I made myself a cup of tea and sat down. I didn't have long to wonder how much to tell the cops before they arrived.

As I buzzed them into the complex and again into my building, Klaus was already on sausage security detail, barking at the door from the moment I hit the button.

Amidst the happy barkfest when he came in, Andy reached into a pocket and pulled out something which he kept hidden in his hand, somehow managing to get my hound to do a spin and a sit before giving him the treat.

Williams lagged behind. 'He made me stop on the way to get them,' he said, with the sort of look that told me this wasn't the first time.

'Good boy,' Andy said to Klaus, then straightened up to shake my hand. 'Good to see you again, Ms Mallory.'

He was being overly formal, either for the situation or for Williams's benefit, but it made me feel about a thousand years old. 'Louise.'

Andy nodded. 'Louise.'

'Come in. I've just boiled the kettle and I've got some cookies – biscuits – although they might be stale. Meg brought them around a few months ago, but they're still unopened.'

Williams looked like he was trying to hold back laughter.

'I know, I'm babbling again. Come in. If the biscuits are nasty, you don't have to eat them.'

This time Andy held back a half step.

Figuring out why, I reassured him. 'Irina isn't here yet, but if you have another treat in your pocket, I'm sure Hamish will be grateful.' Klaus perked up at the T-word, and danced around Andy's feet, still barking happily.

My dog was a tart when it came to treats.

I gestured for the detectives to sit on the sofa and prepared the tea and biscuits. 'While we wait for Irina, I need to tell you about an incident that happened last night. I'm not sure if this is connected to everything else that's been going on, but I was verbally assaulted by those yobs hanging out outside Cluckin' Good Chicken.'

'Verbally?'

'It felt like it was going to escalate, but my neighbour happened to be walking past. He stepped in and, well, kind of defused it. We got out of there, before ...'

Before I could open my mouth and get both of us into deeper trouble?

Williams seemed to understand, but was kind about it. 'Before anyone got hurt. No one was hurt, right?'

'Shaken, but not hurt. No.'

'Good. Which neighbour?' he asked, with a glance at the door.

'Jake Hathaway. And his Staffie terrier, Luther. I rather get the impression that the CGC crew aren't keen on dogs – I've mentioned that to you before. Luther's a big softie, but he looks badass.'

'Do they – or does anyone outside the Pack – know your name? Know who you are or what you're looking into?'

It was a good question. I thought I'd been targeted opportunistically, because I was a single woman walking with a barky little dog. But if it was because I was looking into Jonny's death ...

I sat down, feeling sick.

'I don't know. I mean, they probably recognise me – I need to go through that area most days to get on the Tube or the DLR. And I have friends nearby ...'

'I'm not saying they do know who you are, Louise. I'm just trying to figure out what happened. But I'll get a couple of uniforms over there to ask questions.'

'Thank you.'

'Okay. Do I need to warn you – again – about getting involved in police business?'

'No, detective,' I said, looking down. I was still terrified, but I was also just as convinced that what I was doing was the right thing. At least, it felt like the right thing. And just because it was dangerous didn't mean that I could stop. Feeling a bit like Irina must when she split hairs to justify doing whatever she wanted, I kept my eyes lowered so the detectives couldn't guess what I was thinking.

Klaus tilted his head and ran to the door, barking up a storm again. 'Lift,' I explained. 'I'm guessing it's Irina.'

Klaus's bass/baritone solo barkfest turned into a duet with Hammy's excited tenor as Irina pushed open the door.

'Think now's a good time to start locking the door?' Andy commented.

'Too late,' Williams muttered.

'Anyone would be stupid to break into Lou's flat with two detectives on her couch,' Irina said. Her make-up was subtle but expertly applied and her jeans were DL61s, matched with a black silk top, Bottega Veneta earrings and black Adidas Sambas. She'd nailed the casual, I'm-not-trying-too-hard look. I'd bet her bedroom was a disaster as a result, but the effort hadn't gone unnoticed. If Williams was regarding her as if she was an unexploded bomb, then Andy was looking at her as if she was something intriguing, yet exponentially more dangerous.

'I'm not sure why I'm here,' she announced by way of greeting. 'Louise could have told you everything I know about this.' She turned towards my kitchen, looked in the fridge, then poured herself a glass from the half-empty bottle of Valpolicella. 'Want one, Lou?'

'Make yourself at home,' Williams muttered, looking at Andy.

'Right,' I said, taking charge. 'So, we've been nosing around a bit—'

'Which we've asked you not to do,' Williams reminded us.

'Yes, detective. Which you've asked us not to do,' I parroted politely. 'But then you hauled one of my friends off in handcuffs for the murder, which was totally preposterous. She was his *friend*, for heaven's sake. And then another friend was beaten and tossed into the bushes in the park. Left for dead. She's in the hospital, still in a medically induced coma, in case you were wondering. And if that wasn't enough mayhem for the week, we witnessed another killing – a stabbing – on the street outside of the chicken shop a couple of days later.' I was warming to my theme. 'So, we started asking: what if they were linked? All of them.'

'Because of the box of wings by Mr Tang's body?' Andy asked.

'No, detective,' Irina said. 'Because of the number of people who were threatened after lodging bad online reviews. Some took down their reviews; others blocked the company, changed profiles, got off social media. If it were me, I'd have called the police or complained to the council.'

'Probably both,' I murmured, scratching Hammy behind his ears.

'Personally, I'd like to know if anybody did call the police, and what actions the Met has taken to: A, identify the culprit; B, arrest and prosecute them. And if A has not led to B, then the steps taken to ensure the complainants are kept safe.' Irina itemised each point on her fingers, her throaty voice calm, but her expression stony. It made me begin to believe her brags about what a great lawyer she was.

'You know we're not at liberty to share any details with regards to an ongoing investigation, Ms Ivanova.' Williams couldn't have sounded any more formal if he'd tried.

'Crime is an unfortunate fact of life in this neighbourhood,' Andy added.

'Yes, but it's usually yob on yob, like the stabbing in front of CGC. Or theft. Burglary. Maybe even an opportunistic assault.' I held up a hand to head off any interruptions. 'Hear me out. We know that Jonny Tang, who was quite a successful consultant with one of the big guns, wrote a bad review of CGC. Maybe he thought he had some clout. But I'll bet he wrote to the Met and the council as well.'

Klaus padded up the ramp next to the sofa and onto my lap. He didn't sit, but instead kept moving until he was directly above Hammy, then launched himself at his friend.

I pretended not to notice and continued, 'We know Annabel Lindford-Swayne works for one of the local property developers. She'd be well aware of resident and local business complaints. They're two reasonably well-off and well-placed individuals who could cause problems for a new business. Maybe they were each targeted in such a way as to send a warning to anyone who stood in the way of CGC's commercial success?'

Hammy was responding to the stealth attack, trying to roll Klaus. Klaus hated being rolled and only tolerated it from a few dogs, which included Hammy. There was never any malice in their play.

'Which brings me round to the stabbing on Wednesday. From what I've seen and heard, CGC have the same group of youngish men outside every night. I say "youngish" because they're a bit older than the ones you usually see outside of the local chicken shops. They're not just punters. I mean, they are in that they're eating the food, but it feels like they're some sort of security.'

'Intimidation. It's like they're trying to scare off anyone who might object,' Irina interjected.

'Right. They're a new chicken shop, in an area that seems to already have a chicken shop on each street. Maybe they're trying to see off their competition. Maybe they're all owned by the same people? The other chicken shops, I mean.' I shrugged. 'I don't know.'

Irina slanted a glance towards me that indicated that she'd be looking into that next.

'So, you have these men, intimidating people on the street. You have CGC's owners stepping on the toes of people who live in the building by messing around with the exhaust systems—'

'Allegedly.'

'Allegedly,' I conceded. 'But they're also pissing off

other local businesses. Which is never good for, ah, business.'

Irina took a small sip of wine, watching Andy over the rim of her glass. 'I'm also interested in how they got planning permission to open in the first place, with all the existing chicken shops around.'

'Okay,' Williams said firmly, also glancing at Andy. 'First of all, we wouldn't typically comment on an ongoing investigation, but let me share a few things with you. We have Mr Tang's laptop and we are aware of the online bullying he was subjected to.'

'By Jack Daws?'

'Jackdaw. It's the screen name of CGC's manager's sixteen-year-old kid. We've brought him in and read him the riot act—'

'But he's sixteen and still a minor.' I sighed.

'Yes, although he's been cautioned and has – so far – kept the bullying online.'

'Not that that makes it any better,' Andy added. 'Bullying is not something we tolerate.'

'What about the rest of it?'

'The gang-on-gang action is being looked into, as, I'm sure, are the planning permissions. That's not in our remit, I'm afraid.'

'And Annabel?'

'We're investigating all avenues of inquiry.'

Which meant they probably had nothing. I hadn't really been expecting them to share anything with us, but it didn't hurt to try.

'That's fair.' As the two detectives made to leave, I had

one last suggestion up my sleeve. 'But if you find yourself in a position where you can share something with the public, or you need something "leaked", can I suggest you go to Claire and *The Chronicle*?' I met first Williams's eyes, then Andy's. 'After what you put her through, you owe her one.'

46

LOUISE

Indy (Banjo's Mum)

> The swelling on Annabel's brain seems to be going down. Looks like they're going to bring her out of the coma tomorrow, or maybe Monday. They'll know then what sort of damage she sustained.

> Thanks for letting me know, Indy. Hopefully nothing Annabel can't recover from ...

> Let's hope. Head injuries are tricky.

I had no idea how Indy was getting these updates, but I was grateful for whichever connections she was using.

The detectives didn't linger, and there were no warm words, or even looks, when Andy took his leave of Irina.

She refilled her glass. 'You sure you don't want one?'

'Drank too much last night.'

'Yeah ...' There was enough of an inflection to hint that she knew something, which meant that she must have been watching from her window. Again. As much as I cringed inside, I tried not to show it. What had she actually seen? The drinking, fine. But had she seen me lunge at Jake? Or his reaction?

Jesus. Will it never end?

'The docs are planning on bringing Annabel out of the coma,' I said, changing the subject. 'Hopefully once she's awake she'll be able to let the police know who did this to her.'

'And why.' Irina nodded, crunching on one of the stale biscuits. She made a face, but took a second bite. 'Assuming of course that her brain—'

'Don't say it.'

'Right. Then assuming she remembers. Better?'

'Much.' I sealed the biscuit packet up and handed it to her. 'I'm shattered, but take these for later. If you leave now, you might catch Andy.'

'Why would I want to do that?'

'Because he might be lingering in front of your door. Who knows?'

She didn't move quickly, per se, but every move was perfectly engineered to look casual. The slide into her jacket. Tucking Hammy's coat under her arm, rather than spending time wrestling him into it. Clicking on his lead while they waited for the lift. It was a fair amount of effort to mask a speedy exit.

I watched the lift doors slide closed after them before retreating inside and locking my front door. I turned to Klaus and gave him a tired smile. 'Don't judge. If I hadn't done that, she'd have stayed for the next few hours, ordering in more wine when she finished the bottle, and I can't face even the smell of it in the room.'

He padded back to the living room and dropped onto his bed with a sigh.

'Me too. But tomorrow's Sunday, and with a little luck, it'll be uneventful.' I knew that was unrealistic even as the words came out. 'Or maybe we can at least catch a bit of luck on this.'

Sunday

47

IRINA

Partridge Bark

Ejiro (Hercules's Dad)

So you met with the police yesterday? What did they say?

Sweet FA. 'Stay off the case' yadda yadda.

Meg (Tyrion's Mum)

So who do you escalate to if the cops don't want our input?

Yaz (Hercules's Mum)

Come on, **@Irina**. Take one for the team. See what you can do to persuade the cute detective to prioritise the case. Cases. Whatever.

> It's your turn, **@Yaz**.

Claire (Tank's Mum)

You know it's a bad situation when even The Bells installs CCTV.

Fiona (Nala's Mum)

So, they finally did it!

Claire (Tank's Mum)

Yeah. A bit late, considering the contretemps on Wednesday, but I saw the engineers out there early yesterday morning installing it. On balance, it

> actually makes me feel a little better.

> Remind me: who would actually want to break into The Bells?

Claire (Tank's Mum)

> My point exactly. You know the neighbourhood is in trouble when even they're scared.

'You needed to see that to understand how crap it's getting?' Irina said aloud, setting the phone and the coffee down on either side of her laptop. She opened Louise's packet of stale biscuits, stuffing one into her mouth as she waited for the computer to boot up.

Had Lou been winding her up last night, or had she genuinely believed Andy would be waiting for her outside? Even if Andy had wanted to wait, that massive prat Williams would have found some way to prevent it. Irina was under no illusion: from almost the first time they'd met, it had been clear that Williams did not remotely like her.

Well, the ball was in Andy's court, regardless. She'd reached out – twice – and now it was his turn.

Hammy scrambled out from under the sofa and trotted

up next to her. When he had her attention, he rolled onto his back, his little legs in the air, asking for a belly rub.

'Ah jeez, if it was only that easy for humans,' Irina said, but leaned down to scratch his tummy. She caressed his cheek, a silent apology for the too-brief belly rub before she sat up again and brought up the search engine.

'Zoning regs in the area. Let's see if there was a valid reason CGC should have been turned down.' She crunched another biscuit thoughtfully. 'And then I want to have another look at the shop's ownership. Something doesn't feel right there. And—' She glanced back at her notepad, brow furrowed. 'Too bad I can't get his bank records. Unless he's got the mother of all bank accounts, he has to have some vice to spend his dosh on.'

48

LOUISE

Irina (Hamish's Mum)

> I did a bit of sniffing around. I don't think the zoning is a problem legally, but from a commercial perspective, it still doesn't make sense to me.

> No, and yet, they always look busy.

> Because of the same clientele? The men

> outside? Maybe. But it looks like they've breached some regulations by piping their exhaust through the building's ventilation system. Not sure if it'd be enough to close them down though. Breaches like this get raised, and if confirmed to be the case, they tend to have a set amount of time to remediate.

Interesting.

That *was* interesting, but how did it figure into the jigsaw of the current situation? I stopped by the little Tesco on the high street to pick up grapes and chocolates, on the off chance that Annabel might be awake.

As I passed CGC, I saw Angry Caren – the beautician – coming out with a box of food. Her hair was in its usual state, the black-and-white fringe tamed into submission and the rest 'framing her face', à la Einstein.

The salon was closed on Sundays, which meant that she must live locally. Klaus barked a greeting, even though I didn't get my hair cut there.

She glared in response. 'Don't judge.'

Given how hungover I'd been yesterday, I'd have probably nailed a box of chicken myself if I hadn't been leery about going inside. 'Why would I? It smells good.'

She offered a wry smile then, though it made her look only slightly less intimidating. 'If you can't beat 'em, join 'em.'

I wasn't sure I'd gotten to that point yet, but nodded and walked around to the entrance to the flats and buzzed Claire's number.

'Thanks for watching Klaus while I'm out,' I said, by way of greeting.

'No problem.' She stood aside, making space for us to enter the flat. Klaus burst past us, his lead trailing behind, to launch himself onto the sofa and Tank. The chonkster, just waking up, blinked at Klaus and wiggled his non-tail in response.

'Want a cuppa before you go? I stopped at The Nest for grinds and pastries,' Claire said, jiggling a brown paper bag enticingly. Her blond curls were fastened on the top of her head, but without make-up, she looked tired.

'Go on then.' I took off my jacket and strode to the sofa to wriggle Klaus out of his. 'How are you doing?'

'Me? I'm fine,' she said, before redirecting, 'How are *you* doing, after Friday? Sorry again for not getting there ...'

'That's fine, I wouldn't have wanted to put you in danger. My lesson learned is to just avoid the area after dark, where possible. At least until things have settled down a bit.'

'Sensible.' Claire poured two cups of coffee and put them on the table. 'Milk? Sugar?'

'Both, please. We had the cops over last night, sharing with them some links Irina found between people who posted bad reviews of CGC and those who got a nasty message from somebody called "Jack Daws" – who turned out to be CGC's manager's sixteen-year-old kid.'

'She mentioned it. I'm still trying to figure out why I hadn't heard any of this before. Usually we have a tight community in the building.' Claire took down two plates and put a cinnamon bun on one and an apple fritter on the other. 'You choose,' she directed.

Cinnamon bun. Every time.

'Maybe whoever was on the receiving end felt embarrassed? Or scared?' I took a bite, idly wondering why she'd bought two when she lived alone. 'Getting spooked by a teenager?'

'They didn't know it was a teenager. Still, it feels a little too slick to be something new.'

I paused and looked at her. 'You think it's been done before?'

'I don't know. Maybe not with the kid, but yeah. Maybe.'

'Irina's checking up on what we know about the owners. Maybe if you can figure out where they've operated before, you might be able to see if they've done the same thing there?'

Claire picked an end off the fritter. 'Perfume shops? Not sure those are offensive enough to receive bad reviews.'

'So then how can this fit in to . . .' I flicked my hand to indicate 'everything'.

'I don't know,' she said, her mouth full. 'Yet. But I'll check in with the Tsarina and see what she has.'

49

IRINA

Partridge Bark

Claire (Tank's Mum)

Putting some feelers out. Most of you've already heard me whinge about all the crap going on with CGC. Forget about the thugs hanging outside, but the dirt they leave (that our service charges pay to clean), the use of building ventilation for their exhaust, everything else. Has anyone else seen or heard of someone who's gone through something similar?

Fiona (Nala's Mum)

Sorry to say, but I think this might be more common than anyone thinks. Most of the fast-foody type of places tend to have a fair amount of stains left on the pavement outside from all sorts of spills.

Paul (Bark Vader and Jimmy Chew's Dad)

Or worse.

Fiona (Nala's Mum)

Don't go there, @Paul!

'Zoning,' Irina said aloud. She reached for another biscuit, only to find the packet empty. She looked accusingly at

Hamish, napping on the far side of the room. 'Did you finish the cookies?'

If he had, he wasn't confessing to it.

She stood up and stretched. Went to the kitchen and foraged until she found a small bag of lentil crisps in the back of the cupboard. 'Freakin' disgusting,' she said. 'Who actually buys this crap?' She pried open the bag and tossed two into her mouth. Then poured herself a glass of Pinot Noir to wash it down.

While the new chicken shop didn't appear at first glance to have broken any laws, she couldn't see why the landlord for that complex would have approved it, even if the council had.

If Lou's theory was right, and the council had pushed it through, that was one thing.

But Irina wasn't certain. There were other possibilities – maybe someone pressuring the landlord. Or bribing them. Yet her gut feel kept coming back to the council angle. It was part of the story, even if it wasn't the full story.

'I mean,' she mused aloud. 'Why burn a key contact in the council to get the shop set up, when you could do it another way? And once you're in, you're in. Make it hard for the landlord to turf you out, and keep that council contact hot in case you need them.'

The lentil crisps tasted like cardboard. She checked the fridge, but the only thing in there that she could use as a dip was turning green, and she didn't feel like walking down to the little Tesco or News-N-Booze. She crunched a few more crisps as a thought began to take shape.

'What if they lied on the application? The proposal for

the restaurant? Pitched it as something else, hoping no one would find out until after it was open? Maybe some money changed hands at some point, but Dave Najafi, or whoever it was, still kept the council card up his sleeve, to play if he had to?' Irina brushed crisp crumbs from her chest and determinedly began to type.

50

LOUISE

Irina (Hamish's Mum)

> If you're going to see Annabel, ask her if she knew Cluckin' Good Chicken was a chicken shop when they signed the deal. I mean, if they had a different name or something.

> Assuming she's awake, I'm not sure she'll be ready to talk about this. Or even who landed

> her in hospital. But I'm intrigued – what have you found?

> Haven't found anything. Yet. Just a theory. But working on it.

> Getting on the Tube now – keep me posted!

It was the same line of questioning I'd taken with Annabel at La Figa before she'd shut me down. That Irina was also asking the questions confirmed that I might have been onto something. Hopefully Annabel would be up for answering my questions this time around.

I scampered down the stairs, feeling a little guilty for leaving Klaus behind, but knowing that he wouldn't be allowed in the hospital.

The Royal London wasn't far from the Whitechapel Tube station, although it took me longer than I'd bargained on to find the right entrance. When I finally did, I paused in the gift shop to buy a small bouquet of flowers, in case they wouldn't let me leave the snacks, before blagging my way through to the Intensive Care ward. The receptionist looked at me through thick-lensed glasses that magnified her eyes to manga proportions. The waiting area was empty but for a few people. A man, maybe in his late fifties, scrolling through his phone, a folded, waxed Barbour on the seat beside him. And on the other side, an older Asian couple holding hands ignored me while they stared at the empty door, *The Times* crossword puzzle open on the man's lap.

'My name's Louise Mallory. I'm here to see Annabel Lindford-Swayne. I understand that she woke up this morning.'

'Sorry, no guests at this time.'

I wasn't surprised, but still felt crushed. 'All right.' I placed the bouquet on the desk and pulled the grapes and chocolates from my canvas bag. 'Can you please give these to her and let her know that I came to see her?'

The nurse nodded, looking bored, and returned her attention to her screen as I folded my canvas carrier bag and tucked it into my pocket.

'Damn,' I muttered to myself as I turned back towards the entrance. Even though I'd only planned the visit to check in and maybe cheer Annabel up, it'd been a wasted trip.

'*Wait.*'

I stopped and looked over my shoulder, but it wasn't the receptionist. The man who'd been sitting in the waiting area was moving towards me. He had thick dark hair that was more salt than pepper around the temples, dark eyes and a strong, clean-shaven jaw. There was an air of command about him, the way I'd imagine a ranking officer on a battlefield. The sort of air that was probably born of a privileged background, developed at public schools and honed in boardrooms. The sort of man who did little without having a plan that others were expected to comply with.

I'd worked with men like this in the past, and usually

found that they underestimated me. And yet, there was something familiar about him, something more than just his personality type.

'Robert Lindford-Swayne. You know my daughter?' It was a question but it sounded like a demand. One made in cut-glass tones.

'I'm the one who found her, yes,' I said. 'Louise Mallory. Annabel's my friend. I just wanted to see how she's doing.'

'You found her? In the park?'

'Yes, behind the café. Have they told you how she is?' I jerked my head towards the reception desk.

'They woke her up this morning, but the doctors still need to run some tests to see how much damage has been done.'

'I'm so sorry, Mr Lindford-Swayne.'

'Not your fault, you did your best.'

He was trying to be kind, and yet, maybe it was my fault. If I hadn't asked her those questions ...

His eyes narrowed, as if he could sense my thoughts. 'Let me buy you a coffee, Ms Mallory. I think we have a lot to discuss.'

His tone brooked no disagreement, even if I was inclined to defer. I had no doubt that he wanted to know who'd hurt his daughter and why. And that he'd be a formidable foe to whoever it was.

I nodded and allowed him to lead me out of the hospital and to a nearby coffee shop, where he ordered two flat whites to take away. 'I've spent too much time in the hospital,' he said, by way of explanation. 'I need some fresh air. Let's walk while we talk.'

Where we won't be overheard?

I nodded. 'I have more questions than answers, but happy to help.'

His own questions started off predictably: 'Tell me about the night you found Annabel.'

Then came the trickier ones: 'What did you discuss during that lunch?' and 'What makes you think this is all connected in some way to Cluckin' Good Chicken?'

What made it so tricky wasn't that he was asking the same questions we were; it was that Annabel was scared of something, or someone. I wasn't sure how much I could tell her father without alarming him. I also didn't know him well enough to trust him.

Not when misplaced trust could land me in the same place as Annabel.

Or worse.

I gave him the answers that I could, and kept most of my theories to myself. I had no doubt that he knew what I was doing. By what felt like the tenth time he'd asked a question that I'd already dodged, we doubled back and he walked me to the Tube station.

'Look, I know you don't trust me, and that's fine,' he said, giving voice to my misgivings. 'But let me give you my number. If you hear of anything that can help me find who did this to my daughter, or if you need anything from me, let me know.' For a moment before he turned and strode away, an emotion that might have been vulnerability crossed his face. 'I'd be grateful.'

51

IRINA

Hamish sniffed around the empty bag of lentil crisps, and without thinking, Irina picked it up off the floor and added it to the pile of empty bags on the corner of her desk.

She typed CGC's owner's name, Dave Najafi, into the search engine. No returns. Tried the surname alone, in case he'd anglicised his forename. Google delivered more than she'd expected, but nothing that seemed to be linked to the right person. She tried again in a few permutations.

'Damn. He's as elusive as Jake Hathaway. Or Jack Daws.'

Frustrated, Irina opened her phone, answered a few messages. None of which were from Andy – Lou must have misread his interest, damn her.

She went back to her laptop again and tried a few different spellings for Dave's surname. Gav might have heard the name right but got the spelling wrong.

'Or maybe Gav got the name wrong entirely? Would

that be by accident or did someone give him the wrong name? Pointing him in the wrong direction ... assuming of course that he's not pointing *us* in the wrong direction.' That was a different question though, and one that Irina wrote down in her legal pad, banking it for later.

Hammy, huffing at the prospect of no more crumbs to scavenge, retreated to the couch.

'Whatever. Let's try this from the other direction. There has to be an owner listed at Companies House.' Irina's fingers flew over the keyboard.

She frowned at what she saw on the screen. Checked something else.

Ripping off the top pages from her pad, she turned to a fresh page, and started documenting her findings.

52

LOUISE

Partridge Bark

Paul (Bark Vader and Jimmy Chew's Dad)

> Bonjour all, I'm looking to get some yak chews instead of bones/antler for the boys. I need something for heavy chewers, obvs. Has anyone ever given them to their dogs? Pros and cons? Merci, in advance.

Meg (Tyrion's Mum)

> I give them to T — he loves them. But get good quality ones. Sometimes the cheap ones splinter really easily. I can send you links to where I buy mine.

I walked out of the DLR, trying to herd my thoughts, although they seemed to be running in every direction. What I really needed was a quiet moment to sit and think.

Finding a bench outside The Bells, I did exactly that, only pausing to scroll through my messages and add my comments to the yakker conversation.

Partridge Bark

> Buy a couple and try them out with the boys, @**Paul**. They're cheese, so they'll probably love it ... Klaus only likes them when he's stolen them from someone else. Or when I microwave one and it gets puffy. #SpoiledSausage

Leaning back, I considered where we were at. We had one murder and one attempted murder on top of the usual neighbourhood crime. My mind immediately paired the first two and drew a dotted line to the third.

I messaged Irina, asking if she'd been able to find a connection between Jonny Tang and Annabel.

Irina (Hamish's Mum)

> Tenuous. Jonny lived nearby and hated CGC, and Annabel was one of the people involved with the deal getting them into Village Vet's old space. You'd think they'd be at opposite ends of any conflict, right? Not saying that Annabel bumped Jonny off or anything.

> What if Annabel was duped – or strong armed – into agreeing the deal?

> Yeah, I thought of that too, but still no reason to go after her. She's part of the property DEVELOPMENT

> company, not the property MANAGEMENT company.

> Unless she tried to rock the boat? Asked a few awkward questions?

> Yeah, maybe then. But I still think it's more likely that the culprit's someone who's against CGC, not someone who has a vested interest in it.

So did I.

I sat back against the table and stared up at the sky. It was cold out, but at least the sky was still a bright October blue. The sort of day I usually loved.

Across the street CGC was doing a brisk service. 'A modern – but sad – take on the Great British Sunday lunch?' I said aloud.

Further down the street, a group of men were jogging, rucksacks on their backs, masks and bandanas over their faces, protecting them from the cold.

Only, it wasn't *that* cold.

An electric jolt ran through my body, just under the skin. *Something is about to happen. Something important.*

As a group, they turned, heading straight towards me.

'Holy shit,' I muttered, scrambling to my feet. Already poised for trouble, my fight or flight instinct was clear: *run!*

But they weren't after me and passed by, heading towards the pub's entrance.

It didn't matter – I bolted, sprinting after them.

Why attack a crappy dive like The Bells?

A pub that might already have known something was going to happen, given they'd only just installed CCTV yesterday?

One thought popped clearly into my mind: *what if it's a diversion?*

It might be, but I was still running, and not towards The Bells anymore. I skidded around the corner by News-N-Booze and down the alley leading to the little road behind the high street. While the front of the apartment building faced The Bells across the road, the rear backed onto this small street, and the ever-present low hum of a factory.

Before I could make it to the corner, I heard a boom. I stopped and turned. A runner pulled a bottle from his bag, lit it and threw it into The Bells, resulting in a second boom.

Molotov cocktails? Here?

People rushed forward onto the street, their smartphones held aloft to video it.

'Morons, one of you needs to call the fire brigade,' I muttered, but turned and picked up my pace again.

There were more 'runners' ahead. Two were prying the back entrance to CGC open while the third prepared another Molotov cocktail, sailing it through the newly opened door.

Klaus is upstairs, with Claire.

The realisation punched the air from my lungs. I

speed-dialled Claire's number with shaking fingers, terrified that I wouldn't be fast enough. Each moment I waited for her to pick up was torture. Finally, she answered with a tired-sounding 'Hey.'

'Get the boys and get out of the building. *Now!*' I shouted, over the pounding of my heart.

'What?' she repeated, more alert.

'Call the fire brigade! Some idiots are throwing Molotovs.' The 'runners' were racing away; they'd be gone before I could get there, not that I'd be able to do much against a pack of missile-launching men.

'*Shit!*' Claire gasped. 'Okay. Leave it with me.'

I trusted her to get Klaus and Tank out, but couldn't risk the fire preventing their escape, or burning the building down. Hoping there was an extinguisher near the door, I edged inside, feeling my way through a wall of smoke and into what seemed to be a storeroom. The Molotov had hit the floor and I could see fingers of flames reaching outwards in every direction.

Cooking oil. This was a fried chicken shop – there would be cooking oil. If the flames reached it, the whole building, including the flats above, would be in danger.

Including Klaus, Tank and Claire.

Black smoke billowed with increased force, making my eyes tear and my throat close. Still, I pushed forward towards where I'd glimpsed an extinguisher on the wall, grabbing it and fumbling with the mechanism. Foam shot out, and I tried to direct it between the fire and boxes of what could be oil to create a barrier. It felt like a losing battle. Sirens screamed above the growing inferno and water sprinkled from the ceiling in a half-hearted attempt to extinguish the growing flames.

I felt their presence more than I could see it, somewhere behind me. A spark of hope blossomed. 'Help! Someone, help me!'

The door shifted, and I realised the men weren't trying to help; they were closing the door. On me.

'NO!' I shouted, and threw the extinguisher, hoping it would block the closing door. Stumbling my way over, I pushed at the heavy slab of metal, while the person on the other side pushed back. I reached through the gap, groped around and grabbed an arm.

Whoever it was shook me off. Choking and half blind, I grabbed back on, this time managing to seize hold of a strap – maybe the rucksack of one of the runners. I didn't care; it distracted them enough to allow me to slide out of the door.

My eyes teared up and I gasped for air as I crawled onto the pavement, unable to focus on my assailant, but knowing that I had to hold on. They threw a punch that glanced off my shoulder. The second landed, and I flailed out with my left hand. Heard an 'oof'.

Something smacked against my head as my fingers tightened their hold, and everything tilted on its axis. Voices echoed through the scuffle and the pain, and my assailant took a half step back, still held in place by my hands on the rucksack. They tried to pry themselves free.

'Hey, you!' a voice in the distance yelled.

It faded into a low buzz as I fell backwards.

Smoke curled around me until everything went black.

53

CLAIRE

'Call the fire brigade!' Lou shouted. 'Some idiots are throwing Molotovs.'

Claire ran to the window. Flames licked at the tired paint of The Bells. '*Shit!* Okay. Leave it with me.'

She grabbed her wallet and phone, called the emergency line to report the fire and the address while grabbing the dogs' leads and wrapping Klaus in his jacket.

'Stay where you are,' the call operator directed.

'Sod that. I'm not staying in a burning building!' Claire responded, and clicked the end call button.

The fire alarm sounded just after she reached the stairs. 'Down,' she ordered Tank. The pale Frenchie obeyed, trotting down the first flight and waiting for his mum on the landing. Klaus, in Claire's arms, struggled to be put down, but there was no way she was going to allow him to do the stairs on his own. If the fire didn't kill them, Louise would.

'Go,' she told Tank, picking up her pace, cursing the decision to let her gym membership lapse.

Other people were pushing into the stairwell. 'OMG, there's actually a fire this time!' someone screamed. Claire didn't answer, just concentrated on putting one foot in front of the other, tucking Klaus's nose into her jumper and hoping Tank, who had respiratory issues, could still breathe.

Smoke rises, she remembered. But it had to start low in order to rise, and they were moving closer to it, and it was getting thicker. 'Tank?'

He barked, close by. He sounded frightened, but otherwise okay. She focused on that, only that. *He's still okay.* 'Keep going!' She wasn't sure if she was talking to Tank, the others in the stairwell, or herself.

She figured she must be on the second floor by now. She was sweating, swearing and scared.

'Keep moving!'

The smoke and the crowd of people were denser the lower she got, and she coughed into her shoulder. One arm was wrapped around Klaus, holding him to her chest; the other was on the railing, the only way she knew she was moving in the right direction.

One foot in front of the other.

People were screaming, crying.

She tripped. Someone had dropped whatever they'd brought with them. Claire gritted her teeth. She couldn't fall. Klaus would drop; they'd be trampled. Her fingers tightened on the hot metal, holding herself up, moving forward, one slow, inexorable step at a time.

Because there was no other choice.

54

CLAIRE

The door was held open by the press of people. Beyond them, Claire could see that the rally point indicated on the fire escape plan was largely being ignored. Instead, the gathering crowd was moving far enough away from the flames, which seemed to be coming from the back door of CGC, to not get burned, but staying close enough to watch.

Tank was waiting in the doorway for her, not caring that he was tripping people. Klaus's anxiety hit a fever pitch and he scratched until Claire put him on the floor, clipping his lead on before he could escape.

She moved further away from the emergency exit, gulping in fresh air. But instead of trying to run away, Klaus dragged her towards the flames, crying.

Looking back, Claire didn't know why she didn't pick him back up and run in the opposite direction. But if she had, she wouldn't have seen the Asian man wearing jeans and a black puffer jacket dragging a body away from her building, a few doors away. 'Hey! Hey, you!' she called out.

The man didn't seem to hear her. She put on Tank's lead and tied both dogs to a traffic sign, far enough back from trouble, before walking forward on her own, her nose pressed up against the sleeve of her jumper to avoid the smoke. It was a crap mask, but better than nothing.

She picked up her pace and called out again, 'Let me help.' She couldn't have been more than a couple of metres away when she registered that the prone body was a woman. One wearing a similar jacket to the one Louise had been wearing when she'd dropped off Klaus.

'Bloody hell, Louise. Couldn't stay out of trouble for twenty-four hours, could you?' Claire ran the rest of the way and gripped Louise under one armpit, dragging her back, and back again, feeling every muscle scream. Lou's hand was clamped around a small black rucksack.

'It'd be a lot easier if she dropped that,' Claire muttered, but didn't stop to pry it from her friend's fingers, working with the man to drag Louise over to the post where the boys were tied up. The dogs barked as they got close, and he staying well out of range.

'Thank you,' Claire said, gulping clean air in. It did little to soothe her throat, but that could wait. She dropped to her knees, putting her hand in front of Lou's face, making sure she was breathing. Lou's eyelids fluttered.

Claire closed her own eyes for a moment, muttering a prayer of thanks, then opened them to study her fellow rescuer. He wasn't tall, maybe five foot seven or so. His beard was neatly trimmed and his black hair cut to look messy. More telling was the scar that bisected one eyebrow. But his eyes were kind. 'I recognise you. You're one of the men who hang out in front of the chicken shop.'

He shrugged.

'You didn't have to help her. Thank you,' she repeated.

'Yeah, well,' he said, nodding. 'Saw her try to put out the fire.'

She noticed his wary eyes on the dogs.

'You don't like dogs, do you?'

He shook his head. 'Can't touch them. Dogs are *haram*.' When Claire looked confused, he explained, 'My religion forbids it.'

Claire nodded, even though she wasn't sure she understood. 'And still you helped her.'

The man tilted his head to the side, as if she was speaking a different language. 'What's that gotta do with it? She needed help. I helped.'

Klaus moved forward, licking his mother's face until she coughed and weakly batted him away, before patting his head in apology and holding him close to her neck.

She'd be fine.

The Asian man left without another word or a backward glance and Claire sat on the ground beside Louise, pulling her into a half recline, her on one side, Tank on the other. She looked up, hearing the fire brigade arrive, and hoped they could stop the blaze before everything she owned went up in flames.

She shook her head and corrected herself, dropping a kiss on the top of Tank's head. 'Not everything. The most important things are out here.' She wiped a tear away with her shoulder, ignoring the stench of smoke. 'But at least the firemen arrive faster than the cops.'

55

LOUISE

Partridge Bark

Ella (Bark Vader and Jimmy Chew's Mum)

@**Claire** – is that your building that's on fire? Are you OK??

Claire (Tank's Mum)

We're fine. The fire brigade arrived pretty quickly and sorted out the fire downstairs and across at The Bells. @**Louise** is

> being seen to by a couple of hunky paramedics. We're not allowed back in yet – they need to check to make sure it's safe first, so Tank and I will be bunking with Lou and Klaus for a bit. Assuming of course that they don't take her away with them.

Tim (Loki's Dad)

> You think it's bad enough that The Bells will close?

Claire (Tank's Mum)

> I don't know.

Meg (Tyrion's Mum)

> Paramedics? What happened to @**Louise**? Is she OK?

'Stop it, I'm fine,' I told the paramedic, swatting away his hand as he tried to clean the bump on the side of my head.

I was sitting on the top step of the ambulance. As far as anyone knew, there had been no casualties in the two fires – the one in Claire's building and the one at The Bells – and as far as injuries went, there was smoke inhalation, one woman who'd tripped on the stairs and broken her arm and me, with a bump on my head that, according to Claire, was the size of a goose's egg.

'Ouch!' I whinged at the paramedic, a young man with floppy blond hair who looked like he should be holding a surfboard on an Australian beach. 'That hurts.'

Even the effort of whinging hurt my smoke-chafed throat, and I coughed. Klaus, curled on my lap, growled deep in his throat.

'Leave it,' I told my dog. 'He's just trying to help.'

I locked eyes with the paramedic and tried to stifle another cough. 'I'm fine.'

'I think you're concussed,' he said, his voice easy but firm.

'If I am, it's mild. I know what to do for it, and don't worry, I'm not going home alone, I'll have someone nearby for the next twenty-four hours, at least.' I guessed at the number.

'Not just the hound,' Claire said, raising her hand. Wrapped in a light foil blanket the paramedics had provided, she looked like a takeaway burrito. She wiped soot from her forehead with a filthy forearm, and smiled sympathetically at me. 'I live in that building. I'll be staying with Lou until she's okay to be on her own and I can go home.'

'That good enough for you?' I winced at my tone, realising that getting arsey with the paramedic wasn't helping my case. 'I'm fine,' I insisted. 'Really.'

I just wanted to be in my own flat, with a large cup of tea. With honey. A lot of honey.

'With all due respect,' he said. 'You were knocked out. Head injuries are tricky.'

It was the second time in a week that I'd heard that, and it didn't sound any better this time around.

I kept my mouth shut and my jaw gritted as he cleaned the wound on my head.

'When you've got a minute, Miss,' a uniformed PC said. She was about thirty, with dark hair pulled into a low bun, making her look professional, and a bit older.

'She's busy,' the paramedic said.

'My brain is still working,' I croaked.

'Want to tell me your name, address and what happened?' the PC asked, undeterred. She was one of two uniforms who were working the crowd, taking statements.

'Louise Mallory. 801 Colourway House. I was walking down the street to pick up my dog from my friend's place. I saw some men jogging along. They were wearing bandanas over their faces, the sort you see when it's really cold, not like this. They threw something into The Bells.' I pointed and coughed into my shoulder. 'Then they kept running. I went to the back entrance to my friend's building, saw the same thing happen there. I grabbed a fire extinguisher and tried to help.'

'Why?'

'Why what?'

The PC looked confused. 'Why didn't you run?'

'Because my friend lives in that building, and if I could stop the fire before it took hold that'd be a good thing, right? And Klaus was there. If anything had happened to him . . .'

She looked like she wanted to say, *Idiot*. Instead she said, 'Did you see any of their faces?'

'Nope. They were all wearing masks,' I repeated, trying not to snap.

'Did anything stand out to you? Height? Weight? Clothing?'

I suppressed another cough, which came out with a squeak like a constipated rat.

'I don't know. They were all taller than me. They looked like an average pack of men running. Wearing dark running kit, leggings, the works. And the bandanas.'

'Hair?'

I thought about that. 'Dark caps or beanies.' I shrugged, waking Klaus, who'd been lulled into a nap. 'Honestly, they just looked like normal runners. With running rucksacks. You know, the super small ones.'

'Anything else?'

I shook my head. 'I'm sorry.'

She nodded and scribbled something onto the notepad in her hand. 'And your head injury?'

'I must have gotten dizzy from the smoke and bumped it,' I lied. The paramedic snorted and I gave him a nasty look. 'I'm completely fine.'

'Thanks for your time, Miss Mallory,' the PC said, and handed me a card. 'If you think of anything else, call that number and let us know.'

I tried not to exhale my relief too hard as she wandered off to the next person. With a little luck, this incident, and my involvement in it, would go unnoticed by Andy and Williams. I was in no mood to subject myself to another lecture about not getting involved.

The sky had clouded over and the temperature was dropping. The PC was heading towards a nearby squad car, probably keen to make it back to the station to write up her report. I didn't blame her; I was keen to get out of the cold as well.

'Ouch,' I repeated, and looked down. My left hand rested on Klaus's soft head, but the fingers on my right were tangled in the broken strap of the rucksack I'd ripped off my assailant.

That I'd *stolen* from my assailant.

No one had commented on it; maybe they all assumed it was mine. I hadn't had a chance to check inside it yet, and would be damned if I would hand it over to the cops without at least having a look at what someone had wanted back badly enough to try to kill me for.

Because something told me it'd be something weightier than the latest paperback thriller.

56

LOUISE

Irina (Hamish's Mum)

> What did you do this time?

>> Wrong place, wrong time.

>> But if you're going to do a quid pro quo and tell me that I need to talk to the detectives ...

> No chance of that. Just try not to end up dead, OK?

We crossed the bridge over the canal, my assailant's rucksack slung over my shoulder, Claire still wrapped in the tinfoil blanket. 'I have a spare coat at home.'

She looked at me out of the corner of her eye. 'You're what? A size ten? eight? I'm a twelve. On a good day. There's no way your coat would fit over the girls.' She used her chin to indicate her chest, and it was a fair point. Claire was stocky; muscular but *stacked*.

'We'll find something.'

'You know,' she said. 'I'm glad I got out with the dogs, but if I had to take another thing or two, it'd be my laptop. And my coat.'

I had to laugh – that was so Claire. 'Feeling naked without it?'

'A hundred per cent. Though I mean, I have everything backed up to the Cloud.'

'Obviously.'

'Obviously,' she echoed, and then gave a double take. 'Since when do you walk around with a rucksack? Usually you stuff your phone, treats and keys in your jeans pockets. At a stretch, a canvas bag if you're out shopping.'

'I'll have you know, I have a closet of lovely handbags.'

'Which in all the years I've known you, I've never seen you use. What's with the rucksack?'

I looked around, half expecting to see someone in a dark coat and hat trailing me until they could snatch their bag back, but the most intimidating thing I saw was Rocco, the mastiff cross, standing by his owner Jono outside News-N-Booze. And, as far as I knew, Rocco was big but friendly, and his owners were friends of Gav's. That didn't mean they weren't intimidating, it just meant they weren't a threat to us. 'I'll tell you when we get home.'

She gave me a curious glance. 'More mayhem, when my laptop is out of reach? You tease, Lou.'

We pushed through the gates to the complex and rode the lift up to my flat, each holding our breath against the stench of weed, which felt like sandpaper on my already raw throat. 'Jesus,' Claire wheezed.

'We've established a détente. I won't yell out the window at them or let Klaus bark at them if they hold off on the first spliff until lunchtime.'

'They can last that long?'

'No, but at least it's not seven in the morning.'

'That's good. Also, I'm not sure you have enough left in your voice to yell.'

I unclipped Klaus in the lift, knowing that the only thing he'd do when the doors opened was run to my front door. Following him, I unlocked it and watched the boys race through the flat as if it were some sort of playground.

'Talk to me,' Claire said, flopping onto a kitchen chair. 'What's going on and what do you know?'

'Do you want a notepad first?'

'I want my laptop, but that's not going to happen.'

I disappeared into my home office and reappeared with mine, setting it down in front of her. 'You can borrow mine. At least for tonight.'

She looked at it, her expression a cross between gratitude and disgust.

'Okay, so it's a bit old, but it works.' I put the kettle on as she lifted the lid gingerly. 'You don't have to use it. I've got a pen and paper if you prefer?'

Claire snorted. 'No chance. Log me on, and tell me about your latest accessory.'

I considered how best to update her, opting for the direct approach. Klaus had raced up his ramp, and with a stuffing-less raccoon in his mouth, nimbly darted out of Tank's reach.

'What I told the cops was mostly true. I saw the second group of runners pry open the back door of CGC and throw a Molotov cocktail inside. I tried to put out the fire and someone tried to lock me in. We struggled a bit and I grabbed the rucksack.'

'You *mugged* him?'

'No! I hoped he'd drag me out, not lock me in!' I said, my voice rising. 'I grabbed on to whatever I could reach and held on.'

Tank rounded the corner of the coffee table, misjudging how close he was and knocking against it. I grabbed the mug left over from my morning coffee before it fell, rinsed it out and put it in the dishwasher.

'Bet there's just crap in there. Old newspapers, a rotting piece of fruit. Paperback novel, or something. Have you looked inside yet?' Claire's eyes widened as curiosity took hold. 'OMG, maybe there's a wallet. A phone.'

'I don't know. I haven't looked yet.'

'Then let's have a peek, shall we?' She waggled her forefinger in a dish-the-dirt sort of move.

I slung the rucksack onto the table and we stared at it for a moment. It was simple, unbranded. Black with no other colours or markings. There were no tags on the outside, no water bottles in the side webbings.

'Bloody hell,' Claire muttered and pulled it in front of her. She unzipped it with a flourish and looked inside. 'A couple of envelopes.'

I peered over her shoulder. There were indeed a few envelopes, large brown ones like the ones sold at the post office. 'No smoking gun,' she continued, not without a touch of irony. 'But I'll bet whoever had this bag will be in a boatload of trouble for losing these docs. The guy probably wanted the door closed because it was – wait for it, Lou – a fire safety door, designed to keep the fire in and smother it without oxygen.'

I closed my eyes, trying to recapture the scene. Between the smoke and the fire, all I could remember was a stocky shape in the doorway. And a hand reaching in . . .

'No. I'm pretty sure he saw me. Why would he close the door with a person inside?'

'Are you sure he saw you? Maybe he panicked?' She raised her brows. 'Or do you think he set the fire?'

He hadn't looked like one of the joggers, but that didn't mean he wasn't involved.

'Shit,' I swore, reaching for the top file. 'Well, let's see who these belong to and if they're not related I'll return them.'

Claire blinked at me. 'In person? I'd pay to see that.'

'Yeah, well. In my defence, I was fighting for my life.' My hands began to shake a bit. I went to the freezer and pulled out a bag of peas for the bump on my head. 'Do you think the bag belongs to the Asian guy? The one with the scar who you said dragged me out of the fire?'

'Don't you think if it was his he would have taken it with him when he left?'

'Maybe not if he didn't want you to think that he was the one trying to get me killed.'

'But he was the one dragging you out, not keeping you in.'

'I don't know,' I conceded. 'But whether the bag's his or not, I'll try to find him and talk to him tomorrow. He's usually hanging out by CGC. Maybe he saw the person on the other side of the door.'

'Maybe.'

'Let's see what's in here.' I sighed and opened the first envelope, pulling out a thin sheaf of papers. The first page contained lists of names, maybe companies. The next page was a table, full of acronyms and numbers that made no sense. The third page and the ones after were just as cryptic. I handed them to Claire. 'Do these make any sense to you?'

She didn't answer, just handed me the docs from the second envelope. 'These look like the quarterly figures that I just finished,' I said. 'Bigger numbers, though.'

'But no company listed.'

'No,' I mused. The kettle had long since boiled and I retrieved two mugs for tea. 'But we don't usually have logos on our Excel sheets. The ones from the system, sure, but not whatever's produced for internal use.' I put teabags in each mug, added the water and a tablespoon of honey to each, and brought them back to the table.

We both reached for the next envelope. This one held photographs of men I didn't know, taken with a long lens.

Claire and I looked at each other. 'I don't think this is just some guy bringing his work home,' she croaked, wincing as she took a large gulp of the tea. We stared at the pictures for a few seconds. 'Lou, they look like they're professionally done.'

'Jesus.' This was big. Really big. I struggled to get my head around it. I began to search through the bag's many pockets, finding a couple of pens, but not much else. Remembering something I'd read in a spy book, I did a fingertip search along each seam, each piece of fabric, searching for something that didn't feel right. Eventually, I struck gold, and coaxed a slim black thumb drive from the lining.

'I'm almost afraid to see what's on it,' I said, holding it up.

'I'm not,' Claire said, taking it out of my hand and plugging it into my laptop.

'Wait!'

'What?'

'Maybe it has a virus. Or it'll wipe my laptop.'

She rolled her eyes. 'You watch too many crime shows. You have antivirus that'd pick up anything nasty, and I've never heard of anyone having a drive wiped like that in real life.'

The file manager opened as my laptop recognised an external drive, but the drive itself looked blank.

'Hidden files?' Claire suggested.

'Or it's a drive that someone bought but never used. I've got a few in bags to back up presentations, just in case the tech throws a wobbly.'

Claire tied her hair back with an elastic from around her wrist while I slurped at my tea. 'Sure, but this one looks like it's been used a fair bit. And how often do you go back and delete what you don't need anymore? Why carry something... no, why *hide* something that's empty? I'm telling you, there are hidden files on that drive. Maybe something encrypted.'

She tapped a few keys and shook her head. 'Can I hang on to this?'

'Can you make a copy first?'

'Of files we don't know are there?'

Good point. 'Sure,' I conceded. 'You know someone who can do something?'

'Irina Ivanova isn't the only tech-savvy person I know,' Claire said, without a trace of modesty.

'That's good. Irina could win gold in Olympic cyberstalking, but I'm not sure she'd qualify for hacking.'

'Yeah.' She leaned back in her chair, staring as Tank managed to get the stuffing-less raccoon from Klaus and did a victory lap around my living room. 'Look, I know you don't tend to lock your doors when you're home. Klaus is a good intruder alarm and all, but he's all mouth, no trousers. Whoever you took this from will want it back, and even with the best will in the world, I don't think that little boy will be able to stop them. And far too many people in the neighbourhood know who you are and where you live.'

'I live in a gated complex, Claire.'

'Sure. You want me to tell you how easy it is to tailgate into this complex? Or into your building? Jesus, Lou. If they don't tailgate, all they need to do is ring the stoners downstairs; they'd let in Satan if he said he was bringing weed and women.'

I looked into my tea, but it offered no answers.

'I'm not joking, Lou. You've got to start being more careful.' She picked up her phone and started texting.

'Your hacker?' I asked.

'Nope. Fi's a financial analyst, remember? I'll bet you dinner that she'll be able to tell us what we're looking at.'

57

GAV

Gav stretched out his legs. His right hand itched to rub his hip, but instead he tightened it around his beer glass.

'Where's Violent?' Mo asked, placing a fresh round on the table. The short, balding owner of News-N-Booze was unusually jovial tonight.

'Home with Doris,' Gav replied, ignoring Mo's nickname for Violet. Mostly because it wasn't unjustified. Violet was particular about who she allowed into her inner circle. And that list was as small as she was.

'Bet she'll love that.' Mo rolled his eyes.

'Which "she"?' Jono grinned and leaned back. He slung one arm over the back of the empty chair beside him and rested the other on the massive head of his dog, Rocco. 'Ain't no love lost between Gav's missus and his dog.'

Rocco, as if to underscore the differences between Gav's Affenpinscher (who thought she was a T-Rex) and himself (who identified as a lap dog), sighed and rested his head on his front paws, like butter wouldn't melt in his great, jowled mouth.

'Yeah, yeah.' Gav took a large gulp, finishing off his first pint. 'Anyone hear anythin' about that business up the high street?'

'Which part?' Mo asked. 'Got more gangs about since that chicken shop opened.' He wobbled his head left to right, in a gesture that seemed to add, *And with more gangs comes more violence, innit.*

'Not just gang on gang though, right?'

'Man, you know that shit don't stay contained. They act out on each other, sure, but they're just as happy to rough up someone that's only walked past. Don't even have to offend them. You know that.' Jono picked up a chip, raising it halfway to his mouth before relenting and passing it down to Rocco, who took a dainty bite.

Gav did know.

'An' there's that fire, earlier today. At the new block o' flats and The Bells.'

'Any idea who?' Gav asked.

'Nah. If someone knows, they ain't saying. I-ron-y is though, The Bells had some guy out yesterday to install CCTV,' Mo said.

'So the razz can use it to find 'em?' Jono asked.

'As if. Got the kit installed, awright. But seemed there was some problem with some of the parts. Guy said he'd come back to fix it on Monday. They ain't got jack.'

Gav leaned forward. 'The engineer in on it?'

'Doubt it. Local kid: some relative I think.'

'Don't mean they weren't involved.'

'Don't mean they were,' Mo countered. 'Anyone know the owner o' the chicken place?'

'Dave Najafi? Heard he lives in some posh flat in Mayfair,' Jono said.

'Plenty of crooks living in a des res,' Mo added. 'But most have more of an income than a chicken shop can deliver. That place, it does okay, but not enough to pay the council tax for some swish Mayfair place, let alone a mortgage.'

'He's got other shops.'

'Yeah, I know. The sort that never have ...' Mo blinked. 'Oh. That. Half the shops on the high street are laundering.'

'So why give up a sweet deal like that for a chicken shop?'

'To look legit?' Mo giggled, then sobered. 'Haven't seen him around since about the time it opened.'

''Coz he bought it for his nephew to run,' Jono said. 'His sister's son, I think. But he's got his own security on the case, keeping an eye on it.'

'So the Asian kid who was killed?' Gav asked.

'Tang?' Jono shrugged. 'Way I see it, it's one of two things: either it ain't connected to CGC. Or it is, and that kid was a problem that had to go away.'

58

LOUISE

Partridge Bark

Fiona (Nala's Mum)

> @Claire, I just spoke to the police outside your building. They hope to be able to allow people back in tomorrow, or Tuesday at the latest.

Claire (Tank's Mum)

> That's great. And I'm happy to live in borrowed PJs and leggings until I'm

> let back in, but can you bring over a spare coat if you have one? I don't fit into Lou's. Thank heavens she still had some of Tank's food here from last weekend!

Fiona (Nala's Mum)

> Sure, no problem. You need anything else?

Claire (Tank's Mum)

> An order of Chinese food?

Fiona (Nala's Mum)

> Haha – that's what Deliveroo is for. But I'm on my way with a jacket.

Claire put down her phone. 'How was that?'

'Pretty good,' I replied. 'Gave nothing away to the rest of the Pack about why we need Fi here, with the added bonus of making sure you don't freeze your bits off.'

'Yeah. I agree with you, let's keep this—' She waved her

hand over the bag and its contents, spread out across my table. '— confined to just a small group. At least until we know what we're dealing with. Who do you think? Just you, me, Fi? What about Yaz or Meg? Irina?'

'I'm okay with Meg, but Yaz will talk, and I'd rather this doesn't get around.' And Irina wouldn't be interested as it didn't directly impact her. 'Let's leave it at that, at least until we know whether someone's going to be out to get me, or if this was just their school homework.' The bag of frozen peas I'd got out for my head bump was thawing, and I replaced it in the freezer and brought out the next best thing – nuggets of chopped spinach. Winced as I held the new bag up to my head.

'It's not school homework, Lou.'

I ignored Claire's comment, unsure I wanted to explore the alternative. 'I was supposed to meet Meg's friend Connor again tomorrow. Might be best if Fi goes instead. If she's willing?'

She nodded. 'Let's ask her. If she doesn't want to go, I will.'

I eyed her. 'You smell a story, don't you?'

'I always smell a story. But don't worry. I won't print anything until we have proof.'

Monday

59

FIONA

Louise (Klaus's Mum)

I've just messaged Connor. He's happy to meet you for lunch. I'll forward you the photo Meg sent me of him.

You sure you don't want to come?

100%. I feel like 💩 – got a stonking headache, and I look like I've been 10 rounds in the ring with Tyson. And I'd just sit

> there while you two figure out what's going on. But if you're right that one of the men in the file looks like a councillor …

> **Might** look like a councillor. I don't know. But if it's all the same to you, I'm going to leave your rucksack out of the conversation.

> Fine by me. Thank you — and thank Connor again for me. Give a shout when you're done.

Fiona didn't like the situation. Not the obvious gang warfare outside the chicken shop. Not the dead man on the canal bench. Not Lou's friend in hospital after being attacked and left for dead in the bushes. Not this bag that Lou said she'd 'found' — not for a moment did Fi believe that bull — and which contained dodgy documents. When she'd gone round to Lou's, she'd expected to see porn stashed in the bag, not evidence of blackmail or extortion.

Whoever's bag that was, they would definitely be wanting it back.

Fi would bet good money that it was someone who lived in Claire's building. Someone who'd taken what they'd thought was most important and fled the fire. Fi would have grabbed something different: Nala, of course. Phone, passport, jewellery box – she had some good pieces mixed in with the fun stuff – and dog food, although with the credit card on her phone, that could be sorted easily enough.

But this person might not have a passport. Lots of people didn't (even though everyone Fi knew had at least one). Maybe they kept their phone in their pocket – most people did. She didn't know, and it didn't really matter.

She'd called in sick to work and sat at her kitchen table, her laptop in front of her and the documents spread out around it, trying to make sense of everything in her own mind so that she could ask this guy, Connor, informed questions.

And to be honest, she didn't hold out much hope there. She knew Louise wanted details on who had complained to the council about CGC and what had been done about it. She also knew that for Connor to hand over names and contact details would be illegal, and, quite frankly, even if she had the sort of friendship with him where she could ask him for that information (and she didn't), it wouldn't feel right asking him to break the law. If he did have access to the information, he'd be a fool to give it away, especially to a complete stranger. Seriously, it could be a sting operation or something.

Besides, Irina already knew who had left the bad reviews. And she also knew some of the people who'd been harassed afterwards. 'They'd be able to tell any one of us whether they went to the council or the police, and what – if any – protection they were afforded,' Fi said to Nala, who was reclining on a sunny patch of floor by the window. 'And let's face it, we know the answer would be a big, fat zero. I'm not going to waste my time there.'

Nala sighed and rested her head on her paws. Unless she heard the words 'walk' or 'treat', she remained completely uninterested in anything Fi was saying. Fi pushed her glasses back up her nose and flicked one of the photographs from the rucksack Louise had grabbed between her fingers.

On the screen in front of her, Tower Hamlets Council's website was open to a page describing the mayor and councillors by ward. Each entry had a photograph and a bio. More than a few of those listed shared the same couple of surnames, and Fi wasn't sure whether that indicated familial ties, or just that they were really common names.

'No. If I'm going to ask him anything, it'll be about the councillors,' she mused. 'Though I don't want to tip my hand and just ask about one. Let's see, Nala, if he picks an interesting name out of the hat.'

60

LOUISE

I got down on all fours by the window, crouching beside Klaus as he supervised the goings-on in the courtyard. His wet nose touched mine in his equivalent of a high five, happy that I was joining in on his idea of fun. 'Bork,' I said.

Tail wagging, he stared out the window until he spotted a delivery guy, then let loose with a string of deep-chested barks.

Irina (Hamish's Mum)

What in holy hell are you doing?

I glanced at the message that flashed onto my phone screen and crawled backwards, away from the window.

'How the devil did Irina find out about the fire and the rucksack so quickly? We'd agreed to . . .' I spoke aloud and looked at Klaus, still happily barking at hapless passersby in the courtyard below. I glanced out and spotted Irina on her balcony with Hammy, happy and shaggy, at her feet.

'Oh.' I slunk further back, unsure whether to laugh or cry. I settled on an embarrassed giggle. I'd seen some guy on Insta say that, to show his dog that he was taking an interest in the hound's hobbies, he barked with him at the window. I'd tried it once, and Klaus had approved; it was a small miracle that she hadn't spotted me barking at my window before.

'On the plus side,' I mused to Klaus. 'If anyone's going to catch me barking with you, I'd prefer if it was only Irina.' Despite myself, I took a quick look across the canal, but if Jake was home, and if he'd noticed, there was no evidence.

But then, there was never any evidence when it came to Jake Hathaway.

Irina (Hamish's Mum)

> Been one of those days. Weeks. Months. Whatever.

> Yeah? Well, I think I figured out where Jonny Tang was squirrelling away all his dosh.

> That sounds promising. Drugs? Women? Fast car that isn't parked on the high street?

Sadly, no. Looks like he's sending money to his parents to fund his younger siblings' schooling. One just graduated and two more are in university, one here and one in the States.

> He was what? 35? Big jump between him and the younger ones.

10 years between him and the next oldest. Don't ask me what the hold-up was with Mum and Dad Tang between having him and the rest of 'em, but as far as I can tell, both biological parents are still together, and full parents to the younger ones.

> You're sure?

> You're welcome to check my homework, Miss.

Even if she was serious, there was no chance I'd take her up on the offer. Not least because it would require me to:

Understand the crazy way Irina's brain worked.

Witness some of the rather sketchy ways she found answers.

Though given that she was a lawyer, there was probably no way she'd share the full extents she went to in gathering information, which no doubt crossed more than one legal boundary. And I was more comfortable not knowing.

Meg (Tyrion's Mum)

> I think I mentioned ...
> I'm having my hair done tomorrow. Assuming the salon is open, were there any specific questions you wanted me to ask Benny and Caren? Or just fish for whatever goss they might have heard?

> Go for the goss, I think. The more specific you get, the more they'll think we know, and right now, that doesn't feel like a lot.

Gotcha. And let's face it, hairdressers are the modern-day confessors. You go there and chat about every issue that's going on while you get your roots done. If there's goss in the neighbourhood, they'll know it. You know, I can probably ask Benny if he can see me today instead. He's usually happy to go in on a Monday if he doesn't have something else on, and Caren's often in for a few hours doing admin.

> Only if that's possible – probably best not to push.

> We don't want to look desperate.

Agreed. But if I tell Benny that I have a meeting tomorrow and need to reschedule – something that's happened far too often – it won't look like I'm fishing.

> Sounds like a plan. Thanks for your help, Meg.

No problem. How are you doing? Ethan and I were away over the weekend and were shocked to hear about the fire. Is Claire still at yours?

> I have a bit of a sore throat still, but I'm fine. Claire left this morning. Seems CGC *was* piping their exhaust through the building's ventilation system. The whole place smoked up,

> but the fire was pretty well contained to the shop. The fire marshal allowed residents to return today. You should be fine at the salon, but I hear the sitch is a bit worse at The Bells. I haven't been out that way, but I wouldn't be surprised to see Claire poking her nose in at the pub to see what she can learn.

Ah ok. Good. Nothing's up on *The Chronicle*'s website yet. Bet you the next round of drinks that she'll post something later today 😊

> Ha! I won't bet against you on that. You know what Claire's like when she's onto a good story — and this is one that we all have a vested interest in getting solved.

I had no doubt Claire would have something up, keeping any details about the rucksack and our theories out of it, I hoped. We had no proof and no 'smoking gun'; no idea whose bag it was, who exactly was the target of whatever blackmail or extortion was going on, who'd killed Jonny Tang or if any of it was even connected.

At least Meg would tick one box off my to-do list. I only knew Angry Caren and Benny enough to nod at them as we passed on the high street, so any info-fishing from me would look about as subtle as a great white shark in Klaus's paddling pool.

I dropped a message to Annabel, in case she had her phone back, checking in to see how she was doing. I sent one to her dad as well, figuring that he'd be her gatekeeper at least until she was back on her feet and able to tell him to back off.

I brewed another cup of coffee and started working my way through my emails. The quarterly finance figures had been submitted, a team was working on the NHS proposal and my gaze kept straying to the rucksack.

Rolling my eyes at myself, I stuffed it determinedly into a closet behind a couple of heavy winter coats.

'Out of sight, out of mind,' I muttered to Klaus. I'd just have to wait to see what Meg, Fi and Claire found out.

61

ANDY

Williams put down the phone and grinned. 'Finally caught a bit of luck.'

'You got a date for Saturday night?'

'Nah.' Williams reached back, stretching his arms above his head. The chair he was sitting on creaked, and Andy figured that one day, it'd give up the ghost and Scott'd end up flat on his back on the floor. 'Anyone's gonna have a date on Saturday, it'll be you. With that Russian lunatic.'

'Don't.' It was a low warning, not the first and likely not the last. 'What's put that smirk on your face?'

'Your—'

'Don't,' Andy repeated.

'Fine. So that phone the lads found in the canal? Forensics lady just called. They were able to bring the dead back to life.' He waggled his fingers and made a ghostly 'wooo' sound.

'And?'

'And they were able to whack its memory onto a computer. Took a bit longer than she would have liked, but you know, backlog.'

'And?'

It was a familiar dance; Scott's version of I-know-something-you-don't-know. It drove Andy bonkers, but he'd learned to hide that fact. If Scott thought he had an audience, he'd drag things out.

'And it looks like it was the vic's. Jonathan Tang's. Been wiped clean, so no prints available, but the photos seem to have him in there and the email is his.'

'Okay. Want to have a look and see?'

'They're sending up downloads of his most recent emails and WhatsApp conversations, and the tech sent a link to some photos she found. They'll try to get a better look at the other apps next.'

'Anything worth noting?'

'Yeah, but no. Got the info, but from what she says, no smoking gun. No emails, no messages seeming to indicate why he was killed. No rendezvous planned for that evening. No indication of a romantic liaison. Nothing in the calendar.'

So far nothing on this case had been as straightforward as Andy had hoped. 'Damn. Let's find out who he banks with and see if we can get statements. Might be a clue there.'

Doug Harriman, the CCTV officer, pulled up a chair beside them. 'So, you know that fire yesterday, over on the high street near Partridge Park?'

Andy went still, hoping no one noticed. 'Heard about it.'

'Well, for a while everyone was excited. Locals saw CCTV being installed at The Bells on Saturday.'

'That crappy boozer?'

Harriman pointed a finger at Andy. 'That's the one. Right, so we have CCTV, we might have a chance at identifying who was slinging those Molotovs around, right?'

'You'd hope so.'

'You would indeed, Detective Thompson. Only it looks like The Bells went cheap. Got someone's nephew to install it. Kid couldn't figure out how to get it working – said he'd phone a friend and be back on Monday.'

Andy shook his head. 'One day too late.'

Harriman shrugged. 'At least the fire brigade did a spankin' good job saving both the flats across the street and The Bells. Bit scorched around the edges, but not so anyone'd notice. The Bells, that is. Not the flats.'

'You know it's not our case, Harry?' Williams noted.

'You Grieves in disguise?' Harriman said, without heat. 'Yeah, I know. But same neighbourhood, so we're keeping each other in the loop. Plus, there's something else I thought you'd want to know.'

'What's that?' Andy asked.

'Your doggie chum Louise Mallory came close to being an arson victim. Six to one she's pissed off the wrong person.'

62

FIONA

Claire (Tank's Mum)

> Hey darl, I don't need to ask you to let me know if you learn anything today, do I?

> Nope. You've got us all well trained. You get first dibs on any exclusive. But I'm not expecting a lot, even if he knows something. Might have to play a long game here, C.

> If anyone can get him to spill his guts, it'll be you, Fi. Keep me in the loop.

> You know it.

Fi lowered her specs from the top of her head. 'Because girls with glasses are complete badasses.'

Nala sighed, but didn't turn her attention from the window, avidly watching a group of schoolkids kicking around a football. She didn't move from her spot as Fiona put on her jacket and slung her tote bag over her shoulder. 'Bye, babe!' Fiona called, and closed the door after herself.

It wasn't that Nala didn't care, Fi knew. It was just that her fascination with kids and balls was greater than any issue she might have with Fi leaving her alone.

Pity the council's moved from its previous office block in Poplar, Fi thought to herself as the District line inched its way closer to Whitechapel. She exited the station and passed the Royal London – the hospital that Lou's friend had been taken to. She hadn't realised it was so close to the council's offices.

'Convenient,' she noted to herself, and continued to the café Meg had mentioned. Connor, it seemed, was a creature of habit, frequenting the same bar on a Saturday and the same café for lunch every day. He probably had the same sandwich as well, Fi figured.

She spotted him immediately, sitting at a table in the

back of the café, his back to the wall. His eyes were wary as she dropped into the chair opposite him. 'Hi, Connor.'

He froze, his sandwich – a chicken parm melt – halfway to his mouth.

'I'm Fiona. Meg's friend.'

The sandwich lowered back to the plate. 'Oh Christ, not another one.'

Fi ignored that and pushed her glasses back onto the top of her head. 'Oh, we're not such a bad lot.'

'What do you want? I'm having lunch.'

When she opened her mouth to speak, he cut her off. 'I'm gonna tell you the same thing I told your friend. I don't have access to specific council complaints. And even if I did, I'm not allowed to tell you about them.'

'Oh, I'm not here to ask you about that,' Fi said, giving him her most charming smile. 'Sharing customer information is a crime and I wouldn't want to land you in hot water. I was only going to ask you about the planning process. How a business can secure premises and make the adjustments necessary to support their operation.'

Connor grunted and leaned forward. Took a large bite of the parm sarnie. 'Check the website,' he advised, still chewing. Crumbs of bread began to dot the front of Fi's coat.

She pretended not to notice. 'But I'm asking *you*.' Turning up the wattage of her smile, she added, 'And you were the man who implemented the system that supports the process, weren't you?'

'Yeah, so?'

'So, I just want to know what the process is exactly, and

what sort of governance is in place to ensure it's adhered to. Who signs off on each stage. Where the weaknesses are, in case someone cuts corners. That sort of thing.'

'Go away.'

Fi sighed. Usually the smile worked, but this time she needed something bigger. She shrugged and stood up. Looked back at him over her shoulder. 'I thought we could have a simple chat and avoid the tedious paperwork route, but no problem. I'll just raise a Freedom of Information request. Who knows, maybe I can come up with more questions for you before I hit the submit button.'

Connor muttered a curse. Swallowed the mouthful of sarnie and said, 'Sit down.'

63

LOUISE

Robert Lindford-Swayne

> Annabel is doing well. They moved her from the ICU this afternoon. She thanks you for the flowers and chocolates.

> If she's up for it, I'd love to stop by and see her.

> She's still groggy but if you keep it short, I'll clear it with the doctors. 17:30?

> Yeah, that'll work. Thanks. I'll message when I'm on my way.

> 👍

I didn't expect to be gone for long, but I messaged Irina anyway, asking if she'd be okay to have Klaus for an hour or two. No point in having him bored at home when he could be playing with Hammy. As if he agreed, he looked at me and rolled onto his back in his spot in the waning light by the window.

'Got you covered, sweetheart.' I ruffled his ears and dropped a kiss on his cool, wet snoot, then cruised through the remaining afternoon meetings.

When the time came around, I slipped into my jacket, feeling the reassuring metal tube of defence spray in there. Mentally reminding myself not to put my phone, keys or treat bag in that pocket, I called Klaus.

My hound, on the other hand, wasn't as eager to venture out. He stood at the other end of the entrance hall and rolled onto his back again, his tail wagging.

'Nice try, mate. You want to go see Hammy?' That got him up and running past me towards the door. I clipped the lead onto his collar and picked up his coat, figuring it wasn't cold enough to put it on for the few minutes it would take to walk to Irina's.

When we arrived, she opened the door with a finger to

her lips, making it clear she was on a call. She was dressed in her usual Monday WFH attire: full make-up, fair hair in its usual topknot, nice blouse and leggings. I handed her Klaus's lead and coat while Hammy leapt off the sofa and ran to meet his best friend. Irina nodded and closed the door in my face.

Even taking into consideration that she was on the phone, that was rude. Irina's manners were never much to write home about – unless she wanted something – but they seemed to go downhill fast when she was stressed.

A kinder part of me wanted to pin that stress on whatever case she was working on, but I had a feeling that it was related to Andy Thompson. And maybe it was less stress and more regret?

Or was I giving her more credit than she was due?

While I stood in Irina's hallway, I checked my own phone.

Jake (Luther's Dad)

> Ran into Meg. I heard you got yourself into a hot situation. What is it with you?

> I'm OK, thanks for asking. Nothing worse than a bump on my head and a bit of smoke inhalation.

> Could have been a lot worse, from what I hear. You've got to watch out for yourself, Marple. This neighbourhood isn't safe and you're a magnet for trouble.

> I know, I know.

> I know you know. I'm just not sure how far you believe it.

Maybe he was right, but I couldn't stop now. Not when one man was dead, Claire was in the Met's crosshairs and Annabel was in the hospital. Still, it was good to know that he cared, and that I hadn't completely tanked our friendship in one drunken lunge.

Returning the way I came, I crossed the bridge and walked towards the high street, waving when I saw Meg in the chair at the Hands-On salon. Heavy metal music pumped out onto the street while Benny painted dye onto her hair. Caren sat behind a laptop screen at the reception desk. I wondered how her trademark grumpiness would stack up to Meg's charm in her quest for gossip.

The Tube was almost empty – I was going against rush hour – but I took a seat beside an Asian man I recognised from the Three Mills pack. His name slipped my mind, but his dog was a sweet little maltipoo, who Klaus loved to flirt with.

'You're Evita's dad, right?' I asked.

He gave me a strange look and hung on to the carry-on-sized valise at his feet before making the connection. 'Klaus's mum?'

'That's me.'

He nodded. 'Nice to see you. You going to the Halloween do at The Jim and Tonic this weekend?'

I'd forgotten about that. The Jim and Tonic was a pub on the Stratford side of the canal path, not far from the 2012 Olympic Park. They did good pizzas and mean G&Ts, and in the summer it wasn't unusual for the Three Mills crowd to have a Friday night drink there. 'Let's see. We haven't been to Three Mills in a while. It'd be good to see everyone.'

'I got Evie a sweet pumpkin costume. Last year she chewed the legs off the spider outfit and we had to bin it. Hope you can make it.'

We both got off the Tube at Whitechapel; Evita's dad to switch to the Elizabeth line towards Heathrow, while I had a short walk to the hospital.

Annabel was sitting up in bed when I got to her room. Her blonde hair was unwashed and hung lank around her shoulders. Bruises mottled her face, which had a yellowish cast to it that might have been the harsh hospital lights, but was more likely a result of her trauma and the drugs she was being given. It was hard to see her looking so unwell, and for a moment I was at a loss for words.

A glass of water stood on a tray beside her and, despite her pallor, her expression was thunderous as she glared at her father, who sat in a visitor's chair beside her bed, staring at his phone.

'How're you feeling?' I said by way of greeting.

'I'd be better if you've brought wine instead of chocolates this time,' she rasped, sounding worse than I had after the fire. I had a sinking feeling, knowing what a horrible situation she was in, knowing I was about to make it worse with my questions.

'No such luck, my friend,' I said, opening my canvas bag. 'Just a couple of paperbacks.'

'No glasses,' she shrugged. 'They were in my bag...'

'The police haven't found it?'

'Not as far as I know. And Daddy won't go to pick stuff up from my flat.'

'I've cancelled your phone,' he said without looking up. 'A new one will be couriered here later, but you heard the doctors, Bel. You know you're not supposed to strain yourself.'

'Then bring me my iPad. At least then I could watch a movie or something.'

'Your iPad was in your bag, Bel. And even if you had it, you'd work. And you *need* to rest.'

I had the awkward feeling of stepping into a long-running disagreement.

'Want me to come back later?'

'No,' Annabel said. She paused as she seemed to really take me in. 'You look like crap, Lou.'

My fingers flew to the bump on the side of my head,

wincing as they made contact. 'Says the woman in the hospital bed. I like the gown, by the way. Très chic.'

'Yes, it's the latest in hospital haute couture. Bet you're devastated to miss out on one just like it.' She shook her head. 'What a pair we are. What happened to you? Hell, what happened to me?'

'You? I don't know. Crowd-surfing at The Nest and got dropped?' I held up a finger. 'Wait: there were no crowds to surf.'

The ghost of a smile flitted across her face. 'And what about you? I've heard about people who bang their heads against the wall in frustration, but I've never seen it actually happen.'

'There's a fair bit of frustration about, for sure,' I said, settling myself into the other visitor chair. 'Any update from the cops?'

She grimaced. 'Keystone Kops were in earlier asking their mealy-mouthed questions. What do I remember? Who did this to me? Who would have a reason to attack me?'

'And?' I prompted.

'What do I remember? Not much. That whole night is patchy. I remember leaving for a meeting, but I don't remember who with, or even if we had the meeting. I could check my diary, if I had my phone...' She directed a side-eye worthy of Klaus at her father.

'The police have her laptop,' he said, looking me in the eye this time. 'They're going to contact everyone she met or was scheduled to meet that day. With a little luck, they should be able to narrow it down.' His face was expressionless, his piercing eyes darting away, and I had a feeling he was also putting his own feelers out to find out who'd landed his daughter in A&E.

'Who did this to me?' Annabel continued. 'I don't know, but I hope I got a couple of punches in before they got me. Who would have reason to attack me? Well ... how much time do you have?'

'Seriously?'

Her father leaned forward the slightest bit. I got the feeling that his focus on his phone was an act.

'Don't be daft. Sure, there are people I've pissed off at one point or another, but no one badly enough to whack me.'

'You really don't remember anything? Male or female? One or many?'

She closed her eyes. 'Could be male, but could also be female. I keep getting the feeling that I should know, that there's something I need to remember. I keep trying, but I can't. All I know is that they packed a hell of a punch.'

Her long fingers probed at her head. 'They caught me by surprise. All I know is that I think I was supposed to meet someone and then ... boom.'

Like Jonny Tang?

I wasn't sure where that thought had come from, but it felt right. He'd been smartly dressed, in a place he wouldn't normally frequent after dark. Had he been meeting someone?

'I read somewhere that smell is one of the most powerful senses,' I said carefully. 'Do you remember the way whoever it was smelled?'

'In this neighbourhood? Everything smells like weed.' Annabel's blue eyes met mine directly – either she was being honest, or she was a very good liar. 'I couldn't even tell you if there was someone smoking it or if the smell was coming from somewhere else.'

Okay, so whoever had attacked her hadn't smelled of fried chicken, at least.

'When we had lunch that day, I asked you about Cluckin' Good Chicken. Do you think they had something to do with it?'

She tilted her head, giving me a curious look. 'Why would they?'

'There's been an increase in crime since they moved in.'

She shrugged, then winced. 'Nothing to do with me. And from what I understand, you found me in the park, not on the high street.'

'Yeah, so? People can travel.'

'Sure, they can. But there's no reason for them to go out of their way to target me.'

I wasn't so sure of that.

'Were you involved in granting them the contract for the space?'

She raised an eyebrow. 'You're doing the Marple thing again, aren't you?' When I didn't answer, she did. 'You know I was.'

I knew what I needed to find out from Annabel, but I hadn't prepared how I would elicit the information. 'How straightforward was that? Deciding on which business would get that space?'

Robert had put down his phone and was now watching with interest.

Annabel laughed. 'This is East London. And we're not

talking Hackney. How many businesses do you think put a bid in?'

This was an interesting angle.

'One?'

'Close. And CGC was the highest bid. Had all the paperwork in order. A slight delay because the initial contract stipulated a lower percentage of their food being fried, but ...' She pursed her lips and shifted her head from side to side. 'We came to an agreement on that.'

Which meant they were paying her company more money.

'No co-signs or recommendations from, say, the council?'

She looked genuinely confused. 'Which council?'

'Tower Hamlets?'

'Them? Why would they?' She leaned back against the pillows.

'Aren't they the council whose mayor was convicted of corruption, disbarred, banned from running for public office, for what? Five years? Only to be re-elected?' Robert maintained an innocent expression, even under his daughter's glare.

'Yeah,' I agreed, ignoring the glare that was now turned on me. 'That'd be the one.'

'Lou, I love you to bits, so don't hate me when I tell you: you're genuinely barking up the wrong tree.'

'Yeah, well, maybe. I guess you didn't know Jonny Tang, then?'

'*That* guy.' She rolled her eyes and sighed. 'Yeah. I know him.'

64

LOUISE

Fiona (Nala's Mum)

> Want the good news or the bad news?

>> Both.

> I just had an interesting afternoon with Meg's guy Connor. The process, like any other, is more convoluted than you'd think, but there are checks along the way, and not just from the council

side. That's not to say that something couldn't have been bypassed, but I don't know why someone would want to do that when – let's face it – there are enough empty spaces around here.

> Red herring. Bugger.

Heard you went to see Annabel. How's she doing?

> She's up, tired, cranky. Doesn't remember anything from the evening she was attacked.

You believe her?

> I don't know. But there was one thing that was interesting. She knew Jonny Tang.

Oh yeah? How?

> Seems he was the local Karen in the building. Complained about everything, from the service charges, to the cleaning, to who mixed their recycling with the general trash.

He checked?

> Guess so. From what I gather, he pissed off a lot of people. Which didn't make him popular, but didn't mean that someone wanted to kill him. Still nothing concrete.

So back to square 1 then, right?

> Looks like it. Can you let Claire know what we learned? Or rather, didn't learn?

'Damn,' I cursed aloud and stepped off the Tube, onto the platform. We'd learned nothing. No real reason why somebody might have wanted to kill Jonny, or beat up Annabel. No reason for the firebombing of Claire's building and The Bells. And I was beginning to be convinced that I'd been the victim of dumb bad luck instead of some grand plot when it came to my encounter in CGC during the fire. For all I knew, the owner of the rucksack had been trying to help and my smoke-sodden brain hadn't understood.

Okay, so they weren't whiter than white either. Best thing to do was find a way of getting rid of the rucksack and the documents it contained.

Maybe Jake was right. Maybe I should stop wasting my time and leave the whole sorry mess to the detectives.

Meg was still in the chair as I passed the Hands-On salon, with Benny blow-drying her new 'autumn colours' hair. It looked pretty – a montage of reds, russets and golds – and far more conservative than her last few colour changes. Ethan must be getting to her.

I crossed the bridge and fobbed my way through the gates into my complex, wanting nothing more than to order in something decadent and spend the evening on the sofa, cuddling Klaus.

Drizzle began to fall. With a little luck, I'd be able to pick up my boy and make it home before the rain started in earnest. I turned the corner towards the entrance to Irina's building and glanced up at my own.

My flat was dark, the way it should be. The drapes were drawn in my bedroom, and yet ...

Something didn't feel right.

65

CLAIRE

Fiona (Nala's Mum)

> Dead end with Meg's mate. Dead end with Annabel.

>> She's what?

> No, no! She's not dead. But as far as Lou could tell, not much to add. Didn't remember a thing, but did say your boy Jonny was a Karen.

> He wasn't my boy.

Only because he was killed first. You knew he was as keen on you as you were on him.

> Yeah, well. Not going to find out where that would have gone, will we? The only thing I can do is get whoever did this to him. Pls don't tell the others though.

As if I would. You asked me to keep it quiet. 😬

> Thx hon. Nothing ever happened, you know.

Wouldn't matter if it did.

Claire knew she was lucky. She had good friends who had her back, without asking any questions. She also believed in keeping those friends close and potential enemies closer. As far as she was concerned, the jury was still out on Kate, but she couldn't deny that the other woman had good investigative skills, and she'd be a fool not to put them to good use, even if she knew she'd have to check what Kate was doing to make sure she wasn't covering something up.

And to see if she slipped and mentioned something about keying the car. Or at least showed any remorse. Of course, it could have been someone else. It could even have been random, but with the timing? No. It was a message. Only, Claire didn't know from whom.

'All okay?' Kate asked, looking up from where she sat with her own laptop across the table.

'Yeah,' Claire said, and looked away, absently watching Tank try to hump Andromeda the beagle. He had an intent look on his face, as if this time Andromeda would let him have his wicked way, even though she'd told him off countless times already.

Tank had about three brain cells, Claire figured. One was fixed on food, one was fixed on getting his leg over. And the last one – on a good day – was reserved for his mum. But he was a sweet boy; handsome and good company. And she loved him more than she loved life itself. She knew it was highly probable that until the Met found a better suspect for Jonny's murder she'd still be on their list. And the best way to get off it was to find out who actually did it. It was all tied up with CGC and the backpack, and probably went as high as the council, she just knew it.

'So, what connects them?' Claire asked aloud.

'What?'

Claire turned to Kate. 'I can't help feeling that

somehow we're missing something, Kate. It feels like once we can link the various pieces of this puzzle, who actually had a motive to kill Jonny will be obvious.'

'You think it's possible that Jonny originally had evidence of a connection between CGC and the council? Maybe he was killed because he was about to go public?'

Claire's first reaction was: *No way would he go public without telling me. Without letting me break that story.*

The second was: *Holy crap. What if that backpack originally belonged to Jonny and whoever killed him stole it? Maybe to silence him, maybe for their own gain?*

She lightly bounced her head on the desk as realisation dawned. 'I am so stupid,' she said. She closed her laptop and stood up, reaching for her coat and Tank's harness. 'Sorry, Kate, but I've got to run.'

66

LOUISE

Claire (Tank's Mum)

> Hear me out: what if that backpack was Jonny's? What if he was about to blow out some connection between CGC and the council? Bribery or extortion, or something like that. What if he was killed to prevent that happening?

> Was it Jonny's?

> I don't know Lou! I keep trying to think whether I ever saw him with a rucksack, but I can't remember!

> OK. I suppose that's a possibility. Look, I'm almost home, can I give you a call later?

> Yes, of course!

Meg (Tyrion's Mum)

> Just finished at the salon. Catch up later?

Batting aside the distraction of my phone, I squinted up at my building again. Something high up in the shadows caught my eye. The eighth floor, to be precise. Just behind a balcony populated with dying begonia plants.

I turned off the sound on my phone. Then turned off the phone itself. Reached into my pocket, feeling the cold metal tube of my defence spray. I stepped back from the pathway, staring up at my flat. Another few feet and the balcony would have blocked my view. But I hadn't imagined it, I knew I hadn't.

Feeling a white-hot anger pulse through my veins, I was moving before I even realised what I was doing. I took the lift to the seventh floor and edged up the stairs for the last flight, so that whoever was inside my flat wouldn't be warned by the ding of the lift arriving.

It was still early evening – why rob my flat now? Why not during the day when most people would be out working? Or at night while they slept?

Thank God Klaus is still at Irina's.

I eased the stairwell door closed behind me and crept down the hallway. The lock on my door had been jimmied open, apparently by someone who didn't have a clue what they were doing.

I slung my jacket over the wall light to dim the brightness of the corridor. It was the best I could do. I slowly turned the door handle, not expecting it to open, but it did. Whoever was robbing me didn't even have the sense to lock the door after them. Or maybe they couldn't, having broken the lock and worrying about getting trapped inside?

Leaning in, I listened at the door, but there was no sound. Either they'd heard me and were hiding, or they were far enough away that I was safe sliding in. I toed off my shoes, on the off chance that socks would be quieter.

Taking out the silver tube of defence spray, I made sure my finger was on the trigger button. Took a deep breath and slipped through the open door. Caught it with my left hand to slow it down as it swung back, so when it closed it was with no more than a soft click.

There was an intruder in my home. *Violating* my home. Maybe more than one.

Whoever it was might have a knife, but probably not a gun.

I hoped.

Regardless, it was too late to go back now.

I eased down the hall, one step at a time, expecting someone to jump out at me at any moment. I was sweating, despite the relatively cool air. A light shone from under my bedroom door and I paused at the end of the hall, listening. As I moved towards the room, I felt a breeze, a movement, something.

Stomach churning, I turned. Closed my eyes, leaned back and pressed the trigger. Emptied the defence spray in the general direction of the burglar's face.

There was a high-pitched howl – it could have been male or female, I couldn't tell. To me it was pure animal. Angry and hurt. Clawed hands grappled for me, for the spray, for whatever they could reach.

Bits of the spray blew back at me, stinging my eyes and the back of my throat. Tears blurred my vision, but the adrenaline in my veins filled in the blanks. I kept my finger pressing on the button until nothing else came out. Then I tightened my fist around the can and used it to bulk out my hand. Drew in my right arm, then shot it out, eyes still shut tight against the chemicals, but managing to deliver an uppercut to the burglar's chin. They stumbled back. Tripped over one of Klaus's balls and landed heavily on their back.

I lunged forward, grabbed one of Klaus's spare leads,

and acted fast, while they were still blinded, as well as winded. I straddled the writhing body, becoming aware that the burglar was female, but bulky. I grabbed hold of one of her flailing hands and flipped her onto her front. Placing my knee in the small of her back, I grabbed her other hand, quickly wrapping the lead around both as tightly and securely as I could. When I reached for another spare lead, she tried to get up, to move.

'No chance,' I snarled, and tackled her back to the ground. In my mind, it was a graceful leap that brought her down. In truth, I probably looked like a convulsing frog, but it didn't matter.

In the silence I could hear her breathing harshly, although that might have been me, coughing through the defence spray. At least the screams had stopped.

'You okay, Louise?' my neighbour, Geoff, called from the hallway. Light shone through where he'd opened my door. 'Looks like something busted—'

'Call the police, will you? There's an intruder in my flat.'

Geoff opened the door all the way and turned on the lights, temporarily blinding me. 'You what?'

It was the opportunity the burglar had been waiting for. Her hands were tied, but she scrambled to her feet and ran. I focused on her back, the navy-blue beanie on her head.

'Don't let her pass!' I shouted to Geoff, scrambling to my feet.

He went into a boxer's half-crouch. As she got close, he threw a quick jab with his left and a nasty cross. His form wasn't perfect, but it was good enough, and the burglar crumpled at his feet.

'I'll get calling the cops,' Geoff said, idly rubbing his knuckles before pulling his phone from his pocket. As he spoke to the operator, he looked down at the supine woman and shook his head. I grabbed a second spare lead from atop the shoe cabinet by the door and began to wrap it around her feet.

'Do you want to unmask her or shall I?' Geoff gestured at the beanie.

'Go ahead,' I said, dabbing at my streaming eyes with a tissue.

He pulled it off, revealing a wealth of white-and-black hair, like a barcoded Cruella de Vil. 'Kind of feels like she should get up and say, "I would have gotten away with it, if not for you ... and your meddling neighbour".'

'Caren?' I gaped. The *hairdresser* broke into my flat? We weren't friends, but we were acquaintances. It felt like a double betrayal. 'Why?'

She began to move. Or rather, her mouth did. She screamed and swore with the full vocabulary of a truck driver.

My wrist vibrated, my smart watch again informing me of a loud environment.

'Jesus,' Geoff said. 'She's got more volume than Klaus when he's partying with his friends.'

He wasn't wrong, but there was a bigger point here. 'Unless you're about to tell me why you chose my flat to break into, you can shut right up,' I told her. She ignored me, and in the same stern tone I used with Klaus, I ordered, 'Leave it. Just tell me why. Why did you break into my flat?'

She spat at me.

My blood felt like it was about to boil. By the door, Geoff looked at the top of the cabinet and picked up Klaus's blue-and-orange ball. He tossed it into the air and caught it, his cheeky grin giving him an almost boyish look.

'Ever see *Pulp Fiction*, Lou?'

67

LOUISE

Meg (Tyrion's Mum)

> Hey Meg, I hope your hair appt went well – looked good when I passed by on my way home. Quick q for you … did you mention anything about me while you were in there?

No, why?

Oh wait, maybe. We were talking about the fire yesterday. They were

> really excited to be able to open up today. There was some smoke damage – but the worst of it was contained to CGC and The Bells.

> Okay...?

> I said that they had you to thank. You'd grabbed an extinguisher and waded into the storage room to fight the flames. Ended up with a bump on your head for your efforts, but mostly OK. This was just after you passed by on your way to see Annabel, so I said that it was terrible what happened to her. Did I do something wrong?

> No, not at all. Thanks Meg.

'Got anything to say to me, Caren? You can start with an apology. Then take it from there.'

The woman writhing on the floor replied with another

string of epithets. Ignoring Geoff as he whistled his appreciation of her colourful vocabulary.

'I wonder if she was the one who broke into Mrs Latenby's last week. That you?' he asked her.

His question gave me pause. I'd been about to ask Caren if she was here for the rucksack, but maybe that was too much of a stretch.

She flailed against the leads, either trying to move away or to thump me with her trussed-up arms. But there was something there, and a decision was made.

'That's fine. You don't have to tell us. The cops are on their way.' I stood up. According to my watch, it'd only been fifteen minutes since we'd caught her. Too early to expect the police to show up.

'Geoff, I'll go get you that duct tape, shall I?'

'I just buzzed the cops through the gates,' Geoff said, putting his phone down and running his fingers through his thinning silver hair.

'That was fast. Thanks, Geoff. And in case I didn't say it before, thanks for your help. And for staying with me.'

'Most excitement I've had in ages,' he said, air boxing a jab or two.

The lift dinged and we opened the door to two uniformed police officers, a man and a woman. Both were young, under twenty-five if I had to guess. The woman instantly reminded me of Tank – short, muscular, with the same expression he had when the fibre Claire gave him for his constipation hadn't yet taken effect and she was still giving him commands; trying to pay attention but utterly distracted. The male PC wasn't much taller, and seemed happy to let his female colleague lead the way.

'PC Fury,' she said, holding up a warrant card. 'And this is PC Richell. Someone called about a burglar?'

Geoff took an exaggerated step to the side and circled his arm and wrist, like a magician saying, *Hey Presto!*

'And you are?'

'I'm Dr Geoffrey Baggott. I'm the one who called you. This is Ms Louise Mallory. It's her home that was burgled.'

'Do you know what was taken?'

In the excitement of stopping Caren, I hadn't even thought to check.

I ran down the hallway to my bedroom and opened up my jewellery box. 'My jewellery! That cow took my jewellery!' While I was away from the cops, I did a quick check to confirm the rucksack was unmolested.

PC Fury muttered something I couldn't hear, then Caren shouted, 'He planted it on me, he did! The old man planted that on me!'

'And I suppose he carried you here and dropped you in the middle of my flat too?' I yelled back. On the plus side, if she said it was planted, then she couldn't claim the jewellery was hers and not mine.

I did a quick check to see if anything else was missing. Nothing seemed obvious, and although the PCs didn't instil a lot of confidence in me, at least when I emerged outside, they were patting her down. And hopefully they'd get some answers from her.

68

LOUISE

Irina (Hamish's Mum)

> Hey Irina, can you keep Klausi with you a bit longer? Found a burglar in my flat — police are already here.

Police or detectives?

> It was a B&E, not a murder.

Yeah, he's fine here. He and Hammy are having fun.

> Thanks!

It wasn't like I'd expected Irina to ask how I was, and it could have been worse: she could have asked what I had to steal.

Fighting off a stonking headache, I brewed coffee for Geoff and the PCs and mint tea for myself, while the officers, under Geoff's watchful eyes, replaced the leads wrapped around Caren's wrists with government-issued metal bracelets.

'Bet you don't come to many burglary scenes where the burglar's already been caught?' Geoff said to Fury.

'Most have already been and gone,' she admitted. 'Makes it a bit easier that you detained her. You know this woman?'

'Her name is Caren Hansen,' I replied. 'She owns the hair salon on the high street.'

'Crime of opportunity? The salon is closed on a Monday – maybe she thought she'd supplement her income?' Geoff guessed. He was clearly enjoying himself.

'Well, she was in the salon when I went past on my way out. She didn't seem to have a client, though.' Because the only client, Meg, was busy having her hair coloured by Benny.

'One thing at a time. Richell, stay with Ms Hansen.' PC Fury joined me in the kitchen. Geoff remained in the hallway at first, seeming torn between wanting to stay and hear Caren being questioned, or joining me as I was. In the end he followed Fury.

'To confirm: she saw you leave? Knew you wouldn't be home?'

I nodded.

'Any reason she'd want to burgle your flat?' Fury asked.

I forced myself to meet her eyes. Forced myself to remain calm. 'I'm a businesswoman. A lot of people around here know I own my own consultancy firm. Maybe she thinks we're doing better than we are.' I put their mugs of coffee down on the table in front of them. 'But I don't keep much cash in my flat – only enough to pay for Klaus's monthly manicures. They don't take cards—'

'Klaus?'

'My dog.'

'Where is he?'

'With a friend while I went to visit another friend in the hospital.'

'Did Ms Hansen see you? Did she know that your dog wasn't here, that no one was home?'

'Yeah, she saw me. I passed by the salon. They'd opened, despite having a little smoke damage from a fire yesterday, to do my friend's hair.' I realised how that sounded and clarified. 'Different friend. My friend Irina is dog sitting Klaus. My friend Meg had her colour done. By Ms Hansen's associate.'

Fury nodded. 'Eighth floor. Top floor of the building. Not the easiest to break into,' she said.

'I imagine getting into the complex, or even the building, is easy enough during the day, especially if you don't look too dodgy. Just tailgate behind someone coming in. We're not supposed to allow it, but a lot of people don't pay attention. I'd guess getting out is just as easy, especially if she left the TV and just went for my jewellery box. Maybe my laptop, though it's kind of old.'

'Right. Well. You might consider leaving a light on when you're out. A lot of thieves won't burgle a place if they think someone is home. And I'm not including your dog.'

I nodded, understanding what she wasn't saying: some people would break in specifically to steal the dog. But if the dog wasn't considered loot, it'd be considered an obstacle, though one that could easily be taken care of.

I swallowed hard, feeling nauseated.

Fury patted Caren down again before they left, handing me the small bag of jewellery she'd stolen. With one cop on either side, she was escorted into the lift, the doors closing behind her.

Geoff lingered for a few minutes, his sharp eyes bright. I bet he'd be dining out on tonight's experience for the next couple of months. Eventually, he put down his coffee mug, said goodnight and made his way across the hall to his own flat.

Once I heard the door click shut, I phoned a 24/7 locksmith and put in a request for a callback from a home security company.

Finally, having delayed it as long as I could, I opened up a new WhatsApp chat. There was a big thing I'd left out of my statement to the PCs, but only because that information had to go to the right place first.

69

LOUISE

Detective Andrew Thompson

> Hi Andy, just so you hear it from me, I caught a burglar in my flat this evening. Uniforms just left.

Are you OK?

> Yeah. It's been a corker of a week, but I'm fine.

Did they get much before they left?

> The thief was still here when I got home. My neighbour and I stopped her.

> Don't take this the wrong way, but if someone is going to burgle a flat, it's usually a ground or lower ground floor. Maybe first floor. Yours is a big risk on the 8th floor.

> Yeah. That's what the PC said too. Look, this might be a coincidence, but there was a break-in on the 3rd floor last Monday …

> But?

> So I don't know if she's just really enterprising and decided to hit my flat after Mrs Latenby's but, well, I found a rucksack that she might have been after. Maybe.

> And instead of asking for it back, she broke into your flat?

It has some pretty dodgy stuff in there, but yeah, when you put it that way, I would have just written it off.

> Did you return it to her? Or the uniforms?

No. In the heat of the moment I forgot. And tbh, the PCs looked more interested in having a tick in the closed case box, and I don't think they'd do anything with it.

> OK. I'll check in with them and ask Williams to pick up the rucksack in the morning. You'll be OK to be by yourself tonight?

> Yeah. Locksmith's on their way and Irina will be over with Klaus and Hammy in a bit.

👍

The locksmith arrived first and set to work on the door. Irina came up a few minutes afterwards, heralded by the sound of barking dogs.

The locksmith jumped at the sound, and stepped back as the lift doors slid open and Klaus and Hammy erupted from it. Klaus gave him a quick bark, more for form's sake than anything else, and ran straight to me, jumping onto my knee. Hammy licked my arm, then went to investigate Klaus's dinner bowl.

'A new lock's only good if you use it, Lou,' Irina said, stepping over the locksmith's tools. He gave me a strange look.

'I will use it. And the burglar broke in when I was out. When the door *was* locked,' I said from the floor as Klaus crawled into my lap.

She popped her bag on the kitchen counter with a soft *thunk* and pulled a bottle of wine out of it. 'Figured you'd need a glass after today. After the last couple of days, actually.'

It was unlike Irina to bring wine here, and I was touched. Enough to chase away the stray thought: *She just wanted someone to drink with on a Monday.*

At that moment, it didn't matter.

'So, was it one of the kids that hang out outside the News-N-Booze or was it the CGC gang?'

So, she was after some gossip. That was fine; I didn't want to be alone. 'Neither. It was Caren Hansen.'

'Who?'

'The beautician. Hands-On salon?'

'Angry Karen?' Irina paused with her glass halfway to her lips. 'The one who looks pissed off at the world? Why on earth would she burgle *you?*' There was no irony in her voice, and no awareness that the same 'angry' description could – and often was – used to describe her.

For a moment I was about to tell her about the rucksack, but at the last moment I stopped myself. 'I don't know. Maybe she liked the look of Klaus's kibble?'

Or maybe she just wanted her blackmail bag back.

'So, in summary, in the past week we've had one dead body. One gang stabbing. One mugging that could have been fatal, two arson attempts and a B&E. Did I miss anything?'

'No,' I said glumly, not about to add in one botched seduction attempt.

'That's a bit unusual, even for this neighbourhood, isn't it?'

'You know it is, Councillor,' I said, having a feeling I knew where she was going.

'Can't help feeling that at least some of it is connected.'

I grunted my assent. 'But I can't seem to figure out how or why.'

'Look for the lowest common denominator. What connects them all?'

Feeling sick, I looked away.

But Irina wasn't going to let it go. 'You,' she said.

'Don't be daft, Irina. I didn't do anything. In fact, every damn time I got there too late. Too late to help Jonny. Too late to help Annabel. Almost too late to stop that fire.'

'Or the gang action.'

I took a large gulp of wine. 'Ha, that I wouldn't have had a chance of stopping. I can't perform miracles.' I paused. 'But maybe you're on to something. What else connects everything?' I answered my own question. 'Cluckin' Good Chicken. Or at least, the men behind it.'

Tuesday

70

ANDY

Scott Williams

> Louise Mallory had a break-in last night. I'm checking in with the arresting PCs now, but can you pick up a rucksack from hers?

> You left your rucksack at Louise's? I thought you liked the Russian one …

> It's not mine, Scott.

PC Fury was standing at the coffee pot when Andy arrived. It was the end of her shift and she looked tired, her dark hair escaping from the bun at the back of her head.

'Fury?' he asked.

She startled and turned. 'Sir?'

'I heard you attended a burglary in progress last night. Home of a Ms Louise Mallory?'

'That's right. She and a neighbour had the thief on the floor by the time Richell and I showed up. Why?'

'Ms Mallory is involved in a case I'm working on. What can you tell me about the burglar?'

Fury creased her forehead and finished pouring her coffee, dropping in a few sugars and a splash of milk. 'White woman, forty-eight. Gave the first name Caren – spelled like Karen but with a C – and surname Hansen. Local hairdresser. One hundred and sixty-seven centimetres tall. Stocky build. Blue eyes, black-and-white hair, kind of messed up but with a straightened fringe.'

'How was she dressed?'

Fury frowned. 'I can show you the file, but she was dressed like any other burglar. Dark clothes, beanie hat. Didn't bring anything to take her loot out with; said she figured if she used Ms Mallory's luggage, most people would just think she was a friend staying, if they saw her leave.'

Knowing Louise, Andy wondered if even her luggage was decorated with sausage dogs. He kept his thoughts to himself and gestured to Fury to continue. 'Any idea why she targeted Ms Mallory?'

Fury took a sip of coffee, winced and added another

sugar. 'Seems she – Ms Hansen – was strapped for cash. Cost of living crisis and all. She knew that Ms Mallory owned her own company and lived on the top floor of a posh building, and figured that she'd have jewellery, bags, maybe electronics that could be fenced.'

'Where is she now?'

'Bailed. First-time offence and clearly got it wrong. She owns her own hair salon so didn't seem like a flight risk. Her pal Benny Bryce came to bail her out. Poor man was almost crapping himself being in the station.'

Andy remembered the video Williams had sent him of the woman wearing a fedora walking with a tall man on the Sunday Jonny Tang was killed. 'Can you describe him?'

'Wasn't a suspect, sir.'

'Bear with me.'

'One hundred and eighty-six, maybe one hundred and eighty-seven centimetres. White, with longish dark hair. Seemed a bit twitchy, as I said – might be having to pick his friend up here.'

'You get any sense that they were a couple?'

'Hell no, sir. That man's gay.'

'You sure?'

'One hundred per cent. Also, I'd peg him as a bit of an introvert. Not confident. Kind of hunched into himself.'

'Genuine? He wasn't trying to change his shape or anything?'

'Doubt it. Looked like that was his usual posture.'

Andy nodded; that didn't sound like the couple in Williams's video.

Scott Williams

> Got the rucksack, and you're not going to believe what's in it.

>> Porn?

> Close. Some dodgy pics but at least everyone's got their kit on. Some other bits as well though. Taking it over to the lads in Forensics and giving a heads-up to Major Crimes. Although it looks like that dog pack still have their paw prints all over the case.

>> Damn. Which ones?

> Not your girl, don't worry. Louise didn't mention her.

>> It's not like we're not telling them to leave it alone. You think it's bad enough that someone'd go after Louise?

> Possible. Looks like the sort of thing that leads to blackmail. They'd probably want it back – at the very least, they're not going to want it traced back to them. Least of all by the dog park dog gang. You think whoever broke into her flat is involved?

'Can you send me the mug shot of Ms Hansen?' Andy asked Fury. 'Send it to DC Williams too.'

Fury nodded, still cupping her coffee. 'Will do.'

'Now, please.'

The PC blinked and put down her coffee. 'Right away, sir.'

Andy waved her away, already busy texting again.

71

IRINA

Partridge Bark

Emma (Flash's Mum)

> A bit of a non-dog topic for a Tuesday morning ...

> Some of you might have noticed that the boy racers speeding down the roads — especially the high street — are particularly awful at night time. Some neighbours in my block set up a session with the police and council last night to

discuss this antisocial behaviour.

It went pretty well and they recognise that it is high risk and dangerous to pedestrians – as well as other drivers – and encourage all residents to send photos and videos and report whenever this happens.

I kind of hope that the more we report these things – with evidence – the more chance there is that they might do something.

Yaz (Hercules's Mum)

That's great. Do you have any idea how often I send them videos of those boy racers? You wanna know what they've done so far?

> Hey @**Louise** – speeding cars seem to have a thing for you. You think Dr Cooper's speeding sidekick is back out and looking for blood?

Louise (Klaus's Mum)

> Thanks for the concern, @**Irina**. Pretty sure she – and Dr Cooper – are still locked up, but as we all know, she's probably not the first or the last person I'll piss off ... 😳

'You really do enjoy winding her up, don't you?' Ella asked Irina, glancing at her own phone.

'She loves it,' Irina responded. And even if she didn't, it served Louise right for not waiting on Irina and Mischka for their morning walk, and subjecting her instead to a long outing with Ella and Jimmy Chew.

Irina didn't have much to talk about with Ella at the best of times, but the Frenchwoman was even more taciturn than normal.

'Where's Bark Vader?'

'With Paul.'

'Where's Paul?'

'With Meg.'

'Why?'

'Meg's still sitting Phoebe, and she wanted to get her more used to bigger dogs before sending her home.'

'Anything interesting over the weekend?'

'No.' (That one had been even more abrupt.)

Honestly, she'd have a better conversation with Jimmy, and that dog had fewer brain cells than Tank the Frenchie. 'Lou's a lightning rod for trouble. You heard she had a break-in last night at her flat?'

That shook Ella out of her reverie. 'No! What happened?'

'Someone broke in.' Obviously. 'Lou and her neighbour stopped the thief. Angry Karen from the hair salon.'

'Caren? Really? What has this neighbourhood come to?' Ella whispered. She looked across the canal, avoiding the park bench where Jonny Tang had been found, blue-and-white police tape still fluttering around it. 'Any idea why?'

Irina shrugged.

As if sensing his human's attention, or rather the lack of it, Jimmy looked over the bank of the canal at a coot and barked at it. The coot looked back at him, unfazed. Someone had once told Irina that if too many coot chicks survived the hatching – there was probably a word for that – then Mama Coot killed off the surplus. A bird like that brooked no bollocks from a dog, even a black labrador as big as Jimmy Chew.

'Enough,' Ella said to Jim.

Even that was almost monosyllabic. And Irina knew that English as a second language wasn't an excuse, just like it wasn't for her either. She was fluent in four languages.

'Are you okay?' she snapped at Ella.

Ella looked up at her, dark eyes confused. 'Yes, of course. Why do you ask?'

Irina looked at the sky in a silent appeal for help. *Why oh why couldn't Lou have waited five bloody minutes for me this morning?* She couldn't be that much ahead along the canal, and at this point, Irina didn't care if Louise was walking with Jake or with a squad of X-Men.

She heard a jogger coming from behind and gently pulled Hammy to the side of the path, out of the way. 'Ella . . .'

The jogger didn't sound like they were about to slow down. Irina glanced over her shoulder, saw the runner's arms and legs pump with stocky determination.

As she drew closer, small details jumped out, like the beanie on the woman's head – she was dressed for the street, rather than for exercise. Then there was the expression of anger, rather than euphoria, on her face.

Jim turned to bark at the jogger and, as if in slow motion, Irina saw her arm rise.

'Ella!' she shouted.

Ella turned, and the heel of Caren Hansen's hand caught her in the centre of her chest, thrusting her backwards.

Ella's arms windmilled as she lost her balance, letting go of Jimmy's lead. Instead of lunging at the jogger, Jim launched himself into the canal, maybe after his mother, maybe after the coot, splashing into the water a split second after Ella did.

Something clicked in Irina's mind, and she understood: Caren wasn't jogging, she was going after Louise.

But Ella was in the water. Irina desperately looked between the path ahead and the canal, her heart pounding. The water was cold, and heaven only knew what lived in there. There wasn't a ladder nearby, and Ella was weighed down by her heavy coat and scarf. There was no way she'd get herself, much less Jimmy, out without help.

Irina slipped Hammy's lead from her wrist and yelled at him, 'Find Louise!'

Hammy sat down and tilted his head at her.

She pointed ahead, down the canal. 'Go, Mischka! Find Klaus!'

He didn't wait for her to ask again, running ahead as though a gun had been fired, his lead trailing after him.

Irina slipped her phone into her pocket, took off her coat and jumped into the canal after Ella, hoping that Hamish could get to Louise before Caren did.

And that Louise understood what that meant.

72

ANDY

Marple

> The woman who broke into your flat was released this morning. Do not, I repeat, do not approach her.

> Not planning on it. Just taking Klaus for a walk. Then I'll be heading straight home.

> Best to cut the walk short, Louise.

Beside Andy, Williams put his phone on the desk, hitting the button for speaker. 'Say that again, will you, mate?'

A tinny voice erupted from the device. 'Right, so we dusted the bag, the envelopes inside, the contents of the envelopes and the thumb drive for prints.'

'Tell Andy what you found.'

'Right, Detective. So, there were six distinct sets of prints.'

'Who do they belong to?'

'For four of them, it could be the horsemen of the apocalypse for all I know – we don't have them in the system.'

'My money is on Louise and her mates,' Williams said to Andy. 'What about the fifth and sixth?'

'Those we have. One was a new print that was added last night: Caren Hansen.'

'And were Ms Hansen's prints found only on the outside of the bag?'

'No, Detective. They were pretty much everywhere.'

'And the sixth?'

'The dead man. Jonny Tang.'

'Great. Thanks, mate. We'll get prints from the women who found the bag to compare against. Get it over to Major Crimes when you're done, will you? See if they can identify who's being blackmailed and why.'

Williams hit the end call button and sat down in a chair, leaning back until it squeaked. 'Four riders of the apocalypse sounds about right for that lot. Which one do you think your friend Irina is?'

'Leave it alone, Williams,' Andy said, without heat. 'So

far she and her friends have helped us solve one case and, despite every warning we've given them, are doing their best to help us solve another. What's more interesting is that Tang's prints are on the bag.'

Williams's face sobered. 'Funny, he struck me as pretty straight-laced, but blackmail? Mate, this smells like motive to me. Bet you once we know who he was blackmailing, we'll know who killed him?'

'Yeah. And hopefully we'll find out before anyone else gets hurt.'

73

IRINA

'Are you all right?' A couple walking along the towpath had stopped on the bank to look at them.

'Do we flippin' look all right?' Irina was bobbing in the canal, one hand under Ella's armpit, the other one batting Jimmy away. The stupid beast thought it was a game and kept scrambling on top of Ella. The water, while cold, wasn't deep. The greater problem was that the bottom was silty and Ella kept slipping under. 'The Nest has a long rope – can you get it and meet us down there? And take my coat with you.' Irina pointed at it.

The man gave a thumbs-up and he and his partner hurried away along the canal.

Ella was pale and shaking. 'Hold on,' Irina said, tightening her grip. 'We'll get you out of here.' She pulled Ella closer, trying to use her own body heat to keep her warm until they could get to the ladder by The Nest. 'Next time, consider getting a dog that doesn't like the water so much,' she said.

'Retrievers are water dogs,' Ella said through chattering teeth. She gave Irina a weak smile. 'You go ahead, Irina. See if you can get Jim out.'

'No chance. We're going to get you both out. We're all gonna get out. Then we're going to get you a tetanus shot big enough to protect an elephant. Keep swimming. The water's not deep, but don't drink it. You know what colour it goes in the summer.'

Ella wiped her face; she'd already gone under when she'd fallen in, and the cold air on her wet hair was making her shiver uncontrollably. 'What happened?'

'Idiot jogger knocked you into the water. And your idiot dog decided to join you for a swim – get *off*, Jim!' Irina pushed him away, trying to herd them all in the right direction. The water was so cold her toes and fingers were going numb, but she knew better than to stop. On her own, she could climb up the butterfly bush vines that grew along the embankment on the far side of the canal. They weren't in season, but the branches were thick and sturdy.

Only, she didn't think Ella could do it, and there was no way they'd get Jimmy up them.

'It's just ahead,' she said, softening her voice. 'You go up first.'

'Jim . . .'

'We'll get the rope around him and winch him up. No problem.'

A small crowd was forming outside The Nest, and the man Irina could see edging partway down the ladder wasn't the man she'd seen earlier. It was Ejiro, and she breathed a sigh of relief; she wasn't alone.

'Grab my hand, Ella,' Ejiro said, his voice soft, but no less commanding for it. Irina pushed, and could feel Ella making every effort to move forward.

Ejiro moved down a step or two, careless of his shoes and suit. Behind Ella, Irina tried to find some purchase in the sliding bottom of the canal. Wedging her foot against something that seemed solid enough, she pushed with one hand on Ella's waist and the other under her bottom, while Ejiro pulled.

The crowd cheered as Ella clambered out.

'Throw me the rope, Ejiro,' Irina gasped. 'I'll get it around Jim.'

'Good luck,' he said, and tossed the coiled end to her. Behind her, Jimmy splashed around, as if this was all a big lark.

'Come here, Jim,' Irina said. Jimmy ignored her. '*Idi syuda!*' she barked, and he responded to the Russian command, swimming towards her. 'If I get this tied around him, can you lift him out?'

'Yes,' Ejiro said.

'Yes,' two other voices chorused.

'Good enough.'

Jim tried to launch himself at Irina. Still braced, she managed to get the rope underneath him, only to have it slip away.

She waded after it. Grabbed the rope, then went for an easier option, and passed it through Jim's harness. 'I can't tie a decent knot,' she admitted.

'That's fine.' Ejiro handed the end he was holding to someone else. 'Give me your end, Irina.'

'I hope you didn't skimp on a harness, Ella,' Irina muttered, pushing Jimmy towards the side of the canal and the ladder. She handed her end of the rope up to Ejiro and pushed herself out of the way as he and his helpers hauled up thirty kilos of wet, squirming Labrador retriever.

Once safe on the bank, he gave the mother of all shakes, spraying the crowd with canal water. 'Give me your hand, Irina.' Ejiro held out his own paw, and helped her up the ladder.

Ella was sitting on the grass, huddled in a blanket that someone, probably The Nest, had provided, while Yaz towelled off Jim.

There was no sign of Hamish, and Irina could only hope that he was with Louise.

One of the baristas handed her a blanket, but first she reached for her coat and the phone in the pocket, hoping she wasn't too late.

Louise (Klaus's Mum)

> Caren is running down the canal looking for you – be careful!

74

LOUISE

My phone vibrated again, but before I could pull it from my pocket, I heard barking. Beside me, Klaus went still, only his nose twitching. He moved his back legs, rotating his body 180 degrees, facing back the way we'd come.

'What's going on, dude?' I asked, as if he could answer.

And in a way, he did, joining in the barkfest. It only got louder as a small black juggernaut hurtled down the canal towards us, trailing a lead behind him. 'Hammy? What the . . .'

Klaus barked at Hammy.

Hammy barked at Klaus.

'Where's Irina?' I asked, craning my head but not seeing my friend. I picked up Hamish's lead and looped it over my wrist. Still in a half squat, looking down the path where he'd come from, I froze, recognising a familiar shape in the distance. The puzzle pieces clicked into place.

Caren.

I knew I'd shake afterwards, but in that moment, I felt a cold calmness settle over me. I moved Hammy's lead to my left hand with Klaus's and, shortening the lengths, pulled both boys behind me, holding them firmly in place.

I scooped a smooth stone into my hand from the side of the path and planted my feet the way I'd seen Geoff do the night before.

I kept my knees loose and waited while a second juggernaut raced towards me.

Caren was getting close, her arms stretching out, her expression one of fury.

Changing tactic, I pulled the hounds away at the last second and stuck out my foot as she reached me.

The vibration from the impact shot up my leg, but Caren sailed past, arms outstretched, like a middle-aged, overweight, salt-and-pepper Superman. Or Ursula the sea witch.

I jammed my knee into the small of her back and unclipped Klaus, who immediately went to bark in her face.

She tried to swat at him, and Hammy growled, backing up his friend. 'Leave it,' I ordered. 'Both of you. Come here, Klaus.'

For the second time in twenty-four hours, I tied Caren up with Klaus's leash. Once her arms were as secure as one and a half metres of lead, decorated with dancing alligators, could make them, I leaned in close. 'You try to hit him again and you won't have to worry about him biting you. I'll rip your jugular out myself. *Am I clear?*'

I sat on Caren's back and pulled Klaus onto my lap. Fumbled for my phone and checked my messages.

BONE OF CONTENTION

Detective Andrew Thompson

> I've got her. She's secured for now. I'm on the path by the Lidl. I'll send you GPS co-ordinates now.

> You OK?

> Hopping mad. That woman tried to swat Klaus. I should have let him bite her.

> You're almost attacked by the woman and you're worried about a swat?

> SHE ALMOST HURT MY DOG!

> Stay where you are, I'll have a couple of uniforms pick her up.

I took a few breaths to calm myself as Caren started screaming for help. A few walkers gave me a strange look and moved as far away as they could to pass us, virtually teetering on the edge of the canal.

'Waiting for the police to pick her up,' I told them cheerfully. 'Careful you don't fall in there. It's not the cleanest.'

Partridge Bark

> @Irina, I've got Hammy. If anyone has a spare lead, can you please bring it down to me. I'm on the canal path near the Lidl.

Paul (Bark Vader and Jimmy Chew's Dad)

You forgot Klaus's at home?

> Nope. Used it to tie up the woman who broke into my flat last night.

Ejiro (Hercules's Dad)

The same woman who just pushed @Ella and Jimmy into the canal?

Paul (Bark Vader and Jimmy Chew's Dad)

WHAT! Where? Are they OK? I'm on my way!

BONE OF CONTENTION

> In the canal! OMG – I hope they're OK!

Irina (Hamish's Mum)

They're fine. **@Ejiro** has Jim, but **@Paul's** gonna have to buy his wife a new phone. **@Louise**, can you hang on to Hammy a bit longer? I'm taking **@Ella** home for dry clothes, then to the GPs to get checked out. Maybe get a tetanus shot.

Paul (Bark Vader and Jimmy Chew's Dad)

Which one? I will meet you there.

Meg (Tyrion's Mum)

We're on our way!

Indy (Banjo's Mum)

The Hound after work tonight to celebrate @**Louise** catching her burglar?

> Not just my burglar. I'm willing to bet that she's also the one who killed Jonny Tang.

Indy (Banjo's Mum)

Even more reason to celebrate! Can we link her to Annabel?

> I don't know, maybe. I think so. Waiting for the cops to arrive – I should know more afterwards.

Indy (Banjo's Mum)

Tomorrow's open mic so it'll be packed. I'll call now and see if I can book the function room for tonight.

> If it's not too early to drink on a Tuesday?

'You pushed Ella and Jim into the canal?' I said to Caren. 'What's wrong with you?'

Given her criminal CV to date, it wasn't the worst thing she'd done, but it still managed to shock me.

I opened the chat with Andy and added another message.

Detective Andrew Thompson

> You might want to come yourself. I believe that Caren Hansen, frustrated first-time burglar, is also a blackmailer and a murderer.

> Because she tried to swat Klaus? You serious?

> I'm as serious as a heart attack, Andy. And I'm pretty sure we can prove it.

Caren swore furiously beneath me as I typed. 'Do shut up, Karen.' I took slight pleasure in deliberately mispronouncing her name. 'Unless you want to bite down on Klaus's ball? He doesn't like to share it, but I'm sure he'd take one for the team.'

At least she'd stopped outright screaming.

I settled back, trying to get more comfortable perched on her bottom. All I had to do now was keep the boys from attacking her.

At least until the police arrived.

75

ANDY

Marple

> You've got to be kidding – what proof?

> I'll explain when you get here.

> Stay where you are. We're on our way.

'Get your kit, Scott. Looks like one of the four horsemen – actually, women – has landed us a lucky break.'

Williams swivelled on his chair to face Andy. 'Let me guess: our local Miss Marple, Louise Mallory?'

Andy nodded, double-checking to make sure he had a set of handcuffs with him. 'The Hansen woman made a run at her – which we thought might happen.'

Williams nodded and slipped his warrant card into his breast pocket, making to stand. 'And?'

'And Louise managed to get her tied up. Again.' He held up a hand to stave off Williams's question. 'I'm sure she'll explain how. While she also explains why she thinks Caren Hansen killed Jonny Tang.'

'Seriously?'

'Let's hear what she has to say.'

Williams paused, thinking. 'Hansen's about the right height to be the woman with the fedora. Give us a second, let's see if we can get a warrant to search her flat.'

'And to get her phone records. If it was her, I want to know who her accomplice is. We get Hansen behind bars, I don't want to have to keep looking over my shoulder. Or have the Pack looking over theirs.'

'If there *is* a second person,' Scott Williams said as he followed Andy to the door. Muttering to himself, he added, 'Wish I remembered what those horsemen represented. Pretty sure one was death. What were the others? Lunacy? Chaos? Louise Mallory has to be the god of chaos. I can't wait to hear what she's come up with this time.'

76

LOUISE

Partridge Bark

Indy (Banjo's Mum)

> I couldn't get the function room — someone's pre-Halloween party — but got a few tables in the beer garden. By the heaters. Booked for 18:30!

Kate (Percy and Andy's Mum)

> We're in!

The door rattled, but the new lock held it in place. I looked up from where I was lying on the sofa, alarm jolting through my veins. I hadn't buzzed anyone into the complex, let alone the building. Klaus stood beside the door, barking.

I lay still, feeling my heart beat faster. Had I got it wrong? The cops hadn't said anything one way or another when I'd laid out my thoughts.

Was the murderer Caren Hansen . . . or was there someone else?

The door rattled again. 'Open up, will you?' The voice sounded like Eastern European gravel tinged with impatience. 'Since when do you even lock the damned thing?'

My breath expelled with a harsh *whoosh*. Irina. I got off the couch and shook off the last bits of sleep fug; I hadn't registered how exhausted I'd been until I'd returned home. I remembered texting Babs a brief update then sitting down. It was now dark outside and I glanced at my watch, realising that I'd slept for hours.

'Are you coming? And since when do you lock the door?'

I opened up, stifling a yawn and then a grin as Klaus and Hammy greeted each other with barks, sniffs and kisses. 'Since it got fixed, Monday night.'

'Yesterday,' Irina corrected. She wore a camel-coloured Max Mara wool coat with the collar pulled up. Either she'd gone to the office after taking Ella to the GP, or she'd dressed up for The Hound. 'It's not a habit until after twenty-one days. Let's hope you stick to it.'

I nodded. 'Give me five minutes to wash my face.'

'Not like we can start without you. You're the one with

the information.' She gave me an arch look. 'Which you've been rather tight with.'

'Easier to say it once, to everyone. And it's still mostly conjecture.'

'Yeah, well. Did you invite the detectives? Andy can keep a straight face, but Williams is more likely to say what he thinks.' Her voice was deadpan, and I could only imagine what Williams had said to her, though it explained why she was dressed so smartly.

I nodded and retreated to my bathroom, running some cool water. 'How did it go with Ella and the GP?'

'I'll let her tell you.'

Quid pro quo.

I patted my face dry and applied moisturiser and a bit of make-up while I waited for Irina to fill in the gaps. 'They gave me a tetanus shot as well.'

'Good,' I said, unsure whether I was replying to her or to my reflection in the mirror.

When I was ready, we rounded up the boys and walked the short distance to The Hound in amicable silence. Irina continued straight past the beer-swilling skeleton at the door, while Klaus stopped to wee on it. Instead of following her directly to the beer garden, I stopped at the bar.

Sheri, the bartender, leaned forward. 'Louise, what did you *do?*'

I blinked and felt the still-tender bruise on my head. 'Got whacked trying to help in the fire on Sunday.'

'No, not that. Dr Indy was the first to arrive – wait for it – with Banjo!'

'Maybe she didn't want to leave him home alone?'

'How often does she even join your group? With or without that asocial little boy?'

'Good point.' I put my bag on the bar and helped Klaus out of his coat; it would be warm enough for him under the pub's heaters. 'Can I get a bottle of red and some nibbles?'

'Rumour has it you tackled another local crim today,' Sheri fished.

'I'm going to get a reputation, aren't I?'

'You already have one. I'll get you the wine, but the food is on the house tonight.'

I thanked her and she called back over her shoulder, 'You're the only group crazy enough to be outside, so you've got the space to yourself and you can probably go off lead if you want. But brace yourself – it's already a full house, including some super-hot guy with a Staffie.'

Jake was here? He was in the group, but he *never* came to Pack functions. As far as I knew, he didn't frequent any of the local pubs either.

Detective Andrew Thompson

> I know I mentioned it earlier, but we're all at The Hound, in case you and Detective Williams finish up and want to join us. I promise no one will bite you.

> I know. Thanks.

It wasn't an affirmative, and I didn't really expect him to come. Plus, although none of the Pack dogs would bite him, it was tough to bet against Irina.

I took off my watch and tucked it into a pocket; I didn't need it to tell me I was walking into a loud environment. I pushed through the door, into the beer garden.

The area was decorated for Halloween, and the overhead heat lamps made it warm enough not to wear a coat, although several dogs were sporting Halloween costumes.

The Pack exploded into applause when they saw us, and Klaus, thinking it was for him, strutted towards his friends, barking happily.

'Hero of the moment!'

'Whoo hoo!'

Irina pushed a chair towards me with her foot. 'Sit down, for heaven's sake, and just tell us what happened.' I sat down in it, noting that it was directly across from Jake. I hadn't seen my neighbour since drunk-lunging him, but managed a nod and a smile, which hopefully didn't look as embarrassed as I felt.

'Didn't expect to see you here. You never come to pack events,' I said to him.

He gave me an easy grin. 'My usual Tuesday-night plans got scuppered.'

Meaning pizza and a movie with me? He came here to see *me*?

And then another rogue thought: *Maybe his bolting was less about my lunging at him and more about how much wine I'd consumed before that?*

I mentally shook my head at that. Maybe it was, maybe it wasn't, but from the way he was acting, no lasting harm was done and we were in a relatively good place. Feeling more confident, I smiled at my friends. 'I don't even know where to start.'

'Start at the beginning,' Claire said. Her phone was on the table and I was certain she was recording what we were saying.

'Yeah, start with Jonny Tang,' Yaz said. 'Jesus, finding him like that . . .'

'Actually, I'm going to start further back,' I said. 'When Village Vets closed, a very small number of businesses bid for the space. One was a chap called Dave Najafi, who owns a chain of perfume shops around London.'

'Perfume, or money laundering?' Yaz asked.

'I don't know, but no reason it couldn't be both.' I cast a quick glance at Gav to confirm this or not, but his expression was bland.

'Najafi didn't plan on running the shop himself – he has people to do that for him – but he made sure there was security involved.'

'Bought it for his nephew,' Gav chimed in, ignoring Violet, still wearing her grape fleece as she snuck a few laps from his beer. 'The security are the nephew's mates, but they're paid by Najafi.'

'By security, you mean the yobs that hang out outside,' Claire said.

'Yeah.'

'So, you've got a new chicken shop, in an area glutted with them, but the nephew wants it, so maybe Najafi pulls a few strings. Maybe he doesn't need to pull too hard, as there aren't a lot of takers for that shop space,' Kate guessed.

I nodded. 'So, CGC moves in and, in short order, pisses

off the residents. And, whether you want to believe it or not,' I spoke to Claire, 'Jonny was a bit of a Karen. He started unearthing lots of dirt about CGC and Najafi.'

'Wait a second,' Yaz said. 'We have a shit-ton of shops along the high street that I'm pretty sure are money laundering. Why didn't Najafi just open another perfume shop?'

Gav seemed fixated on Tank, who was busy urinating on a pumpkin.

'The nephew,' I reminded them. 'But Jonny Tang wasn't the only one who did their homework. They might have started looking into CGC to close them down, before they realised who they were linked to.'

'Wait, who?'

'The cost-of-living crisis has bitten deep into a lot of small businesses, Yaz. I think Caren Hansen, whose salon was struggling, first wanted CGC closed; the shop smelled of chicken, customers were getting scared away by the yobs, all that.'

But here's where the penny had dropped this morning. 'And then she realised who it was connected to, and instead of fighting a losing battle, buying air fresheners to combat the smell, luring back customers who were moving elsewhere – sorry, Meg – she wanted to get in with Najafi. Get a cushy set-up as another of his money-losing money laundering operations.'

'Shit,' Yaz breathed, but Jake – and Gav – nodded.

'Then there's Jonny. He thinks he and Caren are on the same side. That they both want to get rid of CGC, which, frankly, they feel is bringing down the neighbourhood. He's the keyboard warrior, right? Happy to send flame-o-grams from a safe distance? He's also able to do a bit of hacking. Got some files – don't ask me how – that look really bad for CGC. He doesn't know that she's switched sides, and he tells her what he finds. Now, she wants in on the gig that he's trying to pull down. Which means he's a threat. I think she arranged to meet him, and killed him.'

'But wouldn't the chicken bones and the CGC box point in the wrong direction, if she was trying to suck up?' Paul asked.

'She wasn't trying to suck up,' I guessed. 'Najafi had no reason to grant her any favours. I think she was trying to blackmail him.'

'The rucksack,' Claire said.

'Yeah. The info in it kind of pointed to the "how". The "why" is more my conjecture, but the detectives didn't dispute it when I laid it out for them.'

'Wait.' Jake held up a finger and gave me *a look*. 'Rucksack?'

I cleared my throat to speak, but Claire beat me to it.

'When the fire broke out in my building, Louise ran into it, grabbed a fire extinguisher and tried to put it out.'

'Klaus and Claire and Tank were upstairs,' I interjected, even though I knew it had been more than that.

'When I found out about the fire, I grabbed what was important,' Claire went on. 'I think Caren did too. Anything she left in the salon could be claimed on insurance, but the bag with the evidence against CGC, arguably her way in, couldn't be replaced. I think when she saw Lou in the back room, fighting the fire, she saw an opportunity. She knew Lou was asking questions, and probably didn't want what was happening made public. Especially not before she made it into Najafi's inner circle. So, our Lou became another threat that had to be neutralised, right?'

'Thanks, Claire,' I said, deadpan.

'I mean, obvs not good that *you* cork it, but from her perspective? One hundred per cent.'

'So, you don't think she was involved in starting the fire?' Jake asked.

'No,' Claire and I both said at the same time. She flicked her hand at me in an over-to-you move.

'No, I think that was one of the rival gangs, maybe a rival chicken shop owner.'

'And The Bells? Who would want to see that torched?' Yaz paused and answered her own question. 'Other than half the neighbourhood.'

'And Annabel.' I smiled wryly. 'Before you ask, no, I don't think Annabel had anything to do with that. I think it might have been as simple as people seeing that they were putting in CCTV. But there was a big enough distraction on the street, and Caren took advantage of it. Put it this way: if she'd planned it, wouldn't she have made sure the rucksack was stashed somewhere safer?'

'Pretty stupid to risk that though. If she hadn't tried to close the door on you . . .'

'So then she came after you,' Jake said. There was an added growl to the deep timbre of his voice. 'And the evidence.'

'Well, first she went after Annabel, who wasn't happy with having CGC in an area she was trying to clean up. I don't know what she was up to – she's still being quiet about it – but I'd bet she was looking for legal ways to evict them. A tricky prospect, when you're dealing with people who don't follow the law. But I think it was the same MO. Set up a meeting to discuss the undesirable CGC, and blindside her.'

Indy threw a small tennis ball across the patio of the beer garden. Banjo bounded after it, as did Jimmy and the beagles. Banjo, far smaller than the others, bolted under the table for it and came out triumphant, before trying to hump Percy the beagle. It was the most I'd ever seen him engage with another dog, and I'm pretty sure Indy noticed it as well; her jaw dropped before her expression morphed into a beaming smile.

'I checked in with Annabel's doctors,' she said, turning back to the group. 'They're still running tests on her, but things are looking good so far.'

'Thank heavens,' I said. My voice broke and I tried to cover it up. 'Annabel is too strong and too ... well ... determined to let something like that get her down.'

'Not for any longer than she has to,' Indy agreed. 'My contact at the hospital told me she tried to check herself out this morning. When they stopped her, she gave them the dressing-down of their lives.'

'That doesn't surprise me!'

'I'm so sorry for landing you in the hot spot with Caren, Lou,' Meg said.

'Not your fault. She was just looking for an opportunity. She'd have found me sooner or later, and it was best for Klaus that he wasn't home, or with me, when it happened.'

'I hope he took a chunk out of her this morning,' Irina declared.

'He tried – both boys did – but I wouldn't let them.'

'But that ratty red cap? Why put that on Jonny's head?' Yaz interjected. 'It was too out of place.'

'I don't know. I actually don't think it had any meaning

other than to make Jonny Tang look – at a glance – like a homeless person. Maybe Caren brought it with her. Maybe she found it that night.'

'Hold on ... where's *his* hat? The fedora?'

I shrugged.

'So, let me see if I've got this straight,' Kate said. 'Angry Caren the hairdresser gets arrested for breaking into your flat. She doesn't find the bag, and could have played dumb about that, and left it there. But the moment she's free, she comes after you?'

'You're assuming Caren's sane,' Yaz pointed out.

'She came after me because I was still a threat,' I answered. 'I had something of hers, and as far as she was concerned, I was standing in the way of her getting the cushy gig she wanted.'

I made a point of not looking at Jake, distracting myself with Klaus, who had his behind in the air and was doing his I'm-cute-you-must-love-me dance for Nala. I didn't think Fi's cocker spaniel had forgiven him for flirting with Phoebe though, as she looked away.

'And I think I've become predictable,' I continued. 'People in the neighbourhood – even those without dogs – know when I walk Klausi, where I walk him and where I usually tend to work when I'm not in the office.'

'You've got to change that.' Jake and Gav spoke as one.

'Predictability will get your arse kicked,' Gav added. 'Maybe you should start taking kickboxing classes with Meg?'

'Yes!' Meg said. 'I can arrange that!'

'So, wait, I'm confused,' Fiona said. 'There was no direct link to Najafi then?'

'No, I don't think so,' I said, taking a sip of wine. 'I think

Caren was trying to wrangle herself into his inner circle. She'd decided – probably on her own – to be useful to him.'

'It's not useful when it lands too much interest from the razz at his door,' Gav said.

'I'm not sure she thought that far ahead.'

'Or that she realised that Najafi's inner circle are his family. However much she might have wanted to be in there, it would never have happened,' Irina said, around a mouthful of chips.

'If it makes you feel any better, Ella,' I said, turning to my quieter-than-usual friend. 'I don't think she meant to tip you and Jim into the canal.'

'And me,' Irina raised her free hand. 'I needed a tetanus jab too.'

'Yes, but you jumped in after Ella,' Paul said. 'You saved three lives this morning, Irina. Four if you count Louise.'

Meg cocked her head to the side and looked at Paul. 'You mean three, right?'

'*Non*. I mean four.' Paul's face split with the biggest grin I'd ever seen. 'Ella is *enceinte*.'

'What?' Yaz asked.

'*Pregnant*? Oh my goodness, Ella!' I moved over to her and gave her the biggest hug I could manage.

She burst into tears, hugging me back tightly. 'I love you, Lou. I love this group. But I cannot do this,' she whispered.

'Do what?'

She shook her head.

'Do what, Ella?'

Paul slipped his hand into hers. 'Raise a child in this neighbourhood.'

'We've been arguing about this the last few days,' Ella admitted tearfully. 'But this morning. *Non.* I cannot do it.'

Claire's eyes widened and she scooted closer to Ella. 'You have us to help here. The whole Pack. And you know how much you love it here. Both of you.'

'Maybe Paul more than Ella,' Irina said bluntly.

I ignored her and asked Ella, 'What will you do?'

'I'm only two months pregnant, but I'm already throwing up every morning. I'm going to ask my company if I can relocate home for a few months.' Ella spoke, but Paul nodded.

'We'll rent out the flat while we're gone.'

'I – we – don't want to lose you.' Yaz said what we were all thinking. 'But we understand.' She tried for a bit of levity. 'Although The Hound might not after they see how much pumpkin Jimmy can chew.'

We looked over. The black Labrador hadn't limited his munchies to one pumpkin, and there was a small orange massacre in progress, in which his brother, Kate's beagles and Tank were also fully participating. Klaus moved closer, sniffed a bit of orange entrail and moved off – he was more of a meat-and-potatoes sort of dog, and vegetables had to be well hidden to be consumed.

'You're only two months in,' Kate said pragmatically.

'And if what happened this morning had not ...' Paul began, his hand tightening on Ella's, showing a united front, even though we all knew how much he thrived on the chaos of the neighbourhood. He swallowed and went on, 'Even if Ella and the child were not in danger, then we would be thinking of maybe moving closer to the time anyway. To be close to family.'

'But we're family,' Yaz whispered.

'*Oui*, you are. And that is why we will not rush. We will find the right tenants, and then maybe the right people to sell to. And we will not say goodbye. You will visit, we will visit. You'll still be family, but further away. Like most of us have, and we make it work.'

He was right; very few of us were London born; having family abroad was pretty normal among the Pack.

I sat down heavily in a nearby chair, between Kate and Jake, falling back on manners to hide my sadness. 'Do you two even know each other?' Kate had been glancing at Jake, but it was hard not to blame her; dressed in his usual black shirt, black leather jacket and jeans, he was the definition of understated but *hot*.

'Kate Marcovici, this is Jake Hathaway.'

There was an energy between them. It wasn't quite sexual, but it was, maybe, a ... recognition.

'Hathaway, huh?' Kate said with a half smile.

'Marco,' Jake replied, although I'd never heard Kate called by that name.

'Wait, you *do* know each other?'

Jake smiled and shook his head. 'No. We've never met.' He didn't elaborate, and instead put one hand on the back of my chair and leaned around with the other to shake Kate's hand. There was still an undercurrent that I couldn't quite name. I still wasn't sure it was sexual, but I *was* sure it existed.

And it looked like Irina was right; I'd been friend-zoned.

I reined in my disappointment and reached over for my wine. *You can't mourn the loss of something you never had.* If he had to be a friend, then at least he was a very good friend.

77

LOUISE

'Sorry we're late,' a voice boomed.

'Late to the party,' Irina muttered, refilling her wine glass from a bottle on the table. 'Again.'

When I glanced at her, her eyes were on Detectives Williams and Thompson as they walked through the door into the beer garden.

'Here to thank us for solving *another* case?' she added.

As the duo walked over to us, Andy passed out treats to the dogs that approached him, which made him more popular with each step.

'Lots of good *sits* there,' Claire said, marvelling at Tank. 'But some people will do anything for treats.'

''Tis the season,' Yaz said, looking at Irina.

'Thought you'd want to know: we got a confession,' Williams said. 'Uniforms went to search Ms Hansen's flat in Canning Town. We found Mr Tang's fedora there, with both his and her hair in it.'

'She was wearing his hat?' Yaz looked from face to face. 'And *no one* noticed?'

'I didn't see her in it,' Meg said. 'Maybe she wore it away from the crime scene, but I don't think she'd wear it around town much.'

'What exactly did she confess to?' Irina asked, narrowing her eyes.

'Pretty much everything. The murder of Jonny Tang. Assault on Annabel Lindford-Swayne. Breaking and entering, and attempted assault on Ms Mallory.'

'Did she cop to keying my car?' Claire asked.

'Wait, what?' I gasped. 'What happened to your car?'

'Someone wanted to decorate either side. Could have been a coincidence or could have been a warning.' She shrugged as if it were not a big deal, but it was.

'Why didn't you say anything?'

She shrugged again. 'I'm a journo. I piss people off for a living. It could have been anyone, for any reason.' I didn't think she really believed it and, from his expression, neither did Andy.

'I'll ask her.'

'Good. And what about the online bullying?' Claire asked. 'The people in my building who complained about CGC were subjected to quite a lot of grief.'

'No, that wasn't her. That was the sixteen-year-old son of CGC's manager,' Andy said.

'Sixteen, huh? Which means he's too young to get much more than a slap on his wrist.' Irina rolled her eyes.

So did Williams, but I wasn't sure Irina saw it.

The detectives exchanged a glance. 'What aren't you telling us?' Kate asked.

Williams inclined his head towards Andy. *Over to you, mate.*

Andy sighed, making a clear effort to direct his attention to me instead of Irina. 'Williams was right, Ms Hansen has confessed to everything. We've requested her phone records and are questioning her close contacts, just to be sure ...'

'Sure?' Claire leaned forward, her eyes narrowing. 'Be sure of what?'

'That she acted alone,' Kate said, then looked at Williams. 'Did she say she had a partner? Or is this because of how rare female killers are?'

'Or do you have evidence that implies that someone else is involved?' Meg asked.

Andy held both hands up. 'She swears she operated alone, and we have no proof to suggest otherwise. But until we can rule it out, it's best to be aware. Just in case.'

Jake crossed his arms over his wide chest, looked at me and nodded. 'Sensible, Marple.'

'See, he calls her that too,' Williams muttered to Andy.

I was about to protest when Paul interrupted. 'Okay, okay. Frankly speaking, everyone probably calls you that, Louise,' he said. 'But whether or not our detective friends will admit to it as well, we are grateful for it. For your tenacity. For what you are willing to risk to find justice for people.'

'You make me sound like a crusader.' I laughed, embarrassed.

'Every crap neighbourhood needs one,' Irina said. 'Might as well be you.'

Andy gave her a bemused shake of the head. 'And yet, there's a compliment in there somewhere.'

She looked confused. 'Of course there is. Lou knows she's my best friend.'

Williams remained silent, but his expression spoke aloud: *possibly your only friend*.

I regained my composure. 'Thanks for letting us know, Detectives. And you're welcome to join us.'

'Irina will even buy you a drink,' Yaz piped up, laughing at Irina's affronted look.

'She just might not give you her phone to pay for it.' I giggled suddenly, feeling the tension of the past ten days fall from my shoulders. I ignored the way Irina's mouth dropped open, appalled, and the other Pack members' quizzical expressions – some mysteries weren't for solving. Klaus ran up to me, a small pumpkin in his mouth. He dropped it at my feet and nosed it forward, as he would a ball.

I pulled him onto my lap and caressed his short fur, feeling content. In this group, with these amazing souls (both hounds and humans), we could do anything.

Epilogue

BENNY

Benny Bryce was shaking as he made his way home from the police station. He'd answered the questions as honestly as he could without dropping Caren into more crap than she was already in.

'How are you acquainted with Caren Hansen?'

'I've worked for her for five years. Since the salon opened.'

'Would you consider yourself her friend? Her confidante?'

'I thought so.'

'Did you know that she was engaged in blackmailing a Tower Hamlets councillor and local businessman?'

'No.'

'Did you know that she did so because she hoped they would let her in on what she thought was a money laundering operation?'

Benny shook his head. 'No. I didn't know that she was doing that. Any of that. I wasn't involved!'

'Did you know that when she felt that the actions of Jonny Tang jeopardised her goal, she killed him? Murdered him and planted evidence pointing to Cluckin' Good Chicken?'

'I didn't know what she was doing, so how would I know that?'

'Please answer the question, Mr Bryce.'

Benny had shaken his head again, looking back and forth between the two detectives sitting opposite him. 'No. Although I do think that would be a really dumb way of getting tight with anyone.'

Dumb maybe, but Caren's brain worked in ways that Benny didn't understand. Like a chess player, sometimes. Three moves ahead. So, maybe she'd been trying to impress Najafi and his friends, instead of forcing their hand? Let them know that she knew about them, and that she could be an asset? Or that if they didn't let her in on their business, she'd damage it.

Forcing the hand of powerful people never ended well, did it? He didn't pretend to understand her motivations, and he was being a hundred per cent honest when he said that she hadn't let him in on any of it.

The detectives exchanged a glance that Benny couldn't decipher.

'Did you help her carry out that murder?'

Benny's heart began to pound in his chest, and he desperately sought to calm himself down. He knew he couldn't afford to lose his composure, or everything would be lost; they'd lock him up as well. Still, when he spoke, it come out almost as a shout. 'NO!'

'Were you aware that when Caren Hansen sensed that Ms Annabel Lindford-Swayne suspected what was going on, she assaulted her? Left her for dead?'

'I had no knowledge of that — and no part in whatever was going on,' Benny insisted.

'Did you witness any intimidating behaviours Caren Hansen evidenced towards either Claire Dougherty or Louise Mallory?'

'No. As far as I knew, she liked them,' Benny said miserably.

'Would you like some more water, Mr Bryce?' the stout detective asked, not unkindly.

'No. Thank you.'

The tall detective was less amiable, forging ahead. 'Were you privy to any evidence that Ms Hansen was trying to stoke gang-on-gang tensions in the area, which resulted in the stabbings on Wednesday and — or — the arson on Sunday?'

'God, no! I was there with her both times. She didn't have anything to do with it — I'm sure of that.'

'Because you were behind it?'

'You can't be serious ... No! I had nothing to do with that! We were both terrified. I live in the neighbourhood, and sometimes I walk home by myself late at night. The last thing I want is more crime. Same with Caren.'

'One last question,' the tall young detective said. 'There is some evidence that Ms Hansen had help carrying out

some, if not all, of these incidents. If it wasn't you, who do you think it was?'

That was the question that Benny had most been dreading. He had no evidence himself, of course; hadn't seen anything, witnessed anything or heard anything. But if Caren had help, there was only one person it could be.

And for Benny to say that name would land Benny in jail. Or worse.

So, he answered in such a way that wasn't an outright lie – he didn't believe in lying to the police – but that wouldn't end up with very, very bad things happening.

More very, very bad things, he corrected himself.

'I've never seen Caren with anyone like that. Anyone who might do those sorts of things.'

'Even though you don't think she did any of those things herself?'

'Yeah. But if she did do it, and she did have help, she didn't tell me who, and I've never met any of her friends so I don't know who it could be. Sorry.'

They'd let him go, eventually. He walked home slowly, passing the canal, the pub, the park. They'd close the salon, and he'd need to find a new job. Maybe a new flat to rent, although he knew that he could never run far enough or fast enough.

Danny would come. Danny always came.

And this time he'd be out for blood.

Acknowledgements

My greatest thanks go to my editor, Katherine Armstrong, and agent, James Wills, for believing in me and my crazy idea about a bunch of people who met at the dog park and solve crimes.

While writing the book is a solitary sport, publishing isn't, and I couldn't ask for a better 'Publishing Pack' than Katherine, James, Georgie Leighton, Jess Barratt, Sarah Harwood, Rich Vlietstra (who lies when he says he isn't a dog person), Lily Searstone and Amy Fletcher. This book wouldn't be where it is without them and any mistakes in it are mine alone.

It is, however, fiction. With the exception of a small number of my favourite local bars, pubs and restaurants, all places, people and situations are completely made up. Oh, with one other exception: Klaus is shamelessly based on my own beloved dachshund. The Dude remains the inspiration for this series, and the borky love of my life.

He makes every day an adventure and a pleasure. He's not just my dog, he's my soul.

The Dude and I landed on our feet when we fell in with our Pack: Kalpna Chauhan and Rolo, Cláudia Braglia Hernandez and Preta, Jenna Fong Sing, Jay Ersapah and Cava. I am so lucky to call you my friends. I love you all!

Ongoing thanks to my MoD Squad beta readers, Catie Logan and Gerry Cavanagh, who were happy to trawl through *Bone of Contention*, rooting out plot holes and inconsistencies. I owe you wine ... a lot of wine ...

Even though they're on the other side of the pond, my brother Stephen has been a rock, and his kids Matthew and Alexandra are, as ever, my shining stars.

The trail from manuscript to finished book can be bumpy, and I'm fortunate to have good friends who make sure my glass is half full. Special shout-outs to Kate Bradley, AK Turner, Steve Carter, Sharon Galer, Petra Losch, Sabrina Chevannes, Kelly West, Theo Pavel, Martina Tromsdorf and Monique Mandalia-Sharma.

Last, but never least, I am grateful for my readers. I LOVE hearing from you, so please keep the lovely messages (and pics of your dogs) coming!

Blake Mara x